VERONICA'S SISTERS

Exploring a remote canyon in the wilds of New Mexico Melinda Pink comes upon a rifle and recent human remains in an old cave dwelling. Someone in the area must be waiting for a body to be found, so Miss Pink alerts the small community of Regis and the police, only to find that no one is missing. Miss Pink is intrigued, especially as she knows that rural America can be a dangerous and unforgiving place. And soon she exposes dark secrets and darker suspicions: drugs, an old cabin haunted by snakes and memories of clandestine meetings, brothel-keeping, the English maid who nursed the wife and married the widower...

VERONICA'S SISTERS

Miss Pink in New Mexico

Gwen Moffat

CURLEY LARGE PRINT
HAMPTON, NEW HAMPSHIRE

Library of Congress Cataloging-in-Publication Data

Moffat, Gwen.
    Veronica's sisters / Gwen Moffat.
        p.   cm.
    ISBN 0–7927–1801–1 (HC)
    ISBN 0–7927–1800–3 (SC)
    1. Pink, Melinda (Fictitious character)—Fiction.   2. Women
detectives—New Mexico—Fiction.   3. Large type books.   I. Title.
[PR6063.O4V47   1993]   93–11684
823'.914—dc20   CIP

British Library Cataloguing in Publication Data available

This Large Print edition is published by Chivers Press, England, and by
Curley Large Print, an imprint of Chivers North America, 1993.

Published in the U.K. by arrangement with Macmillan London Limited,
and in the U.S. with Gregory & Radice.

U.K. Hardcover ISBN 0 7451 2043 1
U.K. Softcover   ISBN 0 7451 2055 5
U.S. Hardcover ISBN 0 7927 1801 1
U.S. Softcover   ISBN 0 7927 1800 3

Printed in Great Britain

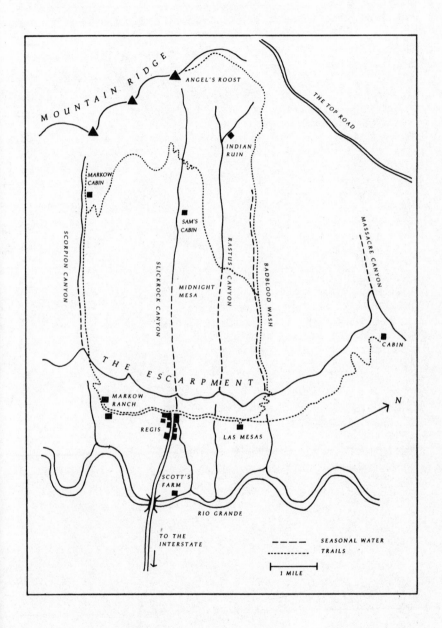

MOUNTAIN RIDGE

ANGEL'S ROOST

THE TOP ROAD

INDIAN RUIN

MARKOW CABIN

SAM'S CABIN

SCORPION CANYON

SLICKROCK CANYON

MIDNIGHT MESA

RASTUS CANYON

BADBLOOD WASH

MASSACRE CANYON

CABIN

THE ESCARPMENT

MARKOW RANCH

REGIS

LAS MESAS

N

SCOTT'S FARM

RIO GRANDE

TO THE INTERSTATE

— — — SEASONAL WATER

· · · · · TRAILS

1 MILE

VERONICA'S SISTERS

CHAPTER ONE

The loose horse scrambled out of the canyon and swung round to face down the slope. A hornet homed in and stung. The horse went plunging across the mesa, startling a jay which took off with alarm calls that could be heard over a mile away.

Two thousand feet above, on the peak called Angel's Roost, the commotion alerted a solitary mountaineer who focused her binoculars and, finding the horse and seeing that it was saddled, started to search for the owner. A riderless horse meant that something was wrong, at the least that its rider would have a long walk home. That is when the horse runs back to its stable, thought Melinda Pink, lowering the binoculars in favour of the naked eye—but this horse was standing still. She guessed that it had been fed and had broken loose because it had been stung, or bitten by a rattlesnake. Now it looked as if it might stand until its owner caught up with it. There was another possibility: that it had already thrown its owner.

She raised the binoculars again, using them at random, panicking because she didn't know where the horse had come from, then, getting a grip on herself, she came back

1

to the animal and saw that it was staring, head up, towards trees in a shallow canyon: Rastus Canyon; she had contoured round its headwall on her way to Angel's Roost. There was nothing for it; she would have to go down there, a man could be lying in the bottom with a broken leg, or worse, and he wouldn't last long on an August afternoon in New Mexico.

She started to gather up her belongings. She had been here only an hour but the shade under the little pinyon pine looked like a campsite, a touch of humanity on a summit that commanded a view down a canyon to the Rio Grande and beyond, to the desert ranges stretching east to Texas.

She fastened her rucksack and, straightening her back, she considered Slickrock Canyon below. No cows had ever been there; it was a box canyon and apparently inaccessible. On either side of it long red walls stretched south-east, decreasing in height to a notch like a gunsight that was no exit but the top of a great escarpment above a village called Regis. Slickrock was a true box canyon; at its head, under Angel's Roost, its walls started from a rock amphitheatre. There were gullies in the walls of course, but they were full of vertical steps and overhangs. It was no place for cows, not even for people, but it must be a sanctuary for wildlife. There was water, that was obvious from the wide ribbon of woodland in the bottom. Momentarily side-tracked, Miss Pink, always eager to explore new ground, studied the canyon walls for a means of descent and to her amazement she found one. There was a system of ledges that might be linked, and a pale speck about halfway up: a lump of quartz? Lime from an eagle's nest? It was moving. Too pale for deer, and there were no bighorn sheep here. She reached for the glasses and gasped, and smiled. She sat down slowly, no longer in a hurry.

A figure was walking up the great wall, not climbing but ascending easily on a diagonal line that had to be a rake. This must be the rider, and small wonder that he had left his horse; his progress was easy only on the diagonal. As she watched, his course changed and he went straight up, using his hands and reaching high. He didn't hesitate so it couldn't be *that* hard but despite the lack of technical difficulty the whole route must be extremely exposed. There was no natural parapet, she could see the man's feet, in orange trainers: curious footwear for a ranch-hand, if he was a ranch-hand. The faded blue jeans were uniform but he wore a white shirt and no hat, and his hair seemed to be long and tied back. He could be a hippie and might have no association with the horse, and this meant she must still go down and look for an injured rider.

The horse was standing in the shade. The man came out on the rim of Slickrock and started to cross the mesa towards Rastus Canyon. His route would take him quite close to the animal which may have whinnied. She saw them come together, almost like two people, then she lost them in the shade. After a while she glimpsed the man, mounted now, moving steadily along the mesa towards the trail that would take him down the escarpment to the village. No one was injured. She could relax.

A new perspective opened for her. She had approached her peak by a wide loop to the north which she now saw might not be necessary on the return. If she could get down to the place where the man was reunited with his horse—Midnight Mesa, she saw from her map—she could cut a corner and see new ground.

At seven thousand feet Angel's Roost was only a small peak as peaks go in America but the trees were ponderosas with plenty of space between the big trunks. The descent to Midnight Mesa was steep and smooth with nothing more for an aged mountaineer to bother about than the lack of friction occasioned by pine needles. After a thousand feet or so the angle lessened and the ponderosas gave way to stunted oaks and juniper: low but dense enough to block the view. Miss Pink wasn't worried; the canyons ran south-east and since the most awesome of them possessed an escape route she knew that her only problem, with the temperature well above a hundred, would be dehydration. She went slowly, conserving energy, feeling some trepidation as she looked around her and saw no sign that anyone had ever come this way before, yet knowing that the trail, the long way home from Angel's Roost, was less than a mile behind her. There was even a highway a further mile or so to the north, probably empty of traffic, but it was always a comfort in a wild place to know that there was a proper road within walking distance, provided you could find it.

The immediate ground was bedrock interspersed with fine gravel. Rock and gravel were white, reflecting the sun. She swallowed and wished that junipers grew closer together or cast longer shadows. She caught a glimpse of rock on her left, higher than her own level. She glanced right and saw more rock looming. The junipers thinned out and came to an end and she found herself looking down a long and totally unfamiliar canyon to the hazy ranges beyond the Rio Grande.

She stepped forward warily and took stock. She had come out on a low point with miniature gorges on either side. There was no way she would risk climbing down a

5

vertical wall even if, as here, it was only twenty feet high; you could die as the result of a broken ankle if no one knew where you were, and she hadn't told the people at her motel of her destination.

She peered over the edge to see what the watercourses were like. Both gorges looked reasonable, once you were down there, unlike the big retaining wall on one side, the north-east side, which was massive, and undercut above its base. Working it out from the map and what she had seen on her approach to Angel's Roost this morning she decided that this canyon must be Rastus. There were aspens not far below and their tops were fairly level. That should mean that there were no big drops and she would be able to walk down the creek.

She retreated for a hundred yards or so, clambered into the little ravine on her right and made her way carefully down the rocks, trusting that as soon as she reached the trees the ground would be easier.

There was fallen timber under the point, bleached white by sun and snow, and wedged in the rocks below the overhanging wall was a rifle.

She froze, open-mouthed, seeming to hear the sound of her last footstep echo back from the wall. Even the birds were silent, but the stillness was in her mind because after a while she heard water talking in the stones.

She picked up the gun, which had bright patches of rust on the metal parts.

There was a slope of sand and flaking scree below what she now saw was a cave under the overhang and there, protected by the rock ceiling, was a stone wall with windows, and a doorway. She had come on the ruin of a cliff dwelling used by the Mogollon Indians, the people who lived in these canyons before the arrival of the Apaches.

For a moment she gloated over masonry which had stood for centuries without change. Eight hundred years and there were the same joints and angles in the shaped stone, the same window apertures and doorway, even the same approach—although not quite, the scree was unstable and strewn with detritus: twigs and dead cactus pads and bits of bone. Some carnivore could be in occupation now.

She put down the gun, picked up a stone and said loudly: 'Come out!'—feeling silly until the embarrassment was superseded by a sense of *déja vu*. Earlier there had been a horse without a rider and here was a rifle as eloquent of its missing owner as a loose and saddled horse.

Articles in stream beds have often been carried there by water, not always, but the knowledge gave her the excuse to stare thoughtfully up the gorge and postpone her next move. The rifle was heavy; it couldn't have been carried far by water and it couldn't be thrown any distance, only dropped. She had been on the rocky point directly above, she had come down the bed of the creek; the second place she must visit was the top of the big overhanging wall. But the first place—reluctantly she brought her gaze back from the rocks in the gorge—the first place was the ruin.

She plodded up the scree. There were a few shrivelled cacti on the slope and a curved bone had come to rest against a prickly pear. It was the shaft of a rib. Near the top of the slope were several vertebrae, still attached to each other, their size indicating a large mammal; not as big as a cow or horse, an antelope perhaps, except that this wasn't antelope country. Mule deer then, and that implied a powerful predator, like a lion. 'No lion,' she said aloud, fingering the stone in her hand, 'would be waiting inside for me.' She listened for movement, her eyes wide with apprehension, and not without cause. Mountain lions, shyest of the big cats, would certainly have slipped away when they heard her on the point above; coyotes too, but there could well be rats come in to feast on the predator's leavings and where there were rats there were snakes.

She reached the ruin and studied a patch of sunlight inside the doorway. All she could see was droppings, possibly those of a ringtail cat. She stamped her feet but she didn't throw the stone; the gesture seemed aggressive, even paranoid. There was no sound, no reaction to her stamping, and a rattlesnake would have given its warning by now. A thought struck her and she smiled in sudden relief. There was no smell. This place hadn't been occupied for a long time, the bones on the slope were old.

She stepped over the threshold and stood aside, concentrating on the gloom. After a few moments the interior became apparent: bulges catching reflected light, bone splinters, a branch, an old boot.

It was a riding-boot but so worn it could have come from a rubbish tip; the upper conformed to the shape of the wearer's foot and the sole flapped. She shook it gingerly. Nothing fell out and there was only the faintest suggestion of odour, as one might expect with very old footwear. There was no sign of its companion.

Looking around, wondering how the branch came to be here, she saw pale nodules near one end, like a fungus. She carried it to the doorway for a better look and nearly dropped it. What she had taken for fungus was the bones of a hand, picked clean of flesh, although not quite: there were brown shreds at the joints and, as she stared at it, a fly landed on a knuckle. There was a slight smell, a processed smell, like pemmican.

She put the branch back where she'd found it and then she searched the one-roomed dwelling as meticulously as was possible without a flashlight but she found nothing further: no more bones, no clothing, not even a belt. Nor, when she left the cave, did she find anything in the creek bed below the rifle, but she hadn't expected to. The predators: bears and coyotes, lions, could have taken the rest of the body some distance. Packrats would have removed any rags of clothing to line their nests. Many people who disappeared in forests did so completely: she was surprised that anything had been left here but then she reasoned that, judging from the scraps of dried flesh on the finger bones, the victim had died comparatively recently, long enough for the rifle to rust but not so long ago that scavengers had quite finished with the body. She wasn't greatly concerned. The lapse of time eliminated horror. And there was a more pressing factor; the incident reminded her that solitary travellers in the wilderness need to keep their wits about them. She intended to get out of this place alive.

She studied the physical features and fixed them in her mind: the confluence of the two streams, the rocky point and the big wall in shades of red, its rock streaked black with mineral stains and massively undercut. But even from a few yards away you had to look for the ruin although it was in plain view. People searching for the missing man would never have known it was there, let alone that their quarry was inside, unless he shouted, unless they had dogs. Hounds would have smelled him a mile away; further when the body decomposed.

She turned to the descent but as she started to clamber down a chaos of boulders she kept an eye on the banks, hoping for game trails. Within a hundred yards she came to the end of the big crag and before she entered the first grove of aspens she saw that the canyon broadened and became comparatively shallow. There were still outcrops of rock but they were isolated, giving the rift a more friendly feel than Slickrock.

The upper slopes were arid however, freckled with pinyon and juniper where even the shade would be hot. The animals had moved down to the creek where they dozed away the daylight hours, scarcely moving as Miss Pink passed by—but she knew they were there. In a place where there wasn't enough breeze to stir a leaf she would sense the turn of a feathered head, a lift of wings and a settling again as she showed no overt interest, didn't even look except out of the corner of her eye. At last she saw what she had been watching for: a glimpse of yellow flank as a deer got up and drifted downstream. She climbed the bank and found a game trail.

She was in mixed woodland, marshy in the bottom where the muddy little path led her through glades of rank grass vivid with lupins and scarlet paintbrush. There was a smell of sap and flowers, of trampled mud and, unexpectedly, the stench of fresh horse dung. She came to an accumulation of droppings about an alder, and stuck in crevices in the bark were coarse brown hairs and pale fibres.

The horse's tracks were obvious, deeply indented as it plunged away, not breaking the halter but evidently pulling loose a badly tied knot. It looked as if the animal might have caught a whiff of scent from the ruin; more likely a vulture had carried a piece of flesh to a tree and dropped it to rot in an inaccessible crack.

The hoofprints led diagonally out of the canyon and she followed, leaving the lush woodland but still in shade because the swell of Midnight Mesa blocked out the light. After a while the angle eased and the sun came blinding through the junipers. Shading her eyes she saw Angel's Roost above the headwall of Slickrock. The place where one might descend into the box canyon must be across the mesa from here. She resolved to come back: when she was fresh, and there was no necessity to report the finding of a body, or the remains of one.

She was no longer following a trail, had lost the horse's track but it was immaterial; on the long whaleback of the mesa the ground was open enough that no one could be lost for long in daylight and the surface was fine for walking, composed of the familiar bedrock and gravel. She worked south-east between the stunted trees and prickly pear and shortly she came to a duck: one small stone balanced on another. Without pausing she turned left.

There was still no trail as such, only a line, the line of least resistance, sensed rather than seen. Occasionally she passed other ducks and then, at a steepening in the ground, a neat cairn of single slabs, stacked like plates, that marked the descent into Rastus Canyon perhaps two miles from where she had left it, where the horse had been tethered. The mud of the creek was deeply trampled by shod hoofs.

There was a mesa on the other side and then a drop to the dry bed of Badblood Wash where she picked up her trail of the morning. This wash led back all the way to the divide, and that in turn had brought her to the foot of the north ridge of Angel's Roost. Looking up the wash now—a wide swath of sand between banks of scrubby vegetation—she realised that there was little more than half a mile between the head of Badblood and the body in Rastus and she wondered why it hadn't been found sooner. If it was known that a man was hunting on these mesas the first place to look for him when he didn't return would be under the cliffs. She frowned and turned to the trail, which was now marked with the signs of cows. She walked slowly down the sand of the wash, staring absently at a troop of gnatcatchers in the mesquite and thinking about closed seasons and poaching. Ahead of her rounded rocks on the skyline indicated the top of the escarpment. She came to it and stopped.

She had left the woodland behind in Rastus Canyon where it had made a delightful contrast to arid slopes but below the scarp was a contrast that was even more marked: acre upon acre of lush jungle with here and there a glint of water that showed the course of the Rio Grande. To the left loops of the river were lost in hazy infinity and to the south the view was obscured by a bulge in the escarpment, but straight ahead, beyond the hardwoods that resembled a rain-forest, the desert started.

There was a break in the cliffs, another system of ledges, and a dusty trail, graded for horses, threatened at intervals by leaning towers that seemed to be wedged in position only by debris, and that was constantly on the move to judge by chunks of scree on the path. The trail descended to a ranch. It was shaded by cottonwoods and only its corrals were visible. Miss Pink wouldn't have known it was there but for having passed it this morning and noted the name on the gate: Las Mesas.

The village of Regis lay to the south and that too was an unknown quantity. She had come here on a whim, attracted by the name of Angel's Roost, having seen from the map that the peak might be approached from Regis. The highway to the north was much closer to the mountain but in that direction there were two miles of forest and no trail: strenuous going and deadly dull; from Regis there was the escarpment, the canyons and the mesas. She had left Palomares, thirty miles away, and arrived here at eight o'clock with the sun high and no one stirring, or at least, no one showing themselves. Regis had impressed her as a place of brilliant light and deep shade, of blind windows and dust and one unpaved street. She had seen no human being since she left the interstate five miles away and it was only the few vehicles parked under trees that told her Regis wasn't a ghost town.

Now, in late afternoon, as she came down from the plateau by way of the zigzag trail she felt a thrill of anticipation. She was about to enter a new world, however small and innocuous, the introduction to come by way of the first person to grant her the use of a telephone. For although she could have telephoned the police from her motel it was curiosity as much as courtesy that dictated she couldn't leave Regis without informing the community of her discovery. Somewhere someone was waiting for a body to be found and it was possible that the missing man, if he didn't actually reside in the village, was known to someone who did.

CHAPTER TWO

'He's not from this village; no one's missing.'

There had been no sign of life at Las Mesas apart from some steers in a corral so, having picked up her car at the foot of the zigzags, Miss Pink continued to Regis and in a window of the first house she came to saw a notice: 'Hacienda del Sol Apartments to Rent'. Getting no reply at the front door she walked round to the back and found a middle-aged woman with some horses in a corral.

The basic report was contained in a sentence: there were human bones in a canyon. Knowing the West Miss Pink wasn't surprised that this woman should seem more

16

concerned with hospitality than with some old bones although she noted that when Pearl Slocum went indoors there was an irregular sound of conversation. She was telephoning.

Drinking iced tea under a walnut tree in the patio they took stock of each other, both surprised and both politely disguising the fact. Miss Pink saw a thin woman in her fifties, smelling of horses, sweat and a tangy scent. The southern sun had been unkind to her but under the papery skin she had good bones. Her hair could once have been a vivid red but it had dried and faded until it was no more than a frizzy bush, yet despite the effects of ageing and heat the first impression was of vitality; she had striking eyes, pale grey above high cheek-bones.

For Pearl's part she saw an elderly and somewhat solid woman dressed like a hired hand but with expertly layered hair and designer glasses with thin mottled frames. She thought that what she could see of the eyes behind the thick lenses was kind but naïve and she was concerned that this old English lady should have been hiking alone in the back-country.

Miss Pink explained that her father had started her climbing in the Swiss Alps and that it was all right if you knew what you were doing, not nearly as dangerous as—sailing, she substituted smoothly. She had been about to say 'riding alone in the high country' but so far she had confined her story to the discovery of the rifle and the bones. As she hesitated, wondering why she didn't mention the solitary rider, Pearl said thoughtfully, showing that her mind wasn't on the danger to Miss Pink of solo hiking, 'He wasn't legal. Whoever he was, he had no right to be there. If there was still flesh on the fingers he hadn't been dead long, and there's been no hunting since March and that was for lion. Deer season ended in January. Your man was poaching.'

'Does it make any difference?' Miss Pink asked innocently.

'Around here it does. Who's bothered about a poacher? He had to be either on Markow land or Avril Beck's, and neither of them couldn't care less. Regis folk are possessive about their boundaries. About most everything,' she added darkly. 'Funny thing though: he must have been working alone.'

'I thought of that. There were no search parties? No one looked for him?'

'I heard nothing. People could have looked and given up—I mean, looked unofficially. If several guys are poaching, even just two, no one's going to call in the Search and Rescue when one doesn't come back to camp.' Miss Pink was silent. 'Perhaps he wasn't popular anyway,' Pearl
18

mused, catching the other's eye and looking away.

'I should phone the police,' Miss Pink said and Pearl, taking this for a request, stood up. 'Phone's in the kitchen. You'll have to excuse the mess, no one's cleaned the place today.' She glanced at her watch. 'Actually I'm expecting my little maid to arrive at any moment.'

Miss Pink followed her across the patio reflecting that the police were going to need her to show them the site of the remains. The prospect of driving up the valley of the Rio Grande this evening only to return first thing tomorrow was daunting. Maybe she could stay here? In the kitchen Pearl tapped out a number and asked for someone called Wayne. 'They're trying to contact the deputy,' she told Miss Pink and glanced round abstractedly. There was nowhere to sit and scarcely room to stand; all the surfaces, even the floor, were cluttered with crockery and saucepans, odd shoes, clothing, mail, a recipe book on a wooden stand, a screwdriver and a broken stirrup on one stool, a saddle minus the stirrup on another. Pearl's eyes sharpened. 'Wayne, Pearl here; I have an English lady at my house. You should hear what she has to say ...' She held out the phone.

Miss Pink introduced herself and a loud male voice responded. She said that she had found human bones in Rastus Canyon.

'What makes you think they're human, ma'am?' The tone could be thought hostile but was probably only bored, suggesting that people were constantly reporting the discovery of bones.

'Because the hand was still grasping a branch,' she said. 'And there was a rifle near by.' This elicited a puzzled: 'No one's been reported missing. How long had he been there?'

Her eyebrows rose but she said gently, 'I couldn't say but there was only a very faint smell.'

'I'll have to come out,' he grumbled. 'Will you be at Pearl's place?'

'At what time?'

'I'll try to make it before eight; it's going to be hot work climbing up that Beck trail. Put Pearl on, willya?'

She handed over the phone and went to stand at the sink under the window just as a slight figure swept into the patio on a bicycle, her coltish legs bare to the crotch. As she propped the machine against the walnut tree it could be seen that she was not, as Miss Pink had supposed, wearing shorts but a flimsy red frock that clung to the gawky body as far as the navel where petal flounces formed the tiniest mini-skirt. The shoes were red too, with extremely high heels. Her straw-coloured hair was cut short and fitted the small skull like a cap. She was about twelve years old and looked like a little girl dressed up in her big sister's party clothes.

'Here's my maid,' came Pearl's voice, exasperated and amused at the same time. 'And whatever has she got on? She can go straight back and tell her dad Wayne wants a horse for tomorrow. No way is that big lump going to get on one of my animals.' The screen door opened and there was an eloquent silence during which they heard someone call from the front of the house: 'You home, Pearl?'

'In back, Kristen.' Pearl smiled and the child in the red dress, whose mouth had drooped at the silence, perked up like a little dog. 'My,' Pearl exclaimed, 'everything's happening at once. Hi, Kristen.'

A second girl appeared at the inner door, an older girl, although in the gloom common to southern houses Miss Pink could distinguish little more than a slim form in jeans and a white shirt, the hair pulled back, and bright orange trainers on the feet. She had to stop herself from gaping.

'This is Kristen,' Pearl was saying. 'And that's Tammy, and this lady's Miss Pink, a visitor from England. I'm going to ask her to stay the night, so we have to get this place organised—'

'Hi,' Kristen said and, lifting her hand, switched on a light, emphasising the

21

kitchen's squalor. She ignored it and stared at the child in the red frock. There was something in her startled eyes that was neither amusement nor exasperation, more like horror. Tammy looked frightened. 'Don't you like it?' she whispered, fingering a flounce.

'It's a neat get-up.' Pearl rushed to the breach. 'But it's much too old for—old-fashioned. Minis went out with the dinosaurs—'

'I saw these girls on television—'

'You look like a hooker,' Kristen said.

'Now, Kristy—'

'My mom said—'

'Your mom don't know what she's—'

'Knock it off, you guys, we got company! And Tammy's going home right now because she has to take a message to her dad, and I can't get him on the phone'—Miss Pink's eyes flickered—'so she has to change anyway because you're going to take the horses out soon's it cools off. I have to clear up here, fix supper for us.'

'That's my job,' Tammy said sulkily, then: 'But I'll ride for you.'

'After you been home. You get on your bike, tell your dad Wayne Spikol's going to be needing that old blue roan of yours early tomorrow, OK? Fact, what you do is bring the roan back with you; I'll run you home tonight.'

Tammy stared. 'Why me? Jay Gatford can—'

Kristen said quickly: 'I'll drive her home now, take your pick-up. Why's Wayne coming here?'

Pearl hesitated, glancing at Tammy. 'Miss Pink found some old bones in a ruin in Rastus Canyon. The police have to see them, take them away.'

'Human bones?' Tammy breathed.

'Rastus?' Kristen repeated on a high note. '*Old* bones?'

'Very old,' Miss Pink said quietly.

'And a rifle,' added Pearl.

'How could you—What were you doing—I'm sorry.' Kristen checked, biting her lip.

'I was hiking.' It was uttered with finality as if no further explanation were needed.

'I didn't know there were Indian ruins in Rastus,' Pearl said. 'Did you, Kristen?' She turned to Tammy. 'That's Beck land, surely, not yours.'

'We stop at Slickrock,' Tammy said. 'Mrs Beck and us both, we stop either side of Slickrock, but there's ruins in all the canyons.'

Kristen opened her mouth, closed it, then said weakly, 'I guess.'

'Everywhere,' Tammy assured her loftily.

Kristen looked at Miss Pink. 'You could have got the canyons muddled.' She had

23

rather plain features, redeemed by her youth but sullen when she was serious. Now, in the glare of the kitchen light she looked quite ugly. 'That's possible,' Miss Pink said cheerfully.

Pearl laughed. 'You're going to have fun tomorrow, trailing in and out of those old canyons. I'd better come with you.' She thought about it. 'And why not? You'll be taking one of my horses. Can you ride?'

'Well enough.'

'What makes you think the bones are human?' Kristen asked.

'There were fingers grasping a branch—and the rifle, of course.'

The girl was fiddling with the broken stirrup, watched by the others. 'How long had they been there?' she asked, picking at a rivet with grubby nails.

'It's difficult to say.' Miss Pink considered the point yet again. 'There's snow at that altitude in winter? Yes, well I would guess that the accident happened since the snow—'

'February,' Tammy put in. 'The last drifts melted in February, but if he was inside a ruin there wouldn't be any snow. Unless a lion dragged him in there outa the cold.'

'He got there under his own steam,' Miss Pink said. 'That's obvious from the branch. He crawled out of the creek: up a slope and into the ruin.'

'How can you tell all that?' Tammy asked, not in the least concerned that they were talking about a dead man.

'His rifle,' Miss Pink said. 'It was lying in the stream bed. He must have fallen from the top of the cliff.'

'What cliff?' Kristen asked.

Miss Pink thought: The one upstream from where you tether your horse, and then she reflected that there could be more than one person in Regis who owned orange trainers. Aloud she said, 'At the head of the canyon two streams come together under a little point and there's a cliff around a hundred feet high. As to when the accident happened'—she shrugged, then committed herself—'perhaps three, four months ago.'

Expressions changed fractionally although they hadn't been illuminating even as they listened. She knew that Pearl and Kristen were thinking back three or four months, pondering, dismissing—but before dismissal she saw a spark of something like recognition. At that moment her eyes were on Pearl and, alerted, she turned to Kristen, but the girl had taken Tammy's arm. 'Come on,' she said roughly, 'I'll drive you home.' She turned back to Pearl. 'Will they need a pack-horse?'

'No,' Miss Pink said, adding as the girls crossed the patio and disappeared round a corner of the house, 'a garbage bag will be

25

adequate. I wonder what happened to the rest of the body?'

'Coyotes. And Wayne Spikol won't be looking for it, that's for sure.'

'Who went missing four months ago?' Miss Pink's voice sounded disembodied as she stared through the window screen. Pearl gaped at the broad back, then swallowed. 'No one. I told you.'

'I didn't mean from here.' Miss Pink turned, her tone placating. 'But someone has to be missing because there he is, what's left of him: up in Rastus Canyon. No doubt the police will know something.'

'We have to clear this mess,' Pearl exclaimed, picking up the saddle and dropping it on a huge chest. 'I guess you think Tammy's too young to be helping out as a maid but school's out for the whole summer and kids get bored, 'sides, she likes doing it and her mom doesn't mind. She won't lift a finger at home so if it keeps her out of mischief it's all to the good, isn't it?' Miss Pink, who was not above using such methods herself, knew that this was a smokescreen obscuring the subject of the missing man.

'She was only dressing up,' she said, smiling. 'So why did Kristen get upset?'

Pearl blinked and tried to reorientate herself. 'They're too close in age, so Kristen doesn't see it that way. It wasn't right to say

26

she looked like a—to say what she said, but she was shocked. Like you said. I mean, that dress was—' She stopped.

'Sexy?' Miss Pink was cool.

Pearl swooped on a saucepan and dropped it in the sink with a clatter. 'She's spoiled,' she said. 'And she probably sneaked out of her home without her mother seeing her. She's all right now; Kristen will take the frock away from her.'

'But why did she get so *cross*?'

'Why—' Pearl was running a tap, pouring a flood of liquid soap on dirty dishes. 'Girlish rivalry!' she announced with a kind of triumph. 'Tammy's pretty, Kristen's jealous.' Her glance at Miss Pink was uncertain as if she wasn't sure how this would be taken.

'Steamy place,' Miss Pink said.

'What! How—steamy?'

'Hot water. Would there be enough for me to have a shower?'

'Oh yes, yes. I should have offered.' She wiped her hands on a dish-cloth, her face suddenly relaxed and almost beautiful. And relieved, thought Miss Pink.

★　　　★　　　★

She telephoned her motel and took a shower and went to sit in the dim living-room. She was ensconced under a lamp with a carafe of wine at her elbow and a *National Geographic* on her lap when there was a gentle tap at the street door, a fluted 'May I come in?' and the screen opened to reveal a soft plump woman in pressed white slacks and a richly embroidered smock. Miss Pink's eyes dropped to the magazine open at a feature on Polynesia. The woman who stepped across the tiles with outstretched hand and a smile of welcome had the flat features and the grey braided hair of a matron from the Cook Islands.

'I'm Marge Dearing,' she said. 'I live across the street.' Pearl appeared in the doorway. 'Miss Pink must be the first English visitor for decades,' the newcomer said pleasantly, revealing the fact that the grapevine was working.

'Find yourself a glass.' Pearl indicated her floury hands. 'Let me finish the biscuits and I'll join you.'

'No hurry.' The woman moved to a sideboard and returned with a glass. 'You'll be company for her,' she said, as if Miss Pink were moving in for a protracted stay. 'We don't see many visitors in August, not till hunting starts.'

'Actually,' Miss Pink said, 'that ties in with my presence in a way. I'm staying at Palomares but I came on some old bones in a cliff dwelling. I have to show the police tomorrow.'

Marge blinked once and slowly; everything she did was deliberate. 'Bones,' she repeated.

'Human bones. Fresh. I mean, not old, as bones go. Three, four months old perhaps?' Miss Pink raised inquiring eyebrows.

The moon face was set. 'What makes you think they're human?'

'A rifle in the creek below and a hand clutching a branch, presumably as a weapon.'

'Then it wasn't an accident? He was beating off a bear, or a lion.'

'That must be it.'

'No one's reported missing,' came Pearl's voice from the kitchen. 'I mean, not a local. Wayne doesn't know of anyone.'

'Gregorio?' murmured Marge.

'He went back to Mexico.'

There was a pause. 'Who's Gregorio?' Miss Pink asked, making conversation.

There was no sound from the kitchen. Marge said coldly, 'He was a hired hand at Las Mesas—Avril Beck's place at the mouth of Badblood—'

'She knows Las Mesas.' Pearl appeared, wiping her hands on her jeans. 'She went up that way. How else would she get to Rastus?'

'He's a Mexican.' Marge spoke to Miss Pink but stared at her neighbour. 'Gregorio Ramirez. He left suddenly.'

There was another pause during which Pearl poured herself a glass of wine and Miss

29

Pink sipped thoughtfully, and sipped again.

'When Kristen comes back,' Pearl said, addressing Miss Pink, 'don't say anything about—you know—three months back? There was a tragedy in the family; her sister—'

'A beautiful girl.' Marge sighed heavily.

'She got into trouble,' Pearl said.

'A baby. Four months gone.' Marge looked across the street at her house which was bathed in evening sunshine. 'Poor Veronica.'

'They were very close,' Pearl told Miss Pink: 'Kristen and Veronica. And Ada Scott—the mother; she's never been the same since, virtually an invalid.'

'Had some sort of stroke,' Marge contributed.

'What happened to Veronica?' Miss Pink asked.

They were startled; they'd thought it was implicit. 'She put an end to herself,' Marge whispered.

'Threw herself in the river,' Pearl elaborated. 'Of course, it was in flood in May, not like now. You couldn't drown in the Rio Grande in August, not till it rains.'

'I see. And—the father—disappeared?'

'Oh no!' Pearl was astonished.

'She means the father of the baby,' Marge pointed out, and smiled indulgently. 'Gregorio disappeared but no one—*no one*

30

ever mentioned the two events in the same breath.'

'Not publicly,' Pearl corrected. 'But everyone knew, and the awful thing was—the worst thing, it was all awful—Veronica was, well, a little immature.'

'She was retarded,' Marge said. 'But so lovely. It was bound to happen, I guess. They couldn't watch her all the time. They tried, God knows, but even Clayton Scott couldn't be with her twenty-four hours of the day. That's her father: a very upright man, it broke his heart, made him fiercely protective of Kristen, and she's a girl won't have anyone protect her, give her orders; always was the wild one, independent—there she was: riding alone today up to the mesas, she's out of control, if her daddy was to know—'

'She can look after herself,' Pearl broke in roughly. 'She's a sensible girl.'

'I wouldn't say that exactly, dear.' They exchanged looks while Miss Pink stared somnolently at a picture of a boy on a donkey. 'You're very quiet,' Pearl told her.

'I was thinking that if they don't find the skull they'll never know who that is in Rastus Canyon.'

'How would the skull help?' Marge asked.

'His dentist could identify him from dental records.'

'Mexicans don't have dentists,' Pearl said,

31

and stopped short.

'They could tell from the rifle,' Marge said.

The silence stretched. 'It's a curious place to be poaching,' Miss Pink mused. 'Surely there's only one trail into the high country. How could he be certain no one would see him riding up the escarpment—and what happened to his horse? He'd need a horse to carry out the carcass.' No one responded to this. 'The map does show a trail up a canyon to the south,' she added diffidently.

'It goes up Scorpion Canyon from the Markow place,' Marge supplied.

'You can't get across Slickrock,' Pearl said. 'Rastus is north of Slickrock.' Marge smiled. Pearl's voice rose. 'I've ridden all over the mesas but there's no way you can get into Slickrock from either side; it's a box canyon.'

'There speaks the townie.' Marge held the other's eye. 'I've hunted the high country all my adult life. I came here as a young bride,' she told Miss Pink, 'a child-bride, you might say: sixteen'—there was a gleam in her eye—'and I was out hunting with Mr Dearing soon's I arrived. We were married in the fall. Mr Dearing taught me all I know about the back-country. Many's the time we shot our deer from the rim and he had to go down into Slickrock and butcher it and pack the meat out on his back while I stayed on

32

top with the horses.'

'Where'd he go down?' Pearl asked.

'The trail's there if you know where to look.' Marge nodded smugly and, having disposed of that argument, turned to Miss Pink. 'It can't have anything to do with the dead man because he'd no more have gone in past the Markow place than past Las Mesas. Like you said, he'd be seen. He had to go in from the top highway. If you're interested in hunting you must come and see Mr Dearing's heads: trophies, all of 'em. I got a barn out back with moose and a coupla old grizzlies and Lord knows how many lions and stuff.'

'She'll love that,' Pearl said coldly.

'It's not the heads,' Marge assured Miss Pink, 'but what they tell you about the hunter. Either Mr Dearing got his beast with the first shot or he followed up and dispatched it.'

'How long have you been on your own?' Miss Pink asked diplomatically.

The plump face sagged. 'Sometimes it seems only a week, other times I can't remember what he looked like.' Pearl stood up and went to the kitchen. Marge sighed. 'Six years, and here I'm still grieving. They say time heals all wounds but it gets worse. I cry a lot at night. He shouldn't have died, he was only seventy. I blame myself.'

'Why is that?'

'Why—' Marge looked surprised. 'Maybe I fed him wrong? It was bleeding into the brain, they said his arteries was coated with fat; there was a powerful build-up of blood and it leaked out in the brain. Well, I mean: all that fat, men love their steaks and fries, don't they? Then there was the bourbon.'

'You can't blame yourself.'

'I did what I could.' A tear fell and glinted on the chubby wrist. 'I tried all kinds of tricks with his feed: sunflower oil and oleo, and I'd invent commissions where he had to take a horse out, like find me some herb or shoot me a squirrel—anything to make him take gentle exercise because he carried a lot of weight, did Mr Dearing, otherwise if I didn't force him out he'd be sat all day on the back porch there, drinking and smoking and watching television. And what does he do after his evening stroll but come home across the patio and drop dead at my feet.'

'Mercifully quick.'

'It shouldn't never have happened. He had another ten years of life in him if he'd been more careful.'

'We can't live with what might have happened.'

'Ah, but it never happened to you. Or maybe it did?'

'Few people get to our age without some kind of bereavement.'

Marge stared at the other's hands. 'You

were married?'

Miss Pink looked up. Pearl was back, grinning, her hands on her hips. 'I'd make a guess,' she said lightly, 'that this lady never suffered for want of gentleman friends. Now we're going to have a venison casserole. You'll stay and eat with us, Marge?'

'No, my dear; I have to walk Pedro.'

'You be sure and take a flashlight.'

'I promise you; I don't want Pedro bit.'

Pearl watched her cross the street and shook her head in exasperation. 'She's getting so careless in her old age.' She shot an apologetic glance at the visitor. 'Not that she's really old, it's just she's aged so much since Mr Dearing—there, now she's got me doing it—since Sam's death. No one around here would go out in the dark without a flashlight, even when there's a moon. You know what she did? Walked her dog along the Markow road with no light and the moon not up yet—and there was a diamondback in the dust. Only the dog warned her. Two nights later it was there again, Ira Markow ran over it. That snake was over six foot: seventy-four inches, can you believe that? I tell you, Marge Dearing walks her dog without a flashlight, she's got a death wish.'

'She was very attached to her husband.'

'You can say that again. Well, married going on fifty years, probably never known another man, what do you expect? And they

35

had no children, just the two of them on their own: unhealthy, I call it.'

'What did he do, I mean for a living?'

Pearl shrugged. 'A bit of ranching, and hiring himself out to the big ranchers: seasonal work. He got by—and he had the lease of some old mines: one-man shows, you know the kind of thing? Guys dig out a few ounces of silver, gold even sometimes: enough to keep them in tobacco and bourbon. Some men go fishing but when Sam wanted to get away from it all he went back in the canyons and shovelled dirt. It's a hobby; sometimes one of these old miners will be found dead in his shack in the hills, but no one's sorry for them, it was how they wanted to go. Never saw the point of it myself; women don't. Marge put a stop to it, of course, but it didn't do any good. He just drank more. The heart went out of him.' Her tone changed. 'Now you come and sit down and I'll bring the food; you must be starving after your hike, and we got a long day ahead of us tomorrow.'

They had finished the casserole by the time Kristen returned with the pick-up. Entering the living-room as if it were in her own home, she collapsed in an easy chair and eyed the women. 'Miss Pink's famous,' Pearl told her. 'She writes books and stories for magazines, and she's a lawyer—'

'A retired magistrate,' Miss Pink

corrected. Kristen stared.

'And she's got a house on a cliff above the ocean in Cornwall,' Pearl enthused, 'and a housekeeper to cook and look after her; isn't that neat?'

'Cornwall is something like Big Sur,' Miss Pink explained.

'What's Big Sur?' Kristen asked.

'This girl's never been further than El Paso and Santa Fe—'

'I have so! We go to Denver for Christmas shopping.' Her voice dropped sharply.

'I'm sorry, sweetie. Did you see Ira?'

'Of course I did. Tammy's on her way.'

'It's getting dark. It's too late to take the horses out but that's fine; they'll have plenty of exercise tomorrow. Will Tammy be all right?'

'It's not quite dark and she was right behind me. No one's going to be curled up in the dirt waiting; I frightened 'em off, didn't I?'

'Oh, you mean rattlesnakes!' Miss Pink smiled at her own obtuseness. No one else smiled. They were intent on something else, their heads raised, and then she heard what they had heard already, and she marvelled at their hearing: the soft thud of hoofs on earth, a click of iron against stone. Kristen pulled herself out of her chair.

'Put the saddle in the wash-house,' Pearl told her.

When the screen door closed Miss Pink said quietly: 'It's comforting to know that places exist where children can be out on their own in the dark—although, of course, people are still at risk from wild animals.'

'Not really. Even kids are safe from rattlers providing they're careful. You have to know that yourself; you've done a lot of travelling in the States.'

'It's like everything else, I suppose: the survivors have learned to be careful. How about yourself? Were you brought up in the back-country?'

'For what are known as the formative years.' Miss Pink was struck, not only by the formality but the hostility in the tone. 'I like to think I'm from San Jose,' Pearl went on: 'in California. I had a beautician's business, but I had this dream of a little place in the country and horses. I love riding. I was put on the back of a horse before I could walk.' She looked away and her voice was distant. 'I was raised on a ranch at the head of the San Joaquin Valley but I left there when I was younger than Kristen and went to the big city.'

'You didn't want to go back there when you retired?'

'No way.' Pearl's eyes were flat. 'They were all dead; there was nothing left. Who wants to remember their childhood?' She brightened. 'And when I'd got enough cash together to retire I realised California ranches cost a fortune, and then someone told me about New Mexico. These old adobes sell for a quarter the price of a place in the Sierra foothills.'

'It must have been a change: San Jose to the valley of the Rio Grande.'

'I love it. I was sick of people and traffic and the rat-race and I'm allergic to smog. Aren't we all? You got room to breathe here, you got *air* to breathe, not fumes. You have to feel the same way; why do you go hiking on the mesas?'

Before Miss Pink could respond the two girls came in, Tammy now in jeans and a shirt. They stood in the doorway, watching her.

'Don't stand there,' Pearl chided. 'Help me clear the table and we'll have some dessert. Did you two eat yet?'

'We had supper.' Tammy moved to collect the plates.

When they were settled with pie and ice-cream Pearl returned to the subject, addressing Miss Pink: 'I was asking, what attracted you to the mesas in the first place?'

'I'm a free agent: just drifting and looking for material for a book'—her eyes gleamed—'and for adventures. Angel's Roost was marked on the Forest map and I liked the name, and I saw you could reach it by way of a trail from Las Mesas.'

'You climbed Angel's Roost!' Tammy was astonished.

'Of course. That's how I found the Indian ruin. I wasn't wandering about up there without a purpose. What did you think I was doing?'

'I'd assumed that looking for ruins was your hobby,' Pearl said.

'No, it was the mountain that was my objective; finding the ruin was pure chance.'

Kristen said: 'I didn't know there was a trail up Angel's Roost. Not that I would know; I'm not a hiker.'

'You ride on the mesas,' Tammy pointed out. 'Horses cover more ground than hikers do.'

'The trail goes up Badblood Wash to the divide,' Miss Pink said, 'then it turns left and approaches Angel's Roost from the north.'

They looked bewildered. 'So how come you were in Rastus Canyon?' Kristen asked. 'Did you see the ruin from the top of the mountain?'

'To tell you the truth, I saw nothing from the top. It was very warm and as soon as I'd eaten my lunch I went to sleep in the shade. When I woke up and looked at the map I saw that I might save myself some miles on the way down if I could get into the head of Rastus. That's how I came on the ruin.'

'I don't believe it.' Pearl was amazed. 'You don't know the country, you were all alone, no one knew where you were; suppose you'd sprained your ankle.'

'I'm careful. You ride up there. Kristen rides on the mesas.' She smiled to show no criticism was intended.

'I was up Badblood today,' Kristen said. 'I didn't see you.'

'Ah, I saw fresh horse tracks. I guessed someone was around.'

'We all ride up there,' Kristen said, 'Pearl and me, and Fletcher Lloyd.'

'He's the hand at Las Mesas,' Pearl put in. 'Avril Beck only has one man now ...' She trailed off, then came back with a rush: 'Avril doesn't ride so Fletcher has to do everything. You have to meet Avril—she's English, did I tell you? She's American now, of course; she married Herb Beck, then he died. This is a village of spinsters and widows.'

There was one of those odd silences until Kristen observed airily, 'So you saw no one all day?' and Miss Pink, accepting it as a question, reassured her. 'No one. Not even in the distance.' If the girl maintained that she went no further than Badblood Wash, it was no business of a visitor to divulge the fact that she'd been seen climbing out of Slickrock.

CHAPTER THREE

At six o'clock in the morning Pearl's kitchen was unoccupied but there were mugs on the table and an enamel pot on the stove. Miss Pink poured herself coffee and stepped outside. The light in the patio was cold and grey but beyond the corral and the wooded creek the sky was flushed with the approach of sunrise. She became aware of movement and realised that the horses were tied to the rail of the corral. Carrying her mug she crossed the patio.

'Good morning. Can I do anything?'

'Morning,' came Pearl's voice from the huddle of solid backs. 'Isn't it lovely and cool? I'm about finished here, thanks.' A saddle was swung high and settled on a blanket. 'I'll be in directly and we'll pick up something to eat. This must be Wayne now.' Miss Pink hadn't heard an engine but she did hear a door close. A bear-like shape ambled round the corner of the house and started for the back door. 'Go in and introduce yourself,' Pearl said. 'I'm right behind you.'

By the time she reached the kitchen the deputy had helped himself to coffee and was spooning sugar into the mug. He was, as Pearl had warned, a very large fellow and, where he had sounded unhappy last night on the telephone, this morning he looked positively morose.

'I'm not at my best at six a.m., ma'am,' he confessed when they had introduced themselves. 'And August's not the ideal time to be riding in them canyons.' He had removed his cap and his bald head shone with moisture. 'It's my day off,' he explained, indicating his jeans and check shirt, mopping his forehead with a handkerchief that was none too clean. He had a clown's face with heavy brows, a blobby nose and a wide mouth—a mobile face that would no doubt change with his mood. At that moment he looked mournful but there were laughter wrinkles at the corners of his eyes and those eyes, framed in fat, were shrewd.

'You look like death,' Pearl said, entering the kitchen. 'I got a good horse for you, he's built like an elephant. I'm coming too so I'll look after you, OK?'

'I don't mind who comes as long as we don't have any problems, any extra problems I mean besides the heat. Are you sure you can find the place again, ma'am?'

'We can't go wrong,' Miss Pink assured him. 'Rastus is the next canyon to Badblood Wash.'

Spikol sighed and lowered his bulk into a chair. 'We can't hang around,' Pearl said

43

quickly. 'The sun's coming up; we should have been on the road half an hour ago. We'll eat on the way.'

They collected canteens and bags of muffins and plodded out to the corral. Miss Pink was amused to see that, far from locking her house, Pearl didn't even close the door, merely latching the screen with a hook. 'Stop the thieves getting in,' she explained, noting her guest's interest, 'like skunks and stuff.'

The sun was streaming through the cottonwoods now, showing three horses at the rail: a blue roan, a chestnut (a sorrel in the West), and Miss Pink's mount: a large dark bay with bulging muscles and a phlegmatic eye. In view of that eye she relaxed, mounted, and followed the others out onto the Las Mesas road, the bay as sedate as an old cow.

Above the village the escarpment was without shadows, every crevice and gully naked in the light: a tiger wall of tawny rock and long black stripes where water poured over the lip in the rainy season.

'You brought slickers,' Miss Pink observed, seeing that they each had a yellow roll behind the saddle. 'Are you expecting rain?'

'Any day now,' Pearl said cheerfully. 'August is the time for storms.'

'We could do with it.' Spikol squinted

towards the river. 'I never seen the water so low.'

'There's someone ahead of us,' Pearl said. There were hoofprints in the dust.

'Early for people to be riding.' Spikol was casual. 'Only one way too. Is he bound for Las Mesas or the rim?'

It was Las Mesas. From the road they could see a saddled horse tied to the fence outside the ranch house. 'That's Clayton Scott's.' Pearl smiled slyly. 'Funny time to come calling.'

'I have to speak to Mrs Beck; it's her land.' Spikol turned in under the crossbar and the others followed. At their approach two people emerged from the house: a well-built man and a plump woman in her forties.

'Good morning you guys!' Miss Pink's eyebrows rose fractionally at the woman's tone which was so high as to sound false. 'We have to go to Las Cruces and take delivery of a new pick-up,' she went on, opening the gate, addressing Pearl. 'Clayton's coming with you.'

Pearl nodded casually and introduced Miss Pink. 'A compatriot of yours,' she said. 'She writes books—and she knows the West better than I do.'

'Pleased to meet you.' Miss Pink murmured a polite response as she tried to place the accent: Texas on a base of urban Sussex? Avril Beck had gone native with a vengeance, and was aiming at an image that was over twenty years too young. She had blue bows in her yellow hair, pink lipstick and too much mascara. She was wearing a frilled blouse, tight Levis and tooled boots. Her cheeks were flushed; she was obviously ill at ease. 'We must get together at a more convenient time,' she said, turning to the deputy before she'd finished, conveying the impression that Miss Pink was of minor importance. 'I should really have someone along with you, Wayne, seeing as it's my property, so I asked Mr Scott if he'd represent me—my interests. That's in order—I mean, there's no objection—' It hung between statement and question.

'It's your land, ma'am, you can send who you like to watch over your interests.' Spikol eyed her companion who had unfastened his horse and mounted. Clayton Scott exchanged a nod with Miss Pink in lieu of introduction. He had an arresting face, what she thought of as a frontier face: a well-shaped mouth, a strong nose and pale eyes that looked as if they were accustomed to far horizons. Under the wide hat brim she guessed there would be a high forehead. She tried to recall what he did for a living: it was most likely ranching; his tack and his clothes were worn but serviceable.

'Don't you have time for coffee?' Avril asked, in the tone of one anxious to be on the

46

road herself.

'Another time,' Pearl said. As far as social graces were concerned, Spikol was leaving them to her. 'It's going to be a hot day for the horses,' she pointed out. 'All right for you'—as a pick-up came round the corner of a barn—'you'll have air-conditioning all day.'

A gangling, bearded fellow in bleached jeans climbed out of the truck and stared at them, his arms hanging loose. 'I'm about ready, Fletcher,' Avril told him, not introducing anyone. 'Do we have plenty of water for the truck?'

'Enough.' The group appeared to fascinate him. He ignored Miss Pink but regarded the others with something that was more than surprise, more like anger; he didn't look like a comfortable man to have around. Spikol watched him impassively. It was Miss Pink who broke an awkward silence, and with her peculiar brand of chattiness. 'It was quite a shock,' she observed, 'coming on human remains when one least expected it; not that there is any time when one might expect it, unless of course, one knows that a person is missing?'

Pearl giggled nervously. The others registered various degrees of amazement. Fletcher Lloyd said quickly: 'No one's missing.'

'As if—' Avril began heatedly, then

47

moderated her tone: 'As if we wouldn't know. He had to be from—well, some distance away. There's no one local missing, is there?' She looked from Pearl to Spikol.

'No one's been reported,' the deputy said. 'Could be some guy disappeared and the wife hasn't reported it.'

'But she would! Oh, you mean a husband may be—there may be another woman.'

'Actually, ma'am'—he drew it out and Miss Pink stiffened—'I was thinking more in terms of the wife being responsible for his disappearance.' The mobile mouth turned up and the laughter wrinkles deepened.

Clayton Scott said weightily, 'It's not a subject to joke about, particularly with ladies present,' and Miss Pink remembered that Avril was a widow. Evidently Spikol remembered too. 'Sorry ladies, it's the policeman's mind: always suspicious.' The suddenly bland eyes met those of Miss Pink and conveyed nothing personal but she felt a charge, as if a connection had been made. Someone *is* missing, she thought, and guessed that sooner or later she would learn his identity, not that it had anything to do with her any more than the sighting of Kristen Scott climbing out of Slickrock Canyon, she was merely intrigued by these people's behaviour.

They left the ranch and took the trail towards the escarpment, riding in pairs, Miss

Pink with Scott. He opened the conversation. 'How did you come to be in Rastus?' he asked curiously, and once again she recounted how she had chosen to try a short-cut on the descent from Angel's Roost, and he displayed the familiar astonishment laced with criticism that a foreigner—and an elderly woman at that—should have the temerity to enter the wilderness, let alone the ability to find her way around in it.

'You need to get high,' she told him. 'Once you have the structure of the area straight, you shouldn't go wrong. These canyons and mesas run north-west to south-east. It's a simple pattern. Of course,' she smiled, 'it doesn't take into account the terrain, but apart from the rim'—she glanced at the escarpment ahead—'there's nothing you can't retreat from, or circumvent. The timber isn't dense and you can always scramble round the crags; they don't go on for great distances.' Excluding Slickrock, she qualified, but to herself; he had the hard look of a man who doesn't relinquish an attitude easily, a man who thought women should know their place.

'You ran into my daughter,' he said.

Her thighs tightened and the bay horse stumbled. 'Pick your feet up,' she snapped, playing for time. And: 'Excuse me'—pushing the bay in front. They had reached the first rise and the trail narrowed. 'That's right,' she called back, 'Kristen and Tammy were over at Pearl's last night.'

There was no response from the rear and she gave her attention to the trail, which seemed much more exposed when viewed from the back of a horse. On foot the walker sees his boots and tracks in the dust, the occasional lizard on a stone. Looking down from a point some eight feet above ground level there was nothing to be seen between her foot and a drop that increased with every stride. She slackened her reins, allowing the bay to see where he was going.

'You've done this before,' Scott said as she rounded the first elbow.

'A little, but he's a steady horse.' With a most peculiar gait, she might have added; she was going to be saddle-sore after this ride.

Halfway up the slope the party stopped for a blow; the horses were big, powerful animals but the roan was labouring under Spikol. Pearl gave them time to calm down a fraction and then chivvied them upwards. People and horses were subdued. The sun was hot on wet backs and the only sound was the slap of hoofs on baked earth and the creak of leather. As they plodded towards the rimrock a bald eagle drifted by, its head as brilliant as new white paint, then they felt the thermal that had lifted the bird from the valley: a warm draught of air on the skin.

The horses quickened their pace and the mood of the caravan changed as the angle eased and they stepped out along the level path that in a few yards brought them to the sand of Badblood Wash.

*   *   *

On Midnight Mesa Spikol stopped and addressed Scott. 'Who's been riding here? I seen no cows since Badblood.' He didn't miss much; on that ground hoofmarks were few and far between.

'I ride on the mesas,' Pearl told him. 'Kristen does.' She glanced at Scott. 'We all do; it's too hot to ride down below in the summer time.'

'You shouldn't come up here on your own,' Scott told her.

'I don't—usually. Often we're all together: Kristen and Tammy and me.' Her eyes gleamed. 'The men come alone. Like Fletcher.'

'Avril Beck will know where he's at. I don't know where Kristen is. She didn't tell me she rides up here.'

'Young girls need their own space, they can't be tied to their parents all their lives. Anyways, the kids are safe with me; I know where I'm at.'

Miss Pink eased her thighs gingerly, longing to dismount. Spikol stared glumly at

51

the bright gravel between the junipers. The horses drooped with heavy heads.

'You saw her yesterday?' Scott asked of Miss Pink. For the second time. He couldn't leave it alone.

'Why, yes.' She blinked and looked to Pearl for help. Pearl said: 'He's talking about up here.'

'Oh. No. I met her at your place.'

'You saw a horse here?' Scott pressed.

'Did I? There were cows in Badblood, I remember, but a horse? No.'

'She was riding yesterday.' He was tight-lipped. 'In the full heat of the sun. That's no way to treat a horse 'less you have to.'

'I don't think what your kid was doing yesterday had anything to do with a guy died months ago,' Spikol said. He took up his reins and sighed. 'So if you'll lead on, ma'am, we'll try to find these remains we're supposed to be looking for.'

Thus directed Miss Pink went ahead, pushing steadily up the mesa, seeing Angel's Roost half-left, the big red cliff showing above the tops of pinyons on the right, and when she calculated that they were past the place where Kristen tethered her horse she diverged sideways until the ground started to drop away into Rastus Canyon. She stopped and the others ranged alongside.

'I'm not going down there,' Pearl said.

'It's all right on foot.' Miss Pink implied that this was the way she'd come out of the canyon herself.

'We'll leave the horses,' Spikol said, and climbed down.

Miss Pink was comfortable in her walking boots but the others had trouble in their high heels and smooth soles, so much so that she felt guilty as Spikol crashed and slithered down the unstable talus and she thought about having to carry him out if he broke a leg. But he reached the creek without injury—although he must be badly bruised—and as he scrambled up the rocks the others held back, as if by rescinding the lead they acknowledged that they had moved into his territory.

They came to the confluence of the two streams. Nothing had changed. There was the rocky point, the talus slope and the ruin under its massive rock ceiling.

'Did you know it was here?' Pearl asked Scott.

'I had no idea.' He shook his head in wonder. 'Herb Beck never mentioned it to me, but then they're everywhere, these old cliff dwellings. Maybe he knew it was here and didn't think nothing to it.'

Spikol, advancing, had seen the rifle. The others stepped forward while Miss Pink studied the overhang, then they all moved slowly up the flaky scree to stop at the rib shaft curved round the prickly pear. 'Well, well,' Spikol breathed, and shook his head. They climbed a little further to the pitiful remains of the spine. No one spoke but Miss Pink caught Pearl's sharp look of inquiry directed at the deputy. His face was wooden. No one suggested that the bones might be those of a deer.

They came to the doorway of the ruin and the others stood aside for Spikol to enter. Pearl turned to Miss Pink. 'I'd have been terrified to go in there! How could you?'

'I shouted, and I was carrying a rock. By the time I reached this spot I was virtually certain that there wasn't even a snake inside.'

'My God!' She looked down the sun-drenched canyon and shuddered. 'Poor guy; it must have been horrifying at night.'

Spikol squeezed out of the doorway, the old boot in one hand, the branch in the other. Pearl's breath hissed between her teeth. 'I didn't believe you,' he told Miss Pink. 'But I guess you're right.' He held out the branch and they stared at the skeletal fingers. 'He wasn't killed by the fall,' he said.

'Unless—' Pearl began, to be interrupted by Scott: 'He coulda been; he coulda grabbed a branch as he felt himself start to slip, he coulda been holding the branch to look over the edge, and it broke.'

Spikol glanced up but the overhang blocked the view. 'Could be. We'll look.'

'Who was he?' Pearl asked, and it wasn't rhetorical; she was looking at Spikol.

'How many times—' He didn't trouble to finish. 'They'll have records in Santa Fe,' he conceded. 'But if he's from out of state, and poaching—he had to be poaching, these bones ain't been here since hunting season—then there'd be no record of him going missing—'

'But if a woman didn't know her husband was poaching—' Pearl began hotly, and stopped as Spikol looked at her. 'Didn't know?' he repeated sceptically. 'Wives know everything.' He transferred his attention to the boot. 'This is old; it's ancient. Was it old when he died, or did it get like this since?'

'Not under cover,' Miss Pink said. 'And animals haven't been tearing at it to try to get the foot out. He took it off before he died. People do that,' she added in the face of their surprise: 'take off all their clothes before the end.'

'So it was already old before he died.' Pearl spoke as if prompted, staring at Miss Pink. 'No one wears boots as old as that. He couldn't have walked in them, for Heavens' sakes! So he rode. So where's his horse?'

'A horse came down without a rider?' Spikol made a question of it. 'But someone surely would have reported *that*.'

'Not if he kept the horse and tack for himself and said nothing about it,' Pearl

55

pointed out. 'A poor person—like a Mexican.'

'Where's the trailer?' Spikol mused. 'A guy comes in from out of state, he don't ride here; he has to bring the horse in a trailer.' He looked down the slope. 'I guess we better try and find the rest of him. We don't have much to go on here '

They separated: Pearl and Scott searching the bed of the stream on the far side of the rocky point, Spikol and Miss Pink clambering up the gorge under the cliff.

'What are we doing?' Miss Pink asked when they stopped for breath. 'Looking for the skull is hopeless; the animal that carried it off could have crushed it anyway. And what with packrats and coyotes you can't expect to find clothing.'

'I can't go back and report that I didn't look at all. And maybe we'll find something by accident.' But his movements had an air of method about them and he was doing what she might have done herself but which now she realised was illogical, except from the point of view of elimination. Looking back at the profile of the cliff she confirmed that it was indeed close to a hundred feet high: convex at the top, then vertical as far as the overhang.

'If he'd come off that,' she said, 'he'd have been too badly injured to crawl up the slope into the ruin.'

'You reckon? Are you a doctor?'

'No, but I've seen the results of a lot of falls. Look at the landing, man!'

The emphasis forced him to study the boulders. 'You're right,' he said at length. 'He'd have been killed.' He looked at the rocky point and its twenty-foot walls. 'And yet that don't seem high enough.'

'It depends on the fall. With the sole flapping on his boot he could have caught his foot in a crack on the edge and landed awkwardly, probably breaking his leg.'

'There are no trees—neither on the big cliff nor on the point.'

'Trees?'

'For him to have grabbed a branch as he fell.'

'Oh, that. The branch could be driftwood he picked up in the stream bed. That's odd.'

'What's that, ma'am?'

'Why didn't he take his rifle into the ruin with him? He needed that for defence against animals. Well, he could have been concussed'—she was speaking her thoughts aloud—'not blinded by blood because he saw the ruin.' Her glasses flashed as she turned to him. 'Is it loaded?'

'No.'

They stared at each other: fat man and elderly woman suddenly on the same wavelength. 'Where are the shells?' she asked.

'He would have fired off all his ammo to attract attention? Yes, so where are the shells?'

'Or—he was carrying the rifle unloaded—like a very correct sportsman—but this is a *poacher*. However—hypothesis: it was unloaded when he fell or otherwise came to grief; in which case, where is his ammunition now? How would a poacher carry bullets? In his pocket or on a belt?'

'Either way the ammo's missing.'

'Now that *is* curious.' She stopped, embarrassed, and shot him a look of apology.

'Let's have a look at that point of rock.' He was addressing her as an equal; he didn't mind her expressing her opinion.

They had climbed to a higher level and they walked down to the point slowly, separating and studying the ground. There were no prints visible because they were back on the bedrock and it was only lightly scattered with gravel; there wasn't even a sign of Miss Pink's presence here yesterday. Arrived at the point they walked round its edge, paying particular attention to the spot immediately above the rifle, which Spikol had replaced in its original position. Pearl and Scott approached; they had found nothing that could possibly relate to the remains in the ruin. The party retreated to the shade and sat down. No one mentioned lunch, they had left the food and the canteens in the saddle-bags.

'We can't do any more here,' Spikol said, summing up. 'We'll take down what we found and that's it. Some day a mother, some relative, will report a guy missing, but there won't be no way of telling if this is him. No way. Hundreds of people go missing every year, probably dozens of bodies are found: drifters, junkies, wetbacks, you name it. No one claims 'em.'

'Of course he was poaching,' Scott said, as if he'd suddenly been convinced. 'This is a perfect look-out; you can see right down the canyon. He'd have been watching for the deer coming to drink.'

'He could have shot himself,' Pearl said. 'Accidentally, I mean. Did you think of that? And the way he got here: he came in from the top road.'

Everyone looked in the direction of the highway. 'How far is it exactly?' Spikol asked.

Pearl said, 'I never rode it, there's no trail. But it's not big close timber like in the Rockies. You wouldn't have much trouble.'

'It's over a mile,' Scott said. 'Mile and a half. He could have done it without a horse, easy: pack the meat out on his back.'

'Then there'd have to be a truck up there, on the highway,' Spikol said. 'It'll be well hidden, but we'll find it if it's there.'

'Not if there was two of them,' Scott

pointed out.

'Ah.' Spikol's eyes came round slowly. 'Now you're putting a different slant on it.'

'They could have quarrelled,' Pearl put in cheerfully, and stopped. No one responded; they were all considering it.

Spikol collected the remains in a plastic bag but he had to carry the branch separately. Scott took the bag from him as they climbed out of the canyon. When they reached the horses no one felt like eating but everyone drank from the canteens, and then Miss Pink announced that she would walk down. Pearl admitted that the bay was a rough ride but that was all right, she said, Miss Pink should ride the sorrel. Miss Pink demurred, urging her to go ahead, leading the bay, she would follow at her own pace. 'No way,' Pearl said, 'I'm not leaving you alone up here, not after what we found today.' At this point Spikol swung himself into the saddle. 'I'll leave you to it,' he said with finality and, to Miss Pink: 'You call me this evening, ma'am, tell me where you're at; we're going to need a statement some time.'

Scott said, 'You going to stay up here?' The women looked blank. 'It's too hot for the horses,' he said, with a touch of bluster. Miss Pink glanced at Pearl who smiled thinly. 'You telling me to come down with you, Clayton?'

'I'm just saying you don't realise how hard

this dry heat is on an animal—'

'I'll see you,' Spikol said loudly, and moved away.

Pearl tightened her cinch with a jerk. 'What we'll do, Clayton,' she said with exaggerated concern, 'is we'll put my horses in the shade where there's a breeze and we'll ride home after the sun's lost some of its strength. We can't come to much harm, the two of us together.'

He gave a grim nod and, mounting, trotted after Spikol.

'Shouldn't trot in this heat,' Pearl mocked. 'Wants to have his hand in everything, that guy. Hell, no wonder Kristen —Ah, forget it! Come on, if you insist on staying up here, let's get over to Slickrock, find us a breath of fresh air. Sorry, you're sore; you want to ride this one?'

'I'm all right.' Defeated in her attempt to be left alone, Miss Pink mounted and followed her companion across the mesa to the rim of Slickrock Canyon where, if there was no breeze, there was space, and an illusion of cool shade imparted by the green canopy below. They tied the horses in a kind of cave formed by a grove of junipers and moved away from the flies to eat lunch under a pinyon. They were thoughtful, even subdued, until Miss Pink, closing her sandwich box and adjusting her back against the tree, returned to the subject of the

Scotts. 'He was pumping me,' she murmured: 'asking me if I'd seen Kristen yesterday.'

'Oh, Clayton! Know what I think?' Pearl sounded sleepy. 'He dreads a repeat, a re-run of Veronica's trouble, what happened to her. Why can't he see Kristen's different, apart from being well, you know: normal? Oh, she'll probably get pregnant, but throw herself in the river? Never. She'd go ahead and have the baby, thumb her nose at her father.'

'How was it she couldn't persuade Veronica to do that: have the baby? You said the sisters were close.'

Pearl was silent for so long that Miss Pink looked to see if she'd fallen asleep but she was staring down the canyon towards the valley, frowning. Aware of the other's scrutiny she said, 'Curious you should ask that question. She never mentioned the baby, and I didn't ask. I don't talk about Veronica to Kristen. She took it hard and that could be the reason: she didn't know about the baby until after Veronica drowned. It didn't show, no one knew; Veronica wore skirts, peasant style, you'd never notice. But probably Kristen thinks she ought to have known, and if she had she'd have done something about it, like you said: persuaded Veronica to go away maybe, have it adopted. Veronica wouldn't have needed any persuading either—that's the worst of it; she was a docile person—and so beautiful. Did I say how lovely she was? Like a Madonna, but thin. Too thin. The bastard!'

'You mean the hired hand. Romero, was it?'

'Gregorio Ramirez. He's a dishy devil; you know the type: more Spanish blood than Indian, slim with small hands and feet, dressed in people's cast-offs and he looked terrific in them: old straw hat, red shirt, torn jeans, boots—coming apart—boots coming—apart.' They stared at each other, then Pearl relaxed and laughed. 'No way. He'd never have dared come back. Not after what happened.'

'How long after Veronica's death did he leave?'

'Shortly after they found the body, a few days, I think. Avril was visiting with friends in Santa Fe, and Fletcher had gone fishing in Colorado. Greg was left alone at Las Mesas to do the chores—they've got a few steers they're fattening and they have to be fed twice a day, and then I guess he was supposed to go up to Badblood to make sure the cows were all right ... When Avril came back the steers were bawling their heads off and Greg was gone. So was a diamond ring she'd left in a drawer of her night table.'

'He'd taken his clothes?'

'What he possessed, yes.'

63

'He didn't own a horse or a pick-up?'

'He didn't own a saddle! Avril won't admit it but he had to be illegal, poor as he was. She'd be paying him starvation wages. She reported the theft of her ring to Wayne but she won't see that again; it'll have been sold in Mexico long ago, or given to a woman. It's not important beside what happened to Veronica.' She gave a twisted smile. 'No, he wouldn't come back; Kristen would kill him.'

A hummingbird hovered for a moment before an Indian paintbrush, its throat more vivid than the flower, then with a flick and a trill it vanished against the glitter of the cottonwoods. Miss Pink said, 'So her father thinks Kristen comes up here to meet a man.'

'Gossip.' Miss Pink waited. 'Fact, actually,' Pearl admitted. 'No real harm in you knowing—everyone else does—including Clayton.'

'And the man comes from the Markow ranch.'

'Tammy talked? No, you just put it together: if she comes up this side of Slickrock then you guessed he comes from the other side—when Ira Markow thinks the guy's putting out salt for the cows, or whatever. That's right, he's one of the Markow hands: Jay Gafford, thirty-seven, the dangerous age and as sexy as they come.

Wouldn't you believe it: the two Scott girls get the dishiest men in the county—and look how it served them, well, Veronica anyway, poor kid. You can imagine what Clayton Scott thinks of Jay—and there's no way he can stop it.'

'Has he tried?'

Pearl opened her mouth, checked, and started again. 'I was going to say: of course he has—because I can't imagine him not trying every which way to stop it; he hates Jay Gafford, and small wonder—but then Kristen never said her father had taken any kind of action. What could do anyway? Lock her in her room, sell her horse? He hasn't. And he hasn't laid a finger on her since she grew up. That surprises you? All the kids out in the boondocks know what their daddy's belt felt like when they were little—and that goes for where I come from too.' Pearl's eyes were sombre in the shade of the pinyon. She went on coldly, 'Clayton didn't do anything drastic to put a stop to it but I guess he had plenty to say.'

'What about Kristen's mother?'

'Poor Ada. She wouldn't worry. She's an invalid, you see: a lovely lady, so kind and gentle; and she adores her girls—adored, I should say. Veronica's death broke her in little pieces. I think Kristen feels as much for her mother as for her sister. After all, Veronica's suffering is over. Where are you going?'

'Just stretching my legs; they're seizing up.'

'Don't go far, and keep away from the edge.'

She moved along the lip of the canyon looking for the natural line that she knew must be there, and that she suspected was unmarked by cairns or even ducks. She discovered it by dint of peering over the crumbling rim until she could see ledges below. Looking back she saw that she was unobserved; Pearl was lying on her back, her hat over her face.

The top of the route was a kind of rock staircase on the wall and its start could be identified by a group of alligator junipers close to the edge. Now she realised that there could well be ruins in this canyon: unrecorded, perhaps as yet unseen by white men. It was an added inducement for exploration. She sat down to watch for birds.

Pearl was packing the saddle-bags when she returned. 'I insist we change horses,' she said. 'It's worse going down.'

'I can walk, and lead the bay.'

'No. It was my fault for putting you on that old mule; I'm going to sell him—heh, watch it, you guys—' Back in the junipers there was a sudden commotion. Pearl had leapt to her feet. 'Oh, it's you, Michael.'

'Michael who?' murmured Miss Pink,

66

glimpsing the figure of a man on foot and wearing a white cotton hat.

'Vosker. You'll like him: the retired neighbourhood professor.'

'What's *he* doing up here on his own?' She regarded the newcomer with resentment. He was thin and he carried a heavy pair of binoculars and a small haversack. She had an impression of the Middle East: dark eyes and a bony nose but a generous mouth that softened what might otherwise have been a predatory face. He had been, still was, handsome, but age showed in the folds of his throat and his finicky progress through the prickly pear. He acknowledged the introduction in a pleasant cultivated accent.

'Did you see anything?' Pearl asked. 'There was a hummer here with a red throat.'

'That could be a broad-tail. Are you birding?' Miss Pink's binoculars were round her neck.

'I'm no expert. And I don't expect to see much in the middle of the day.'

'There's always something to see. There was a whipsnake where I crossed Rastus Canyon.'

'Did you meet Wayne and Clayton?' Pearl asked.

'Yes. You must have been surprised, ma'am, to climb up to a cliff dwelling and find human bones.'

She nodded, thinking that surprise was something of an understatement. Pearl said, 'What do you think, Michael? Michael is an anthropologist,' she explained.

'What connection—Ah, think about what, Pearl?'

'Why, how he died. Accident, suicide or—no, that's wild. What kind of accident: was it the usual kind of carelessness like shooting himself with his own rifle when he slipped, or he fell and broke a leg, or d'you think he got lost in the canyons?'

'What makes you dismiss murder?'

'What! Hell, that's way over the top.'

'It's the formula: accident, suicide or murder; you were about to say that yourself.'

'My big mouth. Come *on*, Michael.'

'If it was Greg Ramirez—'

'*Michael*!'

'Did Spikol suggest that?' Miss Pink asked.

'No. What he did say was that no one was missing and I pointed out that Greg was. This was a Mexican hand working for one of the ranchers.'

'She knows. It's nothing to do with Greg. He went home.'

'How do we know that? And the boot could be his. Spikol showed me, see if I recognised it. I'm surprised you didn't think of it yourself. No one else we know has boots that old.'

68

'But it's not someone we know!' Her tone changed. 'We did think of it, and dismissed it because we—I said Greg wouldn't come back after what happened.'

'You mentioned murder,' Miss Pink reminded him, and the dark eyes turned to her: liquid eyes, like a spaniel's, nothing predatory about them. 'He knew the area,' Vosker said. 'Maybe he didn't go far, holed up with a buddy of his in the valley, or a gang of migrant workers, and came back with one, maybe with two fellows, to a place where he knew there were deer. Scott says it's a good vantage point, above where you found him—and there was an accident or a quarrel, who knows? They abandoned him.'

'Oh, no,' Pearl breathed. 'They left him injured, alive?'

'People commit appalling atrocities,' Miss Pink said, and so quietly that they scarcely heard her, but they caught the gist of it because their heads turned to her slowly, reluctantly on the part of Pearl, but with interest where Vosker was concerned. After a long moment Pearl stooped to her saddle-bags and said gruffly, 'C'mon, the horses'll need a drink.'

'I'd like you to meet my wife,' Vosker told Miss Pink, and her mind lurched to a different plane. 'Will you come to our house this evening for coffee?'

She accepted weakly and they parted,

leaving him on the rim. They rode away through the scattered woodland and neither said a word until they were well out of earshot.

Pearl broke the silence: 'That is one very nasty mind.'

'You had the same thought yourself,' Miss Pink pointed out. 'You were the first person to suggest that if the dead man wasn't alone then there could have been a quarrel.'

'I never suggested the guy was Greg Ramirez.'

'What difference does it make?'

There was another long pause. 'None,' Pearl said.

CHAPTER FOUR

Two men were leaning on the gate of Pearl's corral. They were tall and they wore battered straw hats, jeans and boots, but there the similarity ended; one was paunchy, the other built like a classical sculpture. They turned when they heard the horses and regarded the women with a kind of gentle amusement, a familiarity which disturbed Miss Pink until she realised that she was concentrating on the Greek god, and Pearl was ignoring him, introducing the other man. She blushed furiously and nodded to Ira Markow.

70

He held her horse and she dismounted. The other fellow had moved to Pearl's horse. His back was an elongated triangle: wide shouldered and slim waisted with small buttocks under the thin denim.

'So what do you think of New Mexico?' Markow asked, taking her reins.

She wrenched her attention away from that hard back. 'Primitive,' she said weakly, suspecting his courtesy was assumed, that he knew exactly why this silly old woman was blushing and was laughing at her. 'Uncrowded,' she elaborated. 'Raw. Civilisation passed it by.' She was aware of Pearl staring at her, of Markow's large features registering bewilderment. She said quickly, 'I'm talking about the *country*, the land.' She smiled feebly. 'No fences, those wild canyons'—she gestured at the escarpment 'bears, diamondbacks, lions—why, I haven't seen a tourist since yesterday morning! I love it.'

Pearl gave her a hard look and turned to her saddle-bags. The hired man lifted her saddle as if it weighed a few ounces and strolled towards the wash-house where she kept the tack. At that moment Kristen came out of the house and intercepted him. They stood apart, not touching, probably saying something quite innocuous but the sun had left the patio and in the diffused light the girl's posture appeared abandoned, even

71

wanton. The observer was aware that the light was going and that when the afterglow faded night would come creeping in from the desert like a velvet cat, the frogs would sing and the night birds call, and old people remember what it was like to be seventeen and in love.

*　　*　　*

'So what did you think of Jay Gafford?' Pearl asked as they prepared supper. Kristen had taken Pearl's third horse and ridden to the Markow ranch with Gafford who was taking the blue roan home. 'That's what I thought,' she went on, seeing that Miss Pink was having difficulty with words. 'I told you he was sexy. I could see it got to you.'

'Rubbish.' There was a pause. Miss Pink stared at the window. 'He took my breath away,' she admitted. 'And the age gap! Twenty years. It must drive her father crazy.'

'It's not deliberate.' Pearl was laughing. 'The poor guy can't help having a gorgeous body and bedroom eyes.'

'At your age,' Miss Pink murmured, with just the hint of a question, and Pearl fielded it deftly.

'At any age—but we're as discreet as nuns in Regis.' Her eyes were veiled. 'It helps that we have no street lighting,' she added coolly. 'And that the creek lies at the back of our properties. Kristen usually rides up the creek bed to the mesa road, and she's not one of the discreet people.'

'At night, without street lights, people run the risk of stepping on a rattler.'

'Oh my!' Pearl's eyes were wide in mock consternation. 'I never thought of that.'

'Perhaps you were warning me not to go out in the dark.' Pearl gave a feline smile. 'I have to call Wayne Spikol,' Miss Pink said, feeling that the conversation was out of control.

Spikol asked her if she would come to Palomares in the morning. When she put down the phone she suggested to Pearl that she might pick up her things at the motel and return to Regis for a few days. Pearl was delighted and gave her a shopping list. 'Stay as long as you like,' she urged. 'You can ride either the sorrel or the pinto. I promise I won't put you up on the bay again. I'd forgotten how rough he can be, although I'll swear he's got worse with age. He can go for bear-bait in the fall.'

'Oh no! Sell him as a pack-horse; he's so quiet he'd follow without having to be led.'

'He couldn't carry eggs, that's for sure. You *are* a soft-hearted lady, you know that?'

'Nonsense.'

'I guess the English are all the same: stiff upper lip for people but marshmallows where horses and dogs are concerned.'

73

'I'm soft on people too.'
'Yeah, I noticed.'

★   ★   ★

'It sounds like cadaveric spasm,' Michael Vosker said. 'He was dying and the coyotes moved in, he picked up the branch and lunged at them, and the effort killed him. On the other hand—'

'More coffee, Miss Pink?'

'On the other hand, his attacker could have been a man.'

'Michael, you're shocking our guest.'

'I don't think so. She's had twenty-four hours in which to consider hypotheses.'

Miss Pink had been in the Voskers' patio for half an hour and the warm night, the initial exchange of small talk and a good brandy had lulled her into a comfortable state where violence was only a technicality; she was mildly surprised that Marian Vosker should find the subject offensive. But then Marian was a woman of taste. Her old adobe was beautifully furnished, the patio lush with mown grass, the garden chairs padded. She was a large plain woman who exuded hospitality as if her life was dedicated to making other people comfortable: a worthy partner for a busy professor. Retirement to their former holiday home in the back-country must have produced culture shock after social life on campus, and discussion of a man dying of terror might indeed seem offensive to her, particularly over coffee and liqueurs.

'Gregorio *did* leave,' Vosker said, with just a hint of doubt.

'Of course.' Marian was soothing. 'And he took Avril's ring.'

'It wasn't worth much. Wouldn't keep him for long.'

'That's not very kind, dear. It was a diamond.'

'There was stuff lying around that was a sight more valuable. Herb's good saddle, for instance.'

'Gregorio had no transportation. A man walking along the road carrying a saddle would have been conspicuous. That's the last thing he'd want when he'd stolen Betsy's ring. I mean Avril's.'

'Who's Betsy?' Miss Pink asked.

'Ah.' Vosker was pleased. 'Something you don't know. Betsy was Herb Beck's first wife. When she died Avril married Herb. Avril had come to Las Mesas as the maid.'

'Housekeeper,' Marian corrected. Vosker glanced at her but all he said was, 'So originally the ring was Betsy's. That's all.'

Miss Pink asked slowly, 'Am I missing something?'

'I don't see how it could possibly interest her,' Marian said, in the face of Vosker's

75

silence. 'English people don't have class prejudices any longer any more than we do.'

'Housekeepers often marry their employers.' Miss Pink poured oil on the water. 'I mean, in those circumstances. It's a gesture to the proprieties.' She smiled; an anthropologist should know all about that. 'You can't have an unmarried man and an attractive spinster living under the same roof unchaperoned.'

'She wasn't—'

'She wasn't a housekeeper,' Marian interrupted. 'Not always. She came to the States when she was very young to work as a maid. But she climbed the ladder'—she sounded indignant 'and she hasn't had it easy: she had no experience of running a ranch. She can't even ride.'

'Ranch is a rather grand term for Las Mesas,' Vosker put in.

'You have to give credit where it's due. She manages to make a living. It's a hard country'—Marian turned to Miss Pink, her face earnest in the soft light from the house—'even the big ranchers like Ira Markow are having a difficult time in the recession. Local people have to buy in their hay and grain, did you know that? We were in Montana for a time and the ranchers there grow all their own cattle feed. I'm sorry for Avril; it must be a continual struggle to make ends meet.'

'She was able to employ two hands,' Miss Pink pointed out.

'Gregorio wouldn't have got much more than his keep,' Vosker told her. 'I mean, look at his boots!'

'You're sure that was his boot?' Marian asked anxiously. 'Will Avril be involved?'

'I'm not saying it was Greg's boot, not formally. I told Spikol he had boots like that because Spikol asked me. He can take it from there but he's not going to follow it up; he'll get a statement from Miss Pink, file a report, and that'll be the end of it. It would be a different matter if Greg had gone missing from Las Mesas, but we know he left first and then went missing—I mean, if that *is* him, in the cliff dwelling.'

'How do you know he left?' Miss Pink asked. 'This afternoon you were doubtful.'

'I thought about it since. We know he left because the bunkhouse was cleared of his gear, what there was of it, not to speak of the stolen ring—and then how could he have gone missing from Las Mesas? There was no way he was going to walk—what?—eight miles to the head of Rastus, not in those boots. He had to ride, and there are no horses missing from Las Mesas.'

'All right'—Miss Pink was unaware of Marian's disapproval, caught up as she was in speculation—'it looks as if Pearl's theory is the closest: that he reached Rastus from the

77

top road, on a horse, but with a companion who removed the horse—and the truck and trailer which would have been left on the highway, or hidden near it.' She frowned and added slowly: 'That smells of premeditation.'

'How's that?'

'Just that I don't see the other man hanging around to kill a deer after he'd killed—no, after he'd immobilised Gregorio, so perhaps hunting was never the intention, only the stated motive for the trip.' She paused, then added, 'So the other man took Gregorio's ammunition to prevent him firing his rifle to attract attention—'

'Wait a minute; what makes you think he took the ammunition?'

'Spikol didn't tell you that? The rifle was unloaded and there's no ammo and no spent shells around, not that we could see.' He regarded her thoughtfully. She went on, 'Then this other man rode back to the truck leading Gregorio's horse, or rather, the horse he had borrowed from someone. From the other man? Why do I think it was premeditated? It could have been a spontaneous quarrel.'

'You could be thinking that way because people had it in for Greg.'

'Oh, that's nonsense!' Marian was incensed. 'He was a charmer; he had beautiful manners. When he met a woman on the road he stopped his horse and took off his hat, just like a *caballero*. And he was always smiling.'

'You talk about him in the past tense,' Miss Pink remarked. 'Who had it in for him besides the Scott family?'

'I don't think—'

'So Pearl told you about that,' Vosker interrupted. 'Very unfortunate. I meant you might have the impression that people were hostile to Greg but when I think about it he had no rivals. All the men, that is, the others, they were circumspect with Veronica. She was ethereal, like a flower or a moth; she looked as if she would shrivel up if she got too near a flame—' Marian's jaw dropped as she stared at him. Miss Pink was fascinated. He was unaware of them, looking into the shadows beyond the light. 'She was in another league from Kristen and Tammy and Pearl; they're healthy animals with healthy appetites. And then, of course, no one wanted to mix it with Clayton.'

'Keep your voice down,' Marian whispered.

'Someone's not much bothered now,' Miss Pink murmured, 'about mixing it.'

'You're right.' Vosker grinned. 'But if you knew Jay Gafford and you'd known Veronica, you'd realise that a relationship there was most unlikely. Jay needs an alpha woman, and he's got one and Kristen's more than enough for any man to deal with at one time, I'm sure.'

*   *   *

'Nice evening?' Pearl asked, turning off her radio. 'Have fun? You missed Avril, she called in on her way back from Las Cruces to find out what happened. She's quite sure it's not Greg Ramirez up there in the ruin but then she would say that, she doesn't want trouble. Avril's a very respectable lady.' She was deadpan.

'She can't get into serious trouble for employing an illegal alien.'

'It's not that she's thinking of. And trouble's the wrong word, embarrassment is more like it. Avril comes from a good family in England, her father's a Sir Something or other; she's not used to our rough ways. She never gossips, not with anyone, least of all with Fletcher or me. I never heard her say a word about Veronica's death, except she visited with Ada, of course, that was only polite, but then everyone acted like she died of something, like cancer. Avril'd die of shame to think that one of her hired hands was responsible for Veronica's baby, and then the drowning and all. That kind of thing doesn't happen where she was raised.'

'Well, not the drowning part,' Miss Pink conceded. 'Avril seems very refined,' she

80

added, and left it hanging. Pearl looked at her sharply but the eyes behind the thick spectacles were expressionless. Pearl's mouth twitched.

'She has her position to think of: rich rancher's widow. Did I say rich? There are only two ranches here and she's not in the Markows' league but as I understand it, money isn't as important in England as breeding. Thelma Markow may be wealthy but she's got no background—and her kid works as my maid.'

'Michael Vosker says Avril was in service.'

'What's that mean?'

'Domestic service: an old-fashioned term for servants, never used nowadays unless one is disorientated.'

'You're not!'

'I'm groping a little. As I see it Avril has worked her way up from skivvy to rancher. That seems very American: the rags-to-riches syndrome.'

'That may be what you and I think, but not Avril. She can't forget it, and she'd love to do just that: block it out and start over as the rich widow lady.'

'You said her father was titled.'

'She's illegitimate. Her mother was a lady but she was brought up by a housemaid who'd been fired because she was pregnant, and then she lost her baby so the lady's mother, Avril's real grandmother—who was

81

a countess—she gave Avril to the housemaid, make up for the dead baby, see? I got all this from Betsy Beck; they were quite close, her and Avril. Apparently Avril's natural mother is still alive, she married into a family that's related to Queen Elizabeth. What are you smiling at? You don't believe it?'

'Do you?'

'It's a romantic story. Live and let live, I say, and Avril never did me any harm. I don't think she's very happy; she never seems able to get her act together somehow. Her first husband was a Texan; she got her American nationality through him, but she paid for it. He knocked her about. I guess he drank too. Eventually she landed here; Betsy Beck had broken her hip and it never healed right so Herb had to advertise for someone to cook and clean, and take care of Betsy. And when Betsy died Avril up and married Herb, but she never got much joy of that neither; Herb was an alcoholic and drank himself to death. Some women are always attracted to the deadbeats. I don't know if there was any money, but if there was he musta left it to his two sons, out in California someplace. He did leave the ranch to Avril so in the end she got to call herself a rancher, even though all she owns is a few hundred acres of desert with a creek that's dry most of the time, and a tacky old house, another sheet of iron blows off the roof with every storm. And talk of the devil—' the screen door had opened and—not Avril but her man Lloyd stood on the doorstep. 'Had trouble?' Pearl asked, rising smoothly. 'You look like you could do with a beer.'

He sat down without removing his hat.

'Good evening.' Miss Pink was pointedly polite.

He blinked. 'Evening.' Pearl brought him a can of beer and he thanked her in the same tone of surprise. 'You run into any bother?' he asked, fixing her with those eyes which appeared the more intense for his obvious fatigue.

'That was my question, Fletch. Not that it matters, but I can't abide folk who answer questions with one of their own. It's bad manners.'

'Sorry. No, I didn't have trouble. She came home fast because she had the new truck, and my radiator was leaking. Had to stop and top it up, and then I had to eat.'

'There. I could have fed you.'

'No sweat. What happened up there?' He jerked his head, indicating the plateau, and Miss Pink had a sudden image of pale gravel and solid little trees under the brilliant stars. She drew in her breath sharply.

Pearl said, 'Nothing, and we learned nothing we didn't know before.'

'She didn't tell me much.' He glanced at Miss Pink. 'Just these bones had been found, like human bones, and a rifle.' He was painfully shy; not only unable to pronounce his employer's name but having difficulty in deferring to Miss Pink.

'There was a boot too,' Pearl pointed out.

'She says it's not Greg's but she can't know that. I doubt she'd recognise it. I might.'

'The sole was coming off Greg's boots.'

'Yeah, he stuck it with duct tape.'

'There was no tape on this boot.'

'Only one, his other boot were all right.'

The women exchanged glances. 'He could have ripped the sole when he fell,' Miss Pink said. 'Now if we found the other boot and that was mended with duct tape, identification is conclusive.'

'What're you talking about?' It was startling in its harshness. Miss Pink stiffened but Pearl said calmly, 'Most of us think that it's Greg, what's left of him.'

'Who's most of us?'

'Fletcher,' Pearl said to Miss Pink, as the tone got to her, prompting her to make some kind of apology for him, 'is very possessive about his ranch and his boss—' now his eyes were troubled rather than angry. 'Most of us, sweetie, is me and Michael Vosker and Spikol, maybe Clayton—*Did* Scott think it was Greg?' she asked of Miss Pink.

She cast her mind back. 'He suggested two men could have come down from the highway, and quarrelled. He didn't recognise the boot, not to say so.'

'What made him think there were two men?' Lloyd asked, and Miss Pink, pondering, starting to feel fatigue at the end of the day, dismissed the subject of a rifle without ammunition and stated the obvious: 'There was no horse. But'—she caught herself—'Scott did suggest that, after all, the dead man might have been alone because he could have come down from the highway on foot, meaning to carry out a deer on his back. In that case there has to be a truck somewhere. Spikol means to look for it.'

'A truck means it can't be Greg.' Now Lloyd was so subdued that he could have been talking to himself. 'He didn't own one.'

'And that,' Miss Pink said, equally softly, 'was when Scott pointed out that no truck would be found if two men had been poaching—and then someone'—she didn't look at Pearl—'put forward the notion of a quarrel, and we arrived at the traditional formula of accident, suicide or murder.'

'Yes,' Lloyd said in a perfectly normal voice, 'I been thinking along those lines myself.'

CHAPTER FIVE

'There's no vehicle on a five-mile stretch of that top road,' Spikol said. 'And there's nowhere that you can get a truck off the pavement, either the pines are too close together or the ground drops away too steeply. If there ever was a truck it's gone, and that means two men were involved—or more than two.' He leaned back in his chair and regarded Miss Pink doubtfully. 'That is, if he went in that way,' he added.

Miss Pink sipped coffee from a Styrofoam beaker and wondered who laundered policemen's shirts; did they send them to some superb Chinese establishment or had their wives trained as laundresses? And how did bachelors manage to look so clean and pressed, at least at the start of each day?

They were sitting in the diffused light of an office in the sheriff's building, the glare of sunshine muted by plastic blinds.

'Is it possible,' she asked, 'that he was on a long trip: staying out for days, working his way through the forests, not using trails? No'—she answered her own question—'not a back-packer: wrong boots, and hikers don't carry rifles. And he wasn't on horseback because there's no horse—'

'Unless, as Pearl Slocum said, his horse

came down and was quietly appropriated.'

She studied his face. 'You favour that theory?'

'It seems the most reasonable, except we know he isn't a local so he had to bring the horse in by trailer, and we're back where we started. No vehicle.'

'Gregorio Ramirez is a local,' she said slowly. 'In a sense. He lived locally. And he wore very old boots. He could have ridden up from Las Mesas without anyone being the wiser ... No, when he left he took his possessions, and we keep coming back to the horse.'

'He's a stranger,' Spikol said, with a hint of desperation. 'You found some old bones and a rifle. It's a hunting accident—as in poaching. We'll circulate the information, wait for someone to claim the remains, or at least say they're missing a husband or a son, whatever. Nothing else we can do.'

'Understaffed and overworked,' she murmured.

'The story of my life. Fine for—er, you retired, ma'am?'

'Not exactly. I write stories for women's magazines, and travel articles, that kind of thing.'

He nodded; he had guessed it was something like that. 'So, you going to leave us now?'

'I'm staying in Regis for a day or two. I like

the people and I love the country. I shall go out with Pearl.'

'If you find anything else, like more bones, you'll call me?'

'Or the other boot. Of course.'

He looked startled. As she walked across the bright car park she thought: if the other boot is mended with duct tape he'd like me to put it down a hole. A few anonymous bones he can forget about, but Gregorio Ramirez means problems.

★   ★   ★

She shopped for Pearl and paid her bill at the motel and by eleven o'clock she was heading out of town for the interstate. Palomares had been quiet; what traffic there was drifted gently along the wide streets, and there was always room to park, and as she crossed a bridge that gave access to the slip road she was amazed to see an almost empty interstate. Some two miles distant one vehicle was approaching down the ribbon of concrete. She turned left, picked up speed and joined the interstate at fifty miles an hour. She reached fifty-five, flicked the cruise control and the stereo and settled back to revel in the warm breeze and Paganini.

★   ★   ★

'Ada Scott wants to meet you,' Pearl said, unpacking the groceries. 'You'll be good for her, she sees no one in this place; no one ever comes except hunters, and Ada's not a lady who's into killing. We'll go along there after we've eaten if that's all right with you.'

'I shall enjoy it. Is she confined to her bed?'

'Depends. Sometimes she's in bed for days, others she's as right as rain, cooking and stuff—and in case you're thinking she drinks, it definitely isn't that, I promise you. We got our share of alcoholics here, or we have had: Herb Beck and poor old Sam, but that's it. Not too bad a percentage actually, just two drunks in a community of fifteen souls.'

*　　　*　　　*

The Scott place was down the street from Pearl's and on the same side. Between them were two houses on bushy plots stretching back to the creek. Both houses were unoccupied, one being for sale ('Fat chance they have of selling,' Pearl observed), the other used by the owners for hunting in the fall. On the other side of the street and beyond Marge Dearing's adobe was a sagging barn with the just discernible legend: Regis Hay and Grain Store. The building stood on several acres of wasteland.

89

'Probably full of rattlers,' Pearl said. 'It hasn't been used for years, but the snakes'll keep the rodents down. You don't see many rats in Regis.'

After the barn came the Voskers' neat frame-house in its well-kept garden, and opposite was the Scotts' adobe backing on the street. An ochre-coloured wall was set with small windows and a wooden door. This was slatted in its upper half and between the slats sunlight was visible at the end of a dark passage.

Pearl and Miss Pink went along the passage to emerge on a patio of baked earth. A thicket of bamboo cut off any view from the house which on this, the intimate domestic side, consisted of a shaded veranda with rooms opening onto it. The veranda itself was used as a room with tables and chairs and chests, and here they found Ada Scott, sitting in a rocking-chair with Kristen behind her, evidently putting the finishing touches to her mother's hair. The girl palmed the comb smoothly and stood back while Pearl made the introductions.

Miss Pink saw a woman who initially impressed her as being singularly beautiful, yet later she was unable to recall one remarkable feature, except for her hair which was thick and long, drawn back to a high chignon encircled by a narrow band of beads like pearls. Ada smiled at Miss Pink as if she had been waiting a long time for the pleasure of meeting her. She had large eyes with heavy lids; the effect was patrician: serene and elegant, and Miss Pink relaxed in an ambiance that bore no relation to the fierce August heat.

'You're looking great today,' Pearl observed, in the cheery tone used for invalids.

'Kristen likes doing my hair.' Her upward glance was proud and Kristen was obviously embarrassed. 'I'll bring the tea,' she muttered, and went into the house. 'It's feminine,' Ada explained, 'dressing hair— and Kristen's a tomboy. I am glad you came to see me,' she told Miss Pink. 'Pearl says you write stories. That must be exciting.'

She had been prepared to be agreeable but now Miss Pink found herself admitting that, yes, it was exciting, and feeling that this was truly so, not merely an effort at politeness. She started to talk about field-work, about travel, locations, the concept of allowing stories to find her rather than probing in dark corners to find plots. Kristen came back with glasses of iced tea and, glancing at Pearl, said diffidently that she wanted to take her horse out: just an hour, would that be all right?

'You don't have to be back in an hour,' Ada said. 'Away you go and have fun.'

They watched her cross the patio and enter the bamboo thicket and no one suggested that it was too hot for horses. 'I'm getting better every day,' Ada said, staring at the place where Kristen had disappeared. 'She always was too protective.' She changed the subject. 'I would like to read something by you,' she told Miss Pink. 'Are you realistic or traditional?'

Miss Pink hesitated, stumped for a moment. 'Can you be more specific?'

'Ada doesn't like violence,' Pearl explained. 'Me, I don't read much but there's this guy Elmore Leonard, you heard of him? I got a book of his from the thrift store and it's pretty steamy. Ada'd hate that.'

'I have some of my mother's books,' Ada said. 'Do you know Gene Stratton-Porter? I love *Laddie*. I was raised on that book and I read it over and over.'

'I don't write like either of them,' Miss Pink admitted. 'But I don't shock gratuitously and I'm all in favour of keeping private acts behind closed doors.'

'Quite right too,' Pearl said.

Ada, politely attentive, asked, 'Is your home village like Regis? Or maybe you don't live in a village?'

'Outside one, actually, but it's a world away. And yet'—she pondered—'people are the same wherever you go; the same emotions: love, hatred, fear, jealousy. Rural Cornwall and New Mexico will be no different beneath the surface. Isn't that odd?'

She was asking them to share in this revelation.

'Behaviour will be more extreme here,' Ada said. 'Space makes a difference. Remoteness. People turn in on themselves.'

Pearl swallowed. 'You're thinking of people like Marge Dearing.'

Ada's eyes were shadowed. 'I was speaking generally. I wasn't thinking specifically of Regis.'

'The West is still frontier country?' suggested Miss Pink.

Ada was considering that, and Miss Pink was wondering if perhaps it was not frontier country but something other, when Tammy Markow flashed out of the passage on her bicycle, her long brown legs extended as she braked. She got off and dropped the bike on the ground. Her bare head gleamed like gold in the sunlight and she was wearing skimpy shorts and a tank top that exposed bony ribs. She looked amusing and delightful: half-child, half-woman. 'Hi,' she called. 'Where's Kristen?'

'She's in the corral,' Ada said. 'You'll just catch her.'

Tammy whirled away and Pearl shot a helpless look at Miss Pink who said easily: 'Does your husband ranch, Mrs Scott?'

'We have a farm on the river and a man looks after it. He lives there, and we employ seasonal labour when we need it. That's where Mr Scott is this afternoon. We don't have any animals up here, just the two horses.'

Pearl said quickly: 'Clayton's one of the workers. We're mainly retirees in the village: out to grass.'

'We're evenly divided,' Ada corrected. 'The Markows have two hands, and Avril has—one.' Her eyes clouded and the visitors cast about for something to say that would avoid delicate subjects like ranch-hands and daughters. So far they hadn't touched on Miss Pink's gruesome discovery in the Indian ruin, and she was increasingly aware that the bones could be those of the man responsible for the death of Ada's daughter. God, she thought, why on earth did I agree to come here?

'Those remains you found in the canyon,' Ada said calmly. 'Do you think they belonged to Gregorio, the man who worked for Avril Beck?'

Miss Pink's mouth opened but it was a moment before the words came. 'I can have no idea,' she said, her tone almost treacly in an effort at reassurance. 'Wayne Spikol is inclined to think it's a stranger.'

Pearl's features were set in a glare; nothing she could say would alleviate the situation. Miss Pink licked her lips.

'Poor Greg,' Ada said. 'I was fond of him.'

'We all were,' Pearl said, and closed her

eyes in horror at the slip.

Tammy came through the bamboos and loitered across the baked earth. The visitors regarded her eagerly: an interruption.

'She's gone,' she said dolefully. 'Where'd she go?'

'Oh dear.' Pearl was lugubrious. 'You got nothing to do? You can come out with me and Miss Pink later. We're going up Scorpion,' she added wildly, improvising.

'Kristen will be back soon,' Ada said. 'She just took Jack out for a while. Go fetch yourself a Coke.'

'Jack's in the corral,' Tammy said. 'She wouldn't ride in this heat.' She pouted and looked as if she would like to say more but was intimidated by numbers. She slouched indoors and the others exchanged indulgent smiles and resumed the investigation of the guest's background.

The effect of Ada's interest was first to stop Miss Pink dead, and then to divert her into new channels. She was no longer describing her journeys but investigating motivation. When Ada asked her what kind of people she respected and she cited old women living alone, in particular a rancher in Arizona, Ada wondered if she had remained mentally stable. Miss Pink recalled that the woman had shared a boundary with a man who had murdered his neighbour fifty years ago; everyone knew but there was no proof, and the woman sustained neighbourly contact with the killer all that time. 'There was nothing else she could do,' Miss Pink pointed out. 'She could move away, go mad, or accept him. She was a survivor so she stayed there, and stayed sane.'

'Why did she tell you?' Ada asked.

'Because she had to tell someone and she knew no one would believe me, they'd dismiss the story as a traveller's tale.'

'You're full of surprises,' Pearl said. 'Shocks, is more like it. You were visiting with a woman who lived next door to a murderer!'

Miss Pink didn't add that she'd stayed the night there.

Ada said, 'You weren't curious enough to invent an excuse to call on the man?'

'No.' Miss Pink fidgeted in her chair, intrigued and disorientated. 'Curiosity has to stop somewhere. There's a point where you ask no more questions and you move on.'

'What do you do with what you've found out?'

'Sometimes you use it, heavily disguised and with the location changed. Sometimes'—Miss Pink bit her lip, remembering instances—'sometimes you forget.'

'Can you do that?'

'What I mean is: you lock it in some kind of mental back-room and throw away the

96

key. The secret will die with you.'

'Does it affect you? Do you dream about it?'

'You learn to deal with it, like grief. Like the old rancher did.'

'What *is* Tammy doing?' Pearl exclaimed in a flurry of concern. 'I better go and see if she's trying on Kristen's clothes—'

'I have to read your stories,' Ada said as the younger woman went in the house. 'Will you send me something when you go home?'

'I'll do that. You never thought of writing yourself?'

'No.'

Miss Pink looked away, disturbed at what she saw in the other's eyes, something powerful, like passion, or terror, but knowing that eyes are only coloured tissue and a black hole, incapable of expression, of reflecting emotion. There was nothing in Ada's eyes; they were like windows: screened and hiding what appeared to be an empty house. 'I'm sorry,' she murmured.

Ada inclined her head and Miss Pink remembered her mother who employed the same grave gesture when she accepted an apology. Then the woman's face softened. Kristen was crossing the patio.

The atmosphere was heavy as the earth relinquished the stored heat of the day and as the girl approached slowly, her arms loose, her body languid in the bright sun, she was a dream figure. Miss Pink wondered how she could ever have thought the child plain.

Ada said quietly: 'Tammy's here.'

Kristen was suddenly alert. 'Where?'

'Inside. Pearl's with her.'

'What's the time?' Neither wore a watch.

'It's a quarter-past four,' Miss Pink said.

Kristen went quickly indoors. 'It's hot today,' Ada said. 'We're building up for storms. We should have had rain before now.'

'Yes.' Miss Pink was listening for voices but what she heard was the sound of an engine. Ada had heard it too and started to struggle in her chair. 'Can I help you?' Miss Pink asked. 'Do you want to get up?'

'No. I—I'm just wondering—' The dark eyes observed the windows along the veranda. 'Nothing.' She sank back, now staring at the entrance to the street passage. Clayton Scott appeared and strode across the patio.

'No!' came Tammy's voice, loud and clear. 'My bike's out back.'

A curious little struggle was taking place in a doorway: Tammy trying to shake off Kristen who held her by the arm, Pearl stepping back with a yelp as someone trod on her foot. In the patio Scott picked up the bicycle and leaned it carefully against a tree. The figures on the veranda were momentarily still, then Kristen pushed past

98

Tammy and, still holding her arm, pulled her towards the bike.

'Good afternoon, Tammy.' Scott was stern.

The girls halted. 'Hi, Mr Scott.' Tammy dimpled. Kristen dropped her arm and waited, looking sullen. Scott's face darkened and Miss Pink's heart sank. She heard someone sigh.

'That's no way to dress when you come visiting,' Scott said.

Tammy appeared astonished. 'My dad didn't say nothing. My mom bought me this top. What's wrong with it?' She was teasing him.

'When you come to this house you cover yourself.' His voice had risen and there was a shake in it. 'You cover yourself, you look respectable, d'you hear?'

'Oh, come on!' The child was grinning. 'You expect me to wear a *skirt?* I'm only twelve. If you—'

'And time you stopped rapping and got down to work,' Pearl shouted. 'You got three horses to groom, there ain't no free lunches at Slocum's, miss. We're going to show Miss Pink Scorpion Canyon,' she announced generally. 'Tammy has to go and get the horses ready. You too, Kristen: away you go.'

Clayton Scott advanced to the veranda while the girls picked up the bicycle and disappeared through the passage.

'No problems at the farm?' Ada asked.

'No. I wouldn't expect any. That child's getting out of hand, coming here like that when you got company. You'll have to speak to her mother.'

'Kristen has everything under control.'

'I'm sure. Good day, Miss Pink, Pearl. My, we could do with rain.' He sat down. 'I must apologise,' he told Miss Pink, 'I can't abide the way of raising kids these days. Our problem here is that there aren't enough folk who can have an influence on the youngsters. Only two families, and you can see what kind of parental control there is in the other one.' He stared moodily towards the passage.

'Maybe you'd fetch Clayton a glass of lemonade,' Ada suggested to Pearl, who got up with alacrity.

'Dusty work,' Scott told Miss Pink. 'We're hay-making. Did Ada tell you we have a farm on the river? Some of the best land in the county, we get top prices for our hay. You don't look comfortable, honey; can I fetch you another pillow?'

'I have to go indoors.' Ada was plainly embarrassed and Miss Pink stood up, knowing she had stayed too long. 'Oh, don't go,' Ada protested, and Scott smiled warmly. 'Sit down, ma'am; you can't leave just as I come home. I'll be back directly.'

With practised ease he helped his wife to her feet and supported her to the doorway. She hesitated at the sill and, 'Watch the rug,' Miss Pink heard him murmur.

She sighed and leaned back in her chair. She'd outstayed her welcome but Ada had appeared to enjoy the visit. She wondered what Scott wanted from her; surely he couldn't revert to an inquisition concerning the whereabouts of his daughter on that afternoon two days ago? It was possible; the man was unpredictable, he'd been knocked off-balance by Tammy's dress which, after all, was no more revealing than any child might wear on a hot day and, as Tammy said, she was only twelve.

He came back. 'Pearl's taken over,' he said, smiling down at her. 'Can I bring you another glass of tea?'

'No thank you; we have to be going as soon as Pearl's ready.'

'How are you liking Regis?' He sat down: affable, even charming, and as if to emphasise the benign mood, his social sense, he had removed his hat revealing thick grey hair and, as she had suspected, a high forehead.

'I'm used to small communities,' she said. 'I live in one myself, and basically I don't find Regis very different.'

'English villages are as small as Regis?'

'This would be called a hamlet in

England, but then it would have been much larger at one time, when the mines were operating. Do you lease any mines, Mr Scott?'

'No, I'm not interested in mining. All my time's occupied with the farm. You must come and see it; there's a lot of wildlife on the river banks.'

'I can imagine. Water and sunshine—and there'll be plenty of shade with all those cottonwoods: ideal conditions.'

'You're a birder, I take it.'

'Yes, yes I am.' Where *was* he trying to take this stilted conversation? 'You're interested in wildlife yourself?'

'I do a bit of duck shooting in the fall and I used to hunt with Herb Beck when he was alive; I still look forward to getting a buck come November. I'm partial to a good roast of deer meat. My wife's a great cook, but I'm afraid the girls—Kristen don't take after her in that respect.'

'How does she take after her?'

'Oh, Kristen's a good daughter to me; you mustn't go by appearances. There's not much for a young girl to do in a place like this, and she won't leave her mother. That would be one answer to the problem: go and take a job in town, come home weekends. She won't do it. You see, Ada's not been herself since our tragedy—you know about that? We none of us is over it yet, but maybe

102

you can't—can't go back to where you were before it happened. How can you, nothing can bring her back, you have to start over, make a new life without her, but there's this gap. No matter what we do, you can't fill the gap.' He glanced furtively at the open windows and lowered his voice. 'I *hope* she's better,' he murmured, but the tone was full of doubt. 'And Kristy,' he went on, 'she says the wildest things. Sometimes I'm not sure but what it unsettled her mind.'

'We all have to go through it,' Miss Pink said.

'*What!*'

'Everyone has to cope with grief some time.'

'Ah yes, but not like this. Not that way.' His eyes implored her to appreciate the peculiar circumstances, the depths of their tragedy.

'No, that was thoughtless of me. There's always shock and guilt, of course, but violence intensifies it.' He stared at her. There were tears in his eyes and her heart gave a lurch. 'I'm so sorry,' she whispered, glancing at the windows herself. 'I'm sorry for all of you.'

*　　*　　*

'Exhausting!' she exclaimed, entering Pearl's living-room and dropping into a chair. 'Raw emotion. We shouldn't have gone. Why did you take me?'

'You agreed to come, and you knew their daughter had committed suicide. Anyway, Ada enjoyed visiting with you, I'll swear she did. I wasn't to know Clayton would choose to come home early; Ada didn't expect him back till supper-time. You need a drink; we both need a drink. My,' she went on, handing Miss Pink a stiff Scotch, 'but didn't he get uptight about Tammy's shorts? God help us if he'd ever seen her in that red dress—remember: the one she had on the day you arrived?'

'What's wrong with him?'

'Nothing's wrong.' Pearl turned and stared out of the window at Marge's house. 'What can you expect: he sees Kristen going the same way as Veronica: he must be out of his mind with worry.'

'That's what he said about Kristen.' Leaning back, savouring the whisky, Miss Pink was relaxing.

'Kristen?' Pearl turned. 'Kristen—worried?'

'No, unhinged—with grief. "She says the wildest things," was how he put it to me.'

'Rubbish. Kristen's as sane as you are.' Pearl snorted with amusement. 'Except where Jay Gafford's concerned but, you ask me, she'd never let her father see her like we saw her this afternoon. Made me go queer inside, you could see she'd been with him, couldn't you? Blatant. Outrageous, I call it,' but she was smiling, admiring and condoning. 'Of course,' she added seriously, 'if Clayton means she *acts* wildly, that's true in a sense, I mean: from his point of view what she's doing is dangerous, could be fatal.'

'I can understand his concern about Kristen, but taking it on himself to criticise the way someone else's child dresses is way over the top. Kristen's not going to start wearing hot pants and a see-through blouse because a child five years her junior does.'

'It wasn't see-through.'

'A manner of speaking. On Kristen it would be pretty revealing, a tank top. It would be on Tammy if she had anything to reveal.'

'And she will have, she's got fabulous legs already. I see your point, but it's all part of the same picture. Tammy's spoiled, she cheeks her father, she's a bad influence on Kristen.'

'I don't believe it. Of the two of them Kristen's the dominant character by a long chalk; you saw how she took Tammy away. And incidentally, how do the Markows take Scott's criticism of their daughter?'

'For my money they ignore it. You can ask them. We'll call on the way up Scorpion; have to anyway, can't pass the ranch without stopping by. I see the girls saddled the horses. Now they've gone off someplace. You never know with those two what they'll be up to next. If Tammy don't come back we'll leave her the old bay and go ahead on our own.'

CHAPTER SIX

The escarpment decreased in height towards the south and there the Markow ranch was situated at the mouth of a shallow canyon. As they approached the buildings the main divide came into view at the head of the canyon, its timbered spurs side-lit by the low sun.

'Amazing,' Miss Pink exclaimed, 'I'm constantly astonished in this country at the gap between appearances and reality.'

'Meaning?'

'The forest looks exquisite: soft and benign when really it's appallingly rough—when there's no trail, even dangerous.'

'Why do I have the feeling you're not talking about trees?'

Before Miss Pink could answer the sorrel threw up its head and slewed to confront a bunch of young horses which came charging up to the other side of the fence. 'Who lives here?' she asked, glimpsing a mobile home nestling in the shade of big trees. There were roses on a patch of bare earth that was set with small plastic windmills in an effort to deter ground squirrels. A girl came round the side of the house carrying a plastic basket loaded with washing. She walked with the deliberate gait of the heavily pregnant. On seeing them she put down the washing and wiped her forehead.

'The Harpers,' Pearl murmured. 'Hi, Maxine,' she called. 'Meet my friend from England, Miss Pink. You all right? You look shattered.'

The girl shrugged. 'It's not so bad now the sun's going down, but the heat is awful. Pearl, you got no idea; I just laid on the bed all day. Thelma come over and did the wash for me.'

'Never mind, soon be over.'

'The baby's due in about three weeks,' she told Miss Pink as they rode on towards the big house. 'The way she looks it's enough to make you swear off men for ever.'

'You don't go for babies.'

'I don't think you do either. It's like young animals: blind and helpless and dependent on their mothers—yuk, you can keep them *and* the hell of carrying them: nine months feeling like Maxine looks? No thank you. I like them though when they start to think for themselves; puppies, colts, kids: that's when they're fun to have around. And now you're going to meet Thelma Markow who thinks the opposite: likes babies but can't for the life of her cope with 'em once they're out of diapers. Reminds me of an old cat I had once: wonderful mother until the kittens were weaned and then she didn't want to know. Violent, she was: boxed their ears when they wanted to nurse. Poor little things; if it hadn't been for me they'd all have grown up deprived. Surrogate mother I was.' They stopped at a garden fence and she stared at the house on the other side. 'Ira makes up for it though,' she muttered.

They dismounted and hitched their horses to the rail. A dirt path led to a wooden house like an overgrown cabin, all nooks and corners under the ubiquitous sheet-iron roof. The screen door opened on a dim kitchen with a low ceiling and tiny windows. A light was burning, without it they would have seen nothing. A figure turned from the stove and for a moment Miss Pink, prepared for a middle-aged ranch wife, thought that Tammy had a sister whom no one had mentioned. At first sight Thelma Markow looked about twenty-five. She was slight with bobbed hair and delicate features that were too fine for the big glasses she wore. She welcomed them pleasantly and sent them to the living-room while she put the finishing touches to a pie.

The living-room faced north, its windows

draped and netted so that very little light entered and furniture was lumbering dark pieces cluttered with framed photographs and silk flowers in dull vases. Miss Pink knew it was logical in a hot country to exclude the sun but to shroud windows with a northern aspect seemed paranoid and she sighed for higher latitudes and pale walls and pictures and ornaments that were meant to be seen.

Thelma came in with the inevitable iced tea and Pearl inquired after Maxine as if she were family. 'She's going to her mother in Taos next week,' Thelma said. 'We could manage if there was no complications but we can't risk anything. She's not strong.'

'We don't have a doctor nor a hospital nearer than Palomares,' Pearl explained to Miss Pink. 'So where's Tammy?' she asked of Thelma.

'She went out hours ago. Didn't you see her?'

'We saw her; she saddled my horses and then vanished with Kristen.'

There were footsteps in the kitchen and Ira Markow appeared in the doorway. 'Evening, ladies! What're you drinking? Tea? You don't mind if I have a beer?' He came in and sat down, quite at his ease with three women. 'Tammy with you?' he asked.

'I think she's with Kristen,' Pearl told him. 'She may follow us; she was to ride with us this evening.'

'So why didn't she come with you?'

'Miss Pink and me, we were at the Scotts', and the girls left to saddle up, and when we went home they'd done that but they'd disappeared so we came on and left a horse for Tammy. Why're you worried?'

'She's all right,' Thelma said. 'She's just off somewhere with Kristen.'

Markow was staring at the doorway, rubbing his chin with a large hand. 'Can't come to much harm,' he muttered, 'not in Regis.' He addressed Miss Pink: 'I couldn't bear to live in a place like New York,' he explained, as if in extenuation. 'I'd go out of my mind with worry.'

'He would that,' Thelma assured them with a kind of pride.

'I can't imagine any rancher being able to tolerate New York,' Miss Pink remarked with a smile.

He looked absently at his wife. 'You'd never be able to allow her out the front door.'

'They survive,' Thelma said. 'And we don't live in New York so we don't need to borrow trouble. Where's Jay Gafford?'

'He's away somewheres. It's Saturday. I woulda thought Kristen'd be with him.'

'And Tammy will be tagging along—'

'I doubt that—' Pearl said drily, and at that point a telephone started to ring in

110

another room.

As his wife went out Markow turned to Pearl. 'You left her that big bay to ride,' he protested.

'You don't expect folk our age to ride that brute? Tammy's young enough not to care if a horse is a bit rough.'

'She's got her own pony here, she wants to ride.'

'You spoil that kid like you were her grandpa! It never hurt anyone to find out what a rough ride is like. Miss Pink here rode the bay over eight miles the day we went up Midnight.'

'Yes, I wanted to ask you were there any new developments, like—'

Thelma was back. 'It's for you,' she told Markow. 'Your daddy's bad and it's your mom on the phone.'

He pushed past her and she closed the door behind him.

'Serious?' Pearl asked, full of concern.

Thelma nodded. 'We been expecting it. He's been suffering for months. Cancer.' She touched her abdomen. 'Ira'll have to go.' She was abstracted. 'His mom's in a state; they can't get hold of my sister-in-law, she's in Hawaii.'

'Um'—Pearl threw a glance at Miss Pink—'anything we can do—' Feeling superfluous they made movements to rise.

'Don't go,' Thelma said automatically.

111

'I'm thinking what we have to do. Is that Tammy?' Above the thudding of hoofs they heard horses neigh. 'Excuse me,' she said, and went in to her husband.

A screen door crashed and Tammy appeared from the kitchen, breathing hard. 'Caught you!' she exclaimed. 'You coming now?'

'We have a problem,' Pearl said. 'Your Grandpa Markow's sick. Would that be the one in Texas?'

'Yes, way over in Big Thicket. You fly to Houston—'

Her parents came out of the inner room. Thelma hesitated, staring at Tammy as if trying to place her in the scheme of things. 'We going to Houston?' the child asked eagerly.

'Sweetie, you can't come,' Markow told her.

'Oh no!' It was a wail. Miss Pink stood up, taking the initiative. 'If we could run any messages?' she prompted, looking down at Pearl.

Thelma said, 'We both have to go. My mother-in-law's not well herself and she's all confused and there's no knowing whether they'll reach Ira's sister in time. We been expecting it—Tammy, you go down to the Harpers and you help Maxine, you hear? She's got the spare room you can sleep in.'

'I can go to Kristen's; why do I have to—'

'Maxine needs help—' Thelma began but was over-ridden by her husband. 'Why don't you call Ada Scott? She'd be happier with Kristen.'

'I will! I'll call her!' Tammy rushed away.

'Where's Daryl Harper?' Pearl asked. 'You going to leave him and Jay to run the place on their own?'

'They have to. Shouldn't be for long. Providing they feed the stock and don't turn a tractor over on theirselves, there's no problem. Gafford's experienced enough. Harper was putting a bunch of heifers up in Scorpion. He shoulda been back by now. You might keep an eye out for him if you go that way, and if you see him tell him we had to leave in a hurry. I got time to do the chores before we go; that way I'll be sure the steers have one good feed inside 'em. Maybe I can get Clayton Scott over—'

'The men can manage,' Thelma chided. 'Stop worrying.'

'We were going up Scorpion,' Pearl said. 'We'll look for Daryl.'

Tammy returned, furiously angry. She glared at her father. 'That Kristen Scott!' she blurted. 'She's seeing too much of Gafford!'

'Not now, Tammy.' Her mother was firm. 'I want you to—'

'Did you hear what I said?' She was shouting at her father. 'She's *going* with him! They're—they're shacked up!'

'Gafford's down at Scott's?' Markow asked, surprised. 'Right, I'll have a word with him.'

'That's not what I meant. And he's not there. What I'm telling you is they're having it off together.'

'Now that's no way for a young lady to talk—'

'You old *fool!* Don't you listen to what I'm saying? I'm telling you that Jay Gafford—' As her voice rose to a shriek Pearl stepped forward and slapped her face. Tammy stopped as if choked, her hands flying to her cheeks. Thelma blinked, Markow was horrified and bewildered.

'Now,' Pearl said coldly, 'we'll have some order here. Your Grandpa is very sick and your ma and pa are trying to think; they can't do with your temper on top of everything. They gotta pack and they have to catch a plane. You come with me and we'll call the airport, you write down the times as I tell you. Miss Pink can help with the chores, your ma will pack—and that's everything organised—' She was edging the child towards the room with the telephone.

Tammy held back. 'I'm not staying in this house on my own while they're away.' Her voice broke and tears spilled down her cheeks. 'You hit me,' she sobbed.

'Why can't you stay with Kristen?'

'They won't have me! She says her mom

114

won't neither. They don't want me! It's that Gafford, she has him there—'

'Rubbish. They just don't have the room—and Mrs Scott's an invalid. Kristen's trying to spare her. Now you pull your weight, miss, in a family disaster—' She lowered her voice. Thelma had left the room but Markow lingered. 'Come on'—she was impatient, starting to run out of steam—'come and find the airport number, I can't see that small print. Miss Pink, you go and help Ira with chores.'

In the stack yard Markow shovelled barley. 'She's jealous,' he said indulgently, placing full buckets before Miss Pink. 'Kristen Scott has taken a shine to one of our hands—the one was with me when you came down from Rastus two days back—and Tammy idolises Kristen. She's still just a little girl.'

'But growing up.' Miss Pink took a couple of buckets and trudged across the yard to a trough under a fence, and a line of waiting steers. All the same, she thought, it was a pity Ada Scott couldn't agree to help out, particularly in the circumstances.

Tammy sulked. It was understandable. Probably she didn't realise that her grandfather was dying so the trip to Texas was more important to her than its objective. Rejected (as she saw it) by her parents and the Scotts, scolded by Pearl, she shifted her allegiance to Maxine Harper and refused to go for a ride. Nor would she say goodbye to her parents but trudged down the road carrying her overnight bag. 'Oh dear,' muttered Pearl as they stood at their horses' heads. 'We have to change that mood. You start up the trail; I'll overtake you.'

And so for a short while Miss Pink knew perfection: mounted on Pearl's smooth sorrel and riding alone into the wilderness. Never mind that it was only for a few minutes, time was relative; it was the sensation that was important, not its duration. Like sex, she thought: people are obsessed by it for years, society is obsessed, and its perfection is momentary and—now why on earth, surrounded by beauty and the purest air, with a thrasher calling and a cactus glowing with plummy blooms, did sex have to raise its head? There was one answer, she thought, smiling to herself, sex was the serpent in the Garden of Eden and her subconscious was reminding her that she should be on the look-out for rattlesnakes. 'So watch your step,' she said aloud. The sorrel flicked his ears and she glanced sideways, startled by the sound of her own voice.

The horse breasted the easy gradient and from close at hand a great horned owl cleared its throat and delivered its sonorous call. A clump of asters trembled and was

116

still. The sorrel stopped and Miss Pink held her breath. At the top of a pinyon the owl sat motionless. Nothing moved on a slope that was dreaming in the pale shade. Out in the valley the cottonwoods of the Rio Grande blazed with green fire and all the desert on the other side: the plains and the crumbling ranges were brazen in the last rays of the sun.

There was a drumming of hoofs and the sorrel lifted his head. A mile away a flash of white was moving fast through the Markow property and making for the slope: Pearl on her pinto pony. Miss Pink turned back to the pinyon but the owl had gone, quiet as a floating feather.

Pearl arrived and stopped with a slither. The sorrel backed and filled. 'You didn't expect this on an evening ride,' Pearl said.

'It's hard on the Markows. Did they get away all right? I saw a car leave.'

'They're fine. And I left Tammy helping Maxine prepare supper. My, that was some temper-tantrum, wasn't it? Actually, Maxine says Jay went to town, probably felt like a drink with his pals. I guess he went on there after he saw Kristen in the village. Did you see any sign of Daryl yet?'

'No. You don't think he's met with an accident?'

'Not in this canyon. If he'd been thrown his horse would have come down. Don't borrow trouble, as Thelma says. See what I mean about Tammy's parents? Daddy spoils her rotten and Mom's got a blind spot. Remember the red dress? Can you imagine anyone letting a kid go out in that? Tammy told me she got it in the thrift store.'

They reached the top of the slope and traversed sideways above a wash that was the dry bed of Scorpion Creek. A horseman was coming down the wash. 'Here's Daryl,' Pearl said. 'You see, nothing happened to him.'

Harper was a good-looking young fellow but not all that bright. He accepted the news of the family illness phlegmatically and showed no particular pleasure on learning that he wouldn't have to do evening chores. No doubt he was thinking that with the boss gone there would be that much more work for the two hands. Nor did he seem bothered by the information that the Harpers had a house guest for an indeterminate period, and when they parted, unlike most Western men in the circumstances, he didn't tell them to take care. He didn't even watch them go.

'Does he think we're following him down?' Miss Pink asked.

'I wouldn't attempt a guess at what Daryl thinks.'

'He doesn't tell us to be back before dark.'

'Oh, cowboys: all they think about is one thing—well, two; the other one's hunting. They're all the same: Harper, Ramirez, Gafford. Next thing we know, Kristen'll be pregnant.'

'I wondered.' They were pacing through the coarse sand. 'Could it be,' Miss Pink mused, 'that Ada thinks the atmosphere at the Scotts' is a little too heated for Tammy? That's why she doesn't want the child there, she feels she has to act *in loco parentis*.'

'What's that?'

'Substituting for her mother. Her father too, for that matter. Would you say Ira is permissive or unworldly? He doesn't seem bothered by the relationship between his man and Kristen.'

'Why should he be? There's nothing wrong with it. To hell with the age gap; girls grow up far more quickly than boys. Jay's not taking advantage of that girl; she knows where she's at.'

'That's not the way Clayton Scott looks at it.'

'Fathers are all the same. Look at Ira and his little girl—' Pearl stopped suddenly and Miss Pink, glancing sideways, saw that her face had darkened, although it could have been a trick of the light. For a moment Pearl closed her eyes under the scrutiny then, opening them, said coolly, '*I* would have chosen a good man for my kids—' She grinned and now she was certainly flushed, but that could have been at the memory of a specific man. 'I never found him,' she went on, 'so—no man, no kids. I like Michael

119

Vosker,' she added thoughtfully, 'but that's the story of my life, probably yours too: when you find the right guy it's too late; someone else got there first. And I'm not into breaking up marriages; never was.'

Miss Pink stared at her horse's ears and wondered what was making Pearl garrulous. 'Have you planned anything special for tomorrow?' she asked casually.

'I told Tammy I'd take her and Kristen to the fiesta in Palomares. Now I guess it'll just be Tammy. Would you care to come?'

'Thank you but I would like to do some birding. I've not had the chance yet.'

'That's great.' Pearl sounded relieved, making Miss Pink feel ancient, too old for a fiesta. 'You can take the sorrel,' she added, observing the other's seat. 'You have a good relationship with him. Where will you go?'

'I shall go no further than Badblood and I shall keep to the trail.'

'Right. So long as I know where you are. Not that there's anything to worry about, but everyone has to come off some time, don't they?'

CHAPTER SEVEN

Early next morning, before Pearl was up, Miss Pink breakfasted, saddled her horse, and took the mesa trail to Badblood Wash. From there she crossed the higher ground to Rastus, climbed in and out of the canyon and followed the line up Midnight Mesa until she came to a jumble of rocks and junipers. She tied the sorrel to a tree, loosened the cinch and, putting a full canteen and sandwiches in her pack, she walked towards Slickrock Canyon.

She came out on the rim a few hundred yards from the clump of alligator junipers. Below her the cottonwoods were brilliant in the sunshine and she could hear a chorus of birdsong from the trees and from rocks and gullies. Visibility was perfect, the peak of Angel's Roost with its lone pinyon so clear that she realised she would have been visible had Kristen chanced to look that way three days ago. Now she saw, on the opposite side of the canyon, a break where small trees had rooted. That implied cracks and ledges, and she guessed that the route of descent would be there. She could see no cairns at the top but at this distance they would be indistinguishable from boulders. It was immaterial, she was here for the wildlife, not to discover how Jay Gafford reached Slickrock. It was Kristen's route she was proposing to use—and in the knowledge that no one else would be on it today. From a flurry of telephoning last evening it transpired that Gafford and Kristen were going to the fiesta together, leaving Harper at the ranch. Maxine was in no shape to go to town and Tammy, evidently still sulking, had elected to stay with her. Miss Pink had Slickrock and its animals to herself.

She came to the alligator junipers and looked over the edge, feeling all the trepidation of someone about to abseil from a Dolomite tower. In the event, the descent of the pink wall depended on route-finding, not on technical ability; what had appeared vertical from a distance was nothing more than a scramble, the handholds large and incut, and the pitches connected by slanting rakes. These diagonal stretches were quite wide and not nearly as exposed as she'd thought; there were pockets of gravel and prickly gardens of cacti, and wherever the sun's rays touched the rock lizards sprawled with lifted heads trying to warm their blood and watch for hawks at the same time.

Below her the cottonwoods thrummed like a distant city and there were movements in the canopy as birds flitted from tree to tree. She beamed with pleasure, felt a handhold crumble, and brought her mind back to essentials; one could meet disaster only a few feet above level ground. Even when she came to the bottom of the wall she kept a check on herself, alert for loose rocks underfoot. If she didn't return to the village they would search for her first in Badblood Wash, and that was two miles away as the vulture flew.

She paused on the talus slope outside the first trees and studied the ground. There were indentations in the loose surface and a tread-mark in firmer soil. She followed the tracks into the cottonwoods and found herself on a game trail where any human traces had been overlaid by the prints of deer. She took a closer look. The deer had fawns, one good print was little more than an inch in length. She pushed on, the vegetation forcing her to keep to the path, stooping stiffly under alder branches where Kristen would have ducked and the deer would have passed unhindered.

She came to the creek, which was low but still running. She assumed that all the canyons had water in their upper reaches; it was when they reached permeable rock towards the escarpment that they disappeared underground to emerge in the line of springs along the foot of the cliffs. The water in Slickrock must support a host of animals. Those deer; if they were resident in a canyon no more than five miles long, how was it their population didn't explode? There must be predators, and that meant lions. She followed the creek upstream, walking on its miniature sandspits, looking for the mark of big paws.

Her excitement died when she found a boot-print; she'd be unlikely to see a lion where a man had been. It was the print of a small heel and a smooth sole and she should have been ready for it; she was convinced Gafford had been here three days ago. Damn, she thought, staring at the print, if there are lion they're in the opposite direction, downstream. She became aware, above the chatter of water, of faint sounds that were different from what she was accustomed to in the wilderness. She held her breath, listening, sweat running into her eyes.

The sounds intensified. They were the reverse of stealthy; whatever was making them wasn't bothered about intruders. Vegetation rustled loudly, so loudly it sounded as if it were being trampled. Miss Pink's eyes widened, her grip on reality slipping as the mind recalled images, of rhino, water buffalo: big dangerous beasts. It—they—snorted, slashed, screamed—no, not screamed ... Out of the bushes: squealing, red-eyed, bristling, an animal came charging, a brute so startling it was a chimera. 'Ho!' shouted Miss Pink, her body galvanised with shock, waving her arms as if this were a charging bull: 'Ho, ho, ho!'

It stopped, pivoted and bolted back the way it had come. Frenetic squeals and the sound of a stampede told her that they had all gone, fleeing down the canyon. Her hands were pressed to her heart like a heroine in a melodrama. It was her first encounter with peccaries.

When she recovered she left the creek to find out what they had been doing. There was a kind of glade where a tree had fallen leaving space for the sun to penetrate, and evidently something had been growing here which pigs enjoyed. It looked like a bed of catnip after cats have wallowed in it. The squashed plants had a strong smell, vaguely mint-like.

An obvious trail led out of the glade and she found the print of the cowboy boot again. The path took her through a grove of willows to a crag of friable yellow rock with weeds at its base. For a moment she thought she had come to the end of the canyon but then she remembered that the headwall was a great amphitheatre with slabby rock and caves; this was merely an isolated outcrop.

The path contoured the edge of the weeds to a pile of brushwood at the foot of the rock, a pile such as a packrat makes at the entrance to its nest. She prodded it with her toe and a clutch of twigs toppled and fell. She started back; there was a gleam in the depths. She listened for a rattle but heard only the bees in the willows. She looked for a stick, couldn't see one, and stamped. The gleaming thing didn't move. She kicked the brushwood aside to reveal a plastic bucket and a watering-can.

125

She was utterly bemused. She picked them up, turned them over, studied the ground where they had been standing, but she could find no clue as to their purpose. She turned, blinking at the sunshine. What were watering-cans used for? You might use one to rinse off a car or a horse, but horses couldn't be brought into Slickrock, or if they could she had seen no traces. What else, where else, *how* could a watering-can be used? She sat down, her elbows on her knees, and stared at nothing, her mind blank.

Something caught her eye, something to do with the plants, but for a moment she couldn't identify it and when she did she failed to grasp its significance. The plants were clones. In all the riotous growth in the bottom of the canyon, with its range of species and every gradation of age and size, this colony, no more than ten feet square, was not only uniform, it had eliminated every other species. It dawned on her that this was an alien plant, probably brought-in by birds, and now she realised that another stand had been growing where the pigs had been feeding. The herd must have just discovered it and not yet reached this patch. A kind of mint, she'd thought, getting to her feet and crushing a leaf. It felt sticky and the plants were curiously tall. She stared at a growing point level with her eyes, or where

126

the growing point should be; the main shoot was bent in a curve. And so were all the others, every one of them. She looked closer, parting the long green leaves—flowers appearing, she noticed: drab, like nettles. The growing shoot was fastened to the stem with a plastic tie: green, like the plant. She had stumbled on a marijuana garden.

She replaced the bucket and watering-can and rebuilt the brushwood pile. Her tracks were distinctive: the cleated print of a walking boot. She pondered the difficulty of erasing every print without making more, and decided against it. The peccaries would probably discover the second plot before the growers returned, and the destruction of the crop, obviously by pigs, would outweigh other considerations. All the same she thought it prudent to leave the canyon without hanging about. This place, she recalled, was a box, and the discovery had induced in her a definite feeling of claustrophobia.

She retraced her steps down the creek until her incoming track was obscured by a mass of those small cleft hoofprints which she had mistaken for those of fawns. The peccary herd had crossed the creek heading towards the opposite wall of the canyon, in fact towards that break which must provide access from the Markow property. She took to the bank which she had been following initially, found a game trail and continued down it, catching glimpses of that right-hand wall, brilliantly side-lit but, looking up it and with the pinyons throwing black shadows, no route was obvious. At least, she thought, there was no one on it, no one coming down to water his garden.

She came to a marshy patch bright with red and yellow columbine. She'd seen no columbines on the way in. A hummingbird hung at her shoulder, attracted by her red neckerchief, then swooped away to a twig where its plumage caught the light, ruby and emerald. She strolled on happily and when her mind returned to the worrying subject of drugs, of the significance of this canyon, its remoteness, it occurred to her that she had been walking downstream for a long time.

She left the trail and plunged through undergrowth towards the side of the canyon. The belt of woodland was less than a hundred yards wide but the under-storey was dense. She stumbled and sweated and tore her shirt, and emerged at the foot of the slope leading up to the wall—to find that the wall itself was a long way above, and the intervening space was occupied by extremely steep chutes and huge pinnacles of what looked like yellow clay. Some of the pinnacles had table-slabs tilted rakishly on their summits.

She cast about in panic. She had seen no

sign of this weird landscape from Angel's Roost nor from the rim of the mesa. She recognised nothing. She was too low to see the flood-plain of the Rio Grande, even to see the mouth of the canyon. Angel's Roost was hidden and the far wall of the canyon, the one on the Markow side: all obscured by the tall cottonwoods. Midnight's rim was hidden by the nearest pinnacles, and what made the situation even more frightening was that the pale clay reflected the sun, and the heat was intense. She must have passed the foot of the exit route a long way back. There was nothing for it: she must return up the canyon until she intersected her tracks of the morning—and she must stay in the sun where she had a wider view of her surroundings.

She found a stick and started the slow return. Soon her way was obstructed by a ragged reef with trees at its base. Now there were not only rocks and crevices to contend with but vegetation too, much of it thorny. She worked her way round the foot of the obstacle, parting plants with the stick, terrified of spraining an ankle. Several times, as she lowered herself carefully down the far side of a boulder, she heard scurrying and faint squeaks: rodent noises.

A canyon wren burst into song, the notes fading on a dying fall; pigeons erupted from a tree and clattered downstream. Poised on a rock, Miss Pink followed their flight and became aware of a hole in the rock, and a tip below. It was an abandoned mine.

There were baulks of timber scattered about, dried and splintery, but there were no tracks so far as she could see. She wasn't tempted to explore; climbing down into an isolated canyon was a calculated risk but entering an old mine was madness; she knew her limitations. Besides, she wasn't interested in mines.

She turned back to the canyon, glanced at the trees hoping for a game trail at the edge of the woodland, and saw more timber: upright and angled. The miner had built himself a cabin—and he would have cut a trail to provide access.

There were brambles right up to the back wall of the cabin, which was in fairly good condition. There was an unglazed window looking down the canyon and a door facing upstream. The door was closed by a metal hook that fitted a staple on the jamb. She lifted the hook and the door swung inward silently.

There was a bed under the window against the far wall. It was a double bed with a mattress. Straws protruded from holes in drab hessian. In the middle of the mattress, sunk heavily in a hollow, was a coiled snake. It was cream with black blotches like a leopard and it looked as big as a python. The head was towards her, the eyes open but the only movement was the delicate flick of the tongue.

Miss Pink regarded the dark head and the thick neck—no bulging cheeks, so no venom sacs—and she stepped back carefully and waited.

The snake uncoiled slowly and lowered itself to the floor, the length of it seeming to go on for ever, the tail flipping down to raise a spurt of dust, then sliding with infinite grace to vanish without haste into a large hole. She thought it was about eight feet long, decided that had to be an exaggeration but when she entered the cabin and saw the hollow in the mattress at close quarters and considered its weight she thought eight feet was probably correct after all.

She explored the cabin. No rattler would remain in proximity to a gopher snake of those dimensions. She thought the place hadn't been used by men for a long time. There were old rat droppings on the floor and the mattress and on top of shelves in a corner. On the shelves there were some open rusted cans, one containing nails and tacks, another something wrapped in rag which turned out to be a lump of hard putty. There was a cupboard with dusty mugs and plates and old-fashioned billy-cans, blackened with soot. There was a screw-top jar full of large kitchen matches. Behind the cupboard was a sheet of glass; the miner had been intending to glaze the window.

She sat on the edge of the mattress and eyed the hollow left by the snake. She retraced events. The miner had died—Herb Beck? Sam Dearing?—and the rats moved in, or had been there all the time scavenging his scraps; they were followed by snakes, and this big gopher inherited the territory. When she left she latched the door, amused to think that the gopher, having accounted for the rodents in the cabin, must now forage abroad for food, and yet it still returned to the cabin to sleep.

There was no trail leading to the cabin, or if there was it had been overgrown. She had to go back to the open ground, and as she resumed the tiresome progress up the canyon she thought that a snake's territory would be restricted, that she could soon pass into a rattler's sphere of influence. She sighed, she was having a hard day: interesting but wearing. She looked ahead and saw that she was coming to the end of the yellow towers. The big cliffs were in view again coming down to the canyon floor, and at last she could see the rim. Excited, she searched for the alligator junipers but from below she couldn't distinguish them from the common variety; she would have to continue until she found the tracks: Kristen's and her own. She gave one more glance at the skyline and stepped forward, and stopped. Something had moved on the rim.

She focused the binoculars, praying that it wasn't the sorrel, so close to the edge, realising in the next breath that the horse, if it had broken loose, would have run straight home. Deer then, probably deer, or one of those ridiculous pigs. Whatever it was, it had gone and she forgot it in the renewed need for caution as she started forward again.

She found the escape route quite easily, her tracks obvious on the slope. She was tired now and she took the climb slowly. It was also excessively hot, the wall getting the full force of the afternoon sun, the rock painfully hot to the hands. The lizards were gone and the occasional cactus flower drooped like tired tissue-paper.

She staggered over the rim and into the shade of the junipers. She drank some water, reserving a few spoonfuls for emergencies (if the horse had gone she would have to walk back to the village) and then she strolled slowly across the mesa to the boulders where she had left the sorrel. From some distance away she saw a glint of red where the sun was catching his hide and she sighed with relief. 'Good boy,' she called, picking up speed. The sorrel whinnied but she ignored it. She was staring at a drift of white sand in the lee of a prickly pear, a drift which, side-lit as the sun declined, held the clean mark of a boot, smooth-soled and narrow-heeled, and she remembered that she had chosen to leave the horse at this spot simply because it was secluded, unvisited. There had been no tracks here this morning.

CHAPTER EIGHT

'Marijuana?' Pearl said. '*Grass?* I don't believe it.' It was a great joke.

'I'm serious,' Miss Pink insisted. 'There were two plots, about twenty plants in each, I'd say, but the peccaries have destroyed half of them already.'

'Javelinas. Wild pigs are javelinas here.'

'Who d'you think is growing it?' Miss Pink asked, and Pearl sobered, peering intently at a lettuce leaf. They were preparing supper.

Miss Pink had reached home first, had come back to a village that appeared as abandoned as the mesas. She had seen no further sign of the person who left the print of a cowboy boot, the person who may have been on the rim looking into Slickrock. 'There was someone on Midnight Mesa,' she told Pearl now.

'Fletcher Lloyd. Why not? It's Beck land.'

Pearl had come home about an hour after Miss Pink who'd had time to attend to her horse and take a shower at her leisure. She was drinking beer at the kitchen table when Pearl came in to report the fiesta a success: 'Ada enjoyed it. Funny how her turns come and go; maybe it's the change, she was fine today. You ate already?' She eyed the bread-board that was smeared with jam and something brown.

'No, I'm starving; I was about to start cooking.'

Pearl took the bread-board to the sink and rinsed it rather ostentatiously. 'Peanut butter and jelly,' she observed. 'You're becoming quite American.'

Miss Pink frowned but she was too tired to protest and too much intrigued by the marijuana. 'So presumably Lloyd is growing it,' she observed lightly.

'I doubt that. Why don't you forget you saw it: two little plots, obvious it's just being grown for his own use, whoever.'

'Someone from the Markow place then.'

'Naming no names.'

'And if that was Lloyd on Midnight Mesa?'

'So? He found your horse—it would have whinnied when he was near—and he was looking for me; he wouldn't know you were riding the sorrel.'

'Either he or Avril would have seen me riding past Las Mesas.'

'Not necessarily, but if they did then he was looking to see what you were up to.

Nothing sinister about that; out in the sticks we have to know everything that's going on, not just on our own property but the neighbour's as well.' She was smiling.

'What would he have been doing up there in the first place on a Sunday afternoon? Another poaching expedition?'

'Another—? Oh, like Ramirez, you mean.' Pearl fell silent, abstracted. Miss Pink watched her, wondering if they were both considering those remains in the next canyon to Slickrock, quite close really. She was. 'There's no connection,' she said. 'The grass wouldn't have been planted when he died—or would it? How long does it take to mature?'

'If there was a connection, then the marijuana isn't a joke.'

Pearl thought about that and then: 'Ridiculous!' she exclaimed. 'Of course there's no connection.' She smiled and relaxed. 'But Fletcher Lloyd now: I might guess what he was doing up there on a Sunday afternoon. Planning a rip-off.'

'A rip-off? Oh, of the marijuana.'

'Of course. It's an occupational hazard. He'd steal it just as it's ready for harvest. He could have gone up there to see what stage the crop was at, particularly since he knew Jay and Kristen—' She stopped.

'Were safely out of the way at the fiesta,' Miss Pink completed.

'Oh dear. I shouldn't have said that.'

'I didn't hear.'

'And the pigs will destroy the whole crop anyway. A shame, I enjoy an occasional joint. They should have fenced it.' Miss Pink pursed her lips. 'Did you never smoke?' Pearl asked. 'Tobacco?'

Miss Pink shrugged and changed the subject. 'Whose cabin is that in the canyon? Was it Sam Dearing's or Herb Beck's?'

'I believe Sam's mine was in Slickrock.' There was a pause. 'Of course it was! So many old mines about, one gets confused. You found his cabin? What's it like?'

'Just a cabin with a bed and cupboard, and some crocks. There was a gopher on the bed.'

'A gopher? Oh, a gopher snake! Yes, there would be. I mean, he used to stay there before Marge put a stop to it. So the place would be swarming with rodents. What else did you find in Slickrock?'

Miss Pink enthused about the woodland and the yellow towers with their tilted tables, and Pearl listened with a smile that seemed a trifle wistful, as if she were enjoying the canyon vicariously. Miss Pink made no mention of her moments of panic when she thought she was lost, in fact, in retrospect she hadn't been lost, had merely missed the trail. She admitted as much to Pearl, adding that had she not done so she would never

137

have seen the snake nor that fantastic lunar landscape of yellow clay.

'Yes,' Pearl agreed, her eyes soft, 'they—' and the screen door opened to reveal Kristen looking tired and tense. 'Hi, sweetie,' Pearl said. 'Had fun?'

The girl nodded. 'Yes thanks. A good day. Can I come in?'

'When did you ever have to ask? There's Coke in the fridge, Miss Pink stocked up for us. She had a fun day too.' Pearl was slicing tomatoes on the draining-board. 'She climbed down into Slickrock.'

'Neat.' Kristen perched on a stool and popped a can of Coke.

'D'you know what she found there, Kristy? You'll never guess.' The girl blinked and frowned. 'Grass!' Pearl exclaimed. 'Two plots of grass all ready for harvest.'

Kristen nodded. 'Everyone grows a few plants.'

'That's what I told Miss Pink. Who's bothered about the odd joint? It's not as if we're pushing crack here in Regis. She agrees.' Pearl scrubbed a radish carefully. 'Unfortunately,' she went on, 'there's a herd of pigs got into Slickrock, musta got in from the Markow side, and they've trampled one plot. They'll have found the other by now. A shame, I call it.'

'It doesn't matter.'

'Well, that's cool! Someone's going to be

mad as hell.' The tone was loaded.

'Jesus! What's a few plants of grass? I'm not bothered. When will Ira be back, d'you know? Did you hear anything?'

'Not yet, they only just got there. What's with Ira?'

Kristen was staring at her Coke can. Pearl had turned, unable to hide her surprise. Kristen said suddenly, 'Tammy hates it up there, she's climbing the wall. Can't you have her here?'

'Well, I—That would be rough on Maxine; she's not fit, and the baby could come early.'

'She can cope. Tammy can't.'

'That's different! What d'you mean, Tammy can't cope?'

Kristen hesitated. 'Why don't I go up there?' she asked, and answered her own question: 'That means leaving Mom.'

'Why don't you have Tammy?' Pearl asked.

'No room.'

'You have a spare room—'

'We don't. And Mom can't look after her—'

'Tammy looks after herself—and other people. She's my maid!' Bewilderment turned to anger. 'For God's sake, you'd think the kid was retarded—' She clapped her hands to her mouth and her eyes were wide with the horror of what she'd said.

Kristen stood up. She said evenly, cool in the face of histrionics, 'She's never been without someone to take care of her, so now she feels abandoned and she's scared. She's not retarded of course, but she's very young. Someone has to be responsible for her with Ira so far away.'

'Is she frightened of something in particular?' They turned to Miss Pink as if a piece of furniture had given tongue. They had forgotten her.

'What would you expect?' Kristen asked. There was a pause. 'She's scared of the dark—'

'Rubbish!' Pearl exclaimed. 'She rides this track at night all the time and she never said a word to me about being scared.'

'Her folks were here then.' Kristen moved to the door. 'Maybe she infected me with her panic.' She shrugged, as if relinquishing the problem. 'She'll be OK. I'll see you in the morning, right?'

'Storm in a teacup,' Pearl grumbled as the screen door slammed. 'What a fuss to make: Tammy, I mean, not Kristen. The kid's trying to attract attention because she feels she's been rejected. She wanted to go to Texas—who wouldn't—but there was no way they could take her: an old man dying, probably a funeral and all.'

'Kristen was bothered,' Miss Pink pointed out. 'Very bothered if she and Gafford are responsible for those plots in Slickrock. She didn't turn a hair when you said the pigs had destroyed half the crop, let alone the fact that I'd stumbled on it.'

'She doesn't smoke. I mean, she doesn't use grass.'

'Yes, but'—Miss Pink was impatient—'she showed no interest. Tammy was far more important.'

'Before Kristen fell for Jay, she was like a big sister to Tammy—oh God, why did I have to say Tammy wasn't retarded, and remind her of Veronica?'

'Because Tammy does remind you of Veronica?'

'No-o! There's nothing about Tammy is a bit like Veronica.'

'Youth? Innocence?'

'So?' It was belligerent.

'I should think that's enough.'

*　　*　　*

She had a corner bedroom with windows on two sides, wide open day and night. In her dream she was galloping hard across a mesa on a straight trail through the pinyons. At the end of the trail was the rim of a canyon, and space. As she plunged towards the abyss the hoofbeats grew louder, the sound mounting with her panic. She knew she should throw herself from the saddle but she couldn't do it. Perhaps, she thought, since it's a dream I'll survive, I always do; there wouldn't be any pain, and a dream-horse couldn't die. But she was overwhelmed by compassion and woke in a sweat to hoofbeats that thundered, faltered and took up again to fade in the distance. Her eyelids drooped and she was over the edge and falling.

She woke to the song of the mockingbird but even as she revelled in the sunshine and tried to identify the species that the bird was imitating, she remembered the dream: one of those odd times when she dreamed that she was awake. The content, of course, was predictable, she had correlated riding on the mesa with the dangers of a canyon rim.

'We've got trouble,' Pearl said as she entered the kitchen. 'That kid Tammy: didn't sleep in her bed last night, would you believe it. Have some coffee; you're still half asleep.'

Still standing, Miss Pink drank and came to life. 'Kristen was worried,' she remembered.

'I guess so. I don't know about that. She called me earlier to say Tammy didn't sleep at the Harpers', and was she here by any chance? She's not in her own home neither. Daryl went to look.'

Miss Pink sat down. 'Have they tried all the other houses: the Voskers, Marge—who else is there?'

'Only Avril Beck. And the bunkhouses; there's two of those but she couldn't be in 'em because Fletcher occupies one and Jay's in the other. They're searching the barns. Oh, my God, how does that sound? You think of the river—and Veronica.'

'Veronica was pregnant!' exclaimed Miss Pink, and they stared at each other. 'Ridiculous,' she added. 'Impossible.'

'Twelve,' Pearl whispered. 'She's only twelve.'

'Good morning, girls!' Miss Pink tried to orientate herself as Marge Dearing entered, immaculate in pink and smelling of talcum powder. 'Something wrong?' she asked lightly.

'Tammy,' Pearl said. 'She's missing.'

'Oh.' Marge pulled out a chair and sat down. 'May I have some coffee?' Miss Pink reached for a mug and Pearl filled it in silence. 'What do you mean, missing?' Marge asked, her tone flat. 'When did she go?' She knew about the sick grandfather, everyone did.

'Last night,' Pearl said tightly. 'This morning, who knows? She was supposed to be sleeping at the Harpers' and her bed—the bed in Maxine's spare room—hasn't been slept in. They can't find her anywhere.'

'Odd,' Marge conceded. 'So that's why Kristen was up with the dawn.'

'Was she?' Miss Pink asked. 'How do you

know?'

'And in a hurry. She galloped past here as if the devil was after her. You must have heard her. I *saw* her; she went round the corner of my house like she was competing in a rodeo.'

'What time was that?' Miss Pink remembered her dream.

'Before seven.'

'Maxine called Kristen,' Pearl explained. 'She couldn't sleep—Maxine, I mean—so she got up early to get a drink and she peeked in the spare room just to see Tammy was OK and she wasn't there. She sent Daryl up to the ranch house and she wasn't there neither. She hasn't taken her pony nor her bike.'

'She went for a walk,' Marge said with finality, but then she thought better of it. 'Kristen doesn't think that. What does she think? Why was she in such a tearing hurry?'

'She holds herself responsible,' Miss Pink ventured. 'She was here last evening and she was worried then.'

Marge said slowly, 'Tammy was here yesterday.'

'Here?' Pearl asked. 'In the village or in this house?'

'In the village.' Marge was vague. 'You were at the fiesta.'

'What was she doing here? I don't have her Sundays.'

'I don't know.' Marge was affronted. 'I didn't come across to see.'

'Eating,' Miss Pink said, enlightened. 'She was eating peanut butter and jelly. It was on the bread-board,' she reminded Pearl. 'You thought I'd left the board dirty and I was too tired to argue. In fact, I thought you'd left it like that.'

'Sorry.' Pearl shrugged. 'So what? The kid was hungry and came in and fixed herself a sandwich. It doesn't help us find out where she is now. And who's going to tell her folks?'

'I think we should go up there,' Miss Pink said firmly. 'To the Harper place, I mean. There may be some indication as to where she's gone.'

'If there is, Kristen will have found it. What makes you think you can do better?'

'A fresh eye? Age, experience? It can't do any harm and we can lend moral support; they're all young people up there. She's probably not far away, just—er—calling attention to herself, like you said, Pearl. It would put people's minds at rest. You don't have to worry her parents unduly. Yet.'

'You forgot Jay Gafford,' Marge said.

'How's that?' Miss Pink was sharp.

'You said everyone up there was young.' Pearl said, 'She didn't forget him.'

They drove to the Markow ranch, the three of them on the bench seat of Pearl's

145

pick-up. Miss Pink wondered what was in the minds of her companions. They were silent, preoccupied, forgetful of the visitor between them although she had the feeling that they would have been no more communicative in her absence, which was odd in the light of their being not only neighbours, but friends.

'What do *you* think?' she asked Marge.

'My mind's a blank, dear. Let's wait to hear what Maxine has to say.' It was a reproof.

'And you?' She turned to Pearl and saw slim fingers tighten on the wheel.

'She'd be all right,' Pearl said. 'She's just playing up: like runaways, you know?'

'She hasn't gone far,' Marge said.

'She couldn't; she's on foot.'

Every comment carried an unspoken qualification, like: 'Unless someone picked her up,' or 'She could have hitched.' Miss Pink, reflecting that her experience was liable to suggest a sinister element more often than was justified, contracted her mind, withdrew antennae concerned with vibrations and allowed the morning dominance: sunshine, air and naked rock.

At the Harper home they found Maxine drying dishes and in a bad mood. 'It wasn't fair on the kid,' she protested. 'They shoulda took her with them; any normal father would. I was taken to see my Grandpa when

146

he was dying. Ira's not doing that kid any favours, trying to protect her. Now look what's happened—and she was left in my charge!'

'No one's blaming you,' Pearl said as the others murmured agreement. 'You put your feet up, and I'll make us a pot of coffee.'

On the other side of the living-room, beyond slatted blinds and screened French doors the valley trembled in the heat and the desert mountains were insubstantial as mist. 'They have a good view,' Marge said with a proprietorial air as Miss Pink, unable to resist, parted the slats and surveyed the scene. She turned, her face expressionless; a loop of the river came within a mile of the ranch.

'Where's Kristen?' she asked.

'I'm not sure.' Maxine subsided on a chintzy sofa, her face drawn with fatigue and worry. 'They're all riding, looking for her: Daryl and Jay and Kristen. They'll be in different places.'

'They searched the barns?'

'I guess so, and we called everybody: Avril and the Voskers besides you guys, so they'll be looking too. But where do you look? I mean, the professor said he'd go in the old grain store but she'd never go there, she's scared of snakes. And I guess you looked in your place, Marge, and why should she be in an old barn anyways?'

'I didn't look in my barn,' Marge said coldly. 'I didn't know she was missing until I went across to Pearl. No one called me.'

'I did. You didn't answer.'

'Then I was across the road.'

Miss Pink coughed. They turned to her as Pearl came in with mugs on a tray. 'Who saw her last?' Miss Pink asked.

'Us, of course,' Maxine said, 'Daryl and me. We watched a game show and then we all went to bed. I saw her go in the guest-room—it's the nursery really but there's a bed besides the crib. That's the last time I saw her.'

'Did Daryl see her again?' Marge asked sweetly. 'Can he tell us more than you?'

Maxine's jaw dropped. 'What in hell are you suggesting?'

'I'm not suggesting any—'

'Certainly not,' Miss Pink put in firmly. 'Can you recall what she was doing yesterday?'

But the change of subject touched another nerve. 'How can they expect me to watch her all the time?' Maxine protested. 'So she was here all morning, helping me, and we had something to eat and watched TV but you can't expect a kid her age not to be bored with staying indoors, and she went up to her own home. Was I meant to stop her? She's the boss's daughter! Should I have locked her up?'

'She only came to the village,' Marge said comfortably.

'I know. I saw her go by. On her bike.' Maxine was frowning.

'I saw her too.' Marge pursed her lips.

'Where?' Miss Pink asked.

'I told you! In the village of course. She went past my bedroom window. I was lining a drawer in my dresser and she went by.' Again that disapproving look.

'Is that when she came to my place?' Pearl asked.

'I wouldn't know. I didn't watch where she went. I don't even know if she continued to your back entrance or turned down the street. It wasn't my business.'

Pearl, thoughtful, her chin on her hands, said suddenly, 'But this was the afternoon! It was hours later that she went missing.'

'Is it possible'—Miss Pink was diffident—'that her leaving was influenced by something that happened earlier, like meeting someone?'

'If there were strangers in the village,' Pearl said, 'like a boy, or a family, they'd have been noticed.'

'Not a stranger, but someone she knew who made a suggestion, put an idea into her mind.' Silence. 'Such as telling her it didn't cost much to fly to Houston?'

'It costs a sight more than she could lay her hands on,' Pearl said. 'Unless she knew where there was some cash in her own home. Then how'd she get to the interstate? She wouldn't walk, she'd have taken her bike, and her bike's still here.'

Marge said reluctantly, 'I guess I'll go and look in my barn, not that I think she's there for one moment; she'd have come to me for a bed, she wanted somewhere to sleep—'

'What's wrong with my home?' Maxine asked angrily.

'We have no idea why she left,' Miss Pink put in. 'All we can do is look everywhere. May we see your guest-room?'

'Why?'

'Because it was the last place she was seen. By you.' Miss Pink tore her eyes away from the girl, afraid that she would interpret the statement in a way that was extremely unpleasant.

'Pearl can show you.' She was ungracious but, fortunately, not discerning. She felt she was being blamed but as yet, only for irresponsibility. Miss Pink wondered how long it would be before someone suggested to her that something more sinister could be involved.

The guest-room was at one end of the mobile home. It was scarcely more than a cubicle and furnished only with a camp bed, a cot and a chest of drawers. There were windows on two sides and a built-in closet that contained winter clothes. The room was

150

clean and neat except that the cot was piled with baby clothes and packages in gift wrapping which had probably been moved from the bed. The bed itself was unwrinkled and covered with a patchwork quilt. One window was open, nylon net moving in the draught. Miss Pink parted one set of curtains, lifted the next and saw that the screen was firmly in place. The second window was closed and unscreened but the bottom half lifted easily and with hardly a sound. 'This was how she went,' she said.

'And closed it behind her.' Pearl lowered her voice. 'What you were asking in there, about meeting someone in the afternoon? Who did you have in mind?'

Miss Pink didn't answer the question. What she did say was: 'She must have left voluntarily, there was no sound of a struggle or a cry for help. That's a good sign.'

They went back to the living-room. 'Didn't she have an overnight bag?' she asked Maxine.

'Yes, she took it. Did you discover anything?' Maxine was sarcastic.

Miss Pink shook her head. 'We'll go up to the ranch house. Do you have a key?'

She wasn't surprised to learn that the place wasn't locked. Leaving Marge with Maxine they walked up to the main house. Pearl wanted to take her truck but Miss Pink said that if there was anything to be seen they

151

could miss it if they were in a vehicle. On the track Pearl looked around her helplessly: at the corrals and barns, at the steers in the feed-lot. 'You think the answer's here,' she said, and it was an accusation. 'But she's so young! I know these two guys, they're not like that.'

'Like what?'

'They're straight. Look—' She stopped and Miss Pink halted and turned to face her. Behind Pearl was the mobile home and the distant jungle on the banks of the river. She frowned, her eyes on the trees, but she was listening. 'Even suppose Jay wanted novelty,' Pearl said, 'and Daryl—with Maxine—er— inactive—no way would they touch the boss's kid. It's not just their jobs, it's the penalty! Think of it: they'd get life! Besides, she's not here, so how could it be either of them?' Miss Pink had started to walk on. Pearl hesitated and then hurried to catch up. She seized the other's arm. 'Why don't you believe me? Come on, if you know something the rest of us don't, we have a right to know.' Her nails dug into Miss Pink's flesh, she was losing control. 'After all, you're a stranger! What did you say?' as Miss Pink muttered something. 'I didn't catch that.'

'I said I don't like the silence.'

Pearl glanced round wildly. 'Of course it's quiet, there's no one about—'

'I mean, there's no sign or sound of her. Why doesn't she contact someone?'

'She doesn't want to. She's being naughty.'

'I hope so.'

In the house they found Tammy's room without difficulty: a young girl's room that at first sight looked as if burglars had been there, tapes and clothes on the floor and bed, the bed itself, under the clutter, made up, not slept in since it was made. Pearl picked up a black sweatshirt with cartoon cats on the front. 'The little bugger,' she breathed, her gaze going to a pair of jeans. 'Those don't even fit her! She's much smaller'n me.'

'Those are your clothes?'

'The shirt is, and—yes, the Levis are mine. I can't believe it. I give her things she takes a fancy to but this shirt is new, and it cost a fortune. She just walked off with it. Ah, well.' She threw it on the bed in disgust.

They searched the rest of the house even though Maxine had told them that Kristen had done so. 'Kristen was expecting this,' Miss Pink said in the living-room. 'That business about Tammy being scared of the dark and so on, it was a cover for something else. She wanted Tammy at your place last night. We have to find her.'

'We're looking. What else can we do?'

'I mean, find Kristen. She knows something about this.'

There was a pair of field-glasses on a sideboard. Taking them, Miss Pink went outside and studied the valley flats and the rim of the escarpment and the trail that led to Scorpion Canyon but there was no sign of the searchers. They walked back to the mobile home, picked up Marge and returned to the village. Marge went to her barn, Miss Pink walked down the street to the Voskers' house. Marian met her at the door, her face expectant, then anxious.

'You haven't found her? Michael's driving all the tracks between here and the interstate.'

'Why there in particular?'

'It's something to do.' She took Miss Pink to her living-room. 'We can't sit and do nothing. Clayton's searching the creek and Fletcher Lloyd's riding between Las Mesas and Pearl's place. The ditches are overgrown.'

'What's the thinking behind that?'

'Rattlers. Michael says that if she trod on a big diamondback, if she panicked—and she hates snakes—she could—er—'

'Die of shock.' Miss Pink was blunt. 'True, but if she loathes snakes that much she wouldn't go in the creek bed in the dark or in the early morning. But quite right,' she conceded, 'one has to look everywhere. What I came to ask you was, did you see anything of her yesterday afternoon—either you or Michael?'

'Michael was out birding. No, I didn't see her. But she was with Maxine last evening. What makes the afternoon important?'

'She was here in the village. She could have said something, given a hint as to what she intended to do, even borrowed money to fly to Houston.'

'Oh, you think she's gone to her parents.'

'If she has done, everything's fine, and perhaps there's nothing wrong if she's only gone to Palomares, but we ought to know. It's possible she told someone she was going to town and that person doesn't know she's missing, or that we think she's missing.'

'I never thought of it that way—but no—' Marian shook her head decisively. 'Everyone's been contacted. They'd have said.'

'No one's been asked if they saw her—or spoke to her yesterday afternoon. She may have said something that no one thought was important at the time. It may only have been a passing word in the street. She was on her bike. Marge saw her pass but didn't see if she took the road to Las Mesas or came down this way. It was in the afternoon,' she added vaguely.

'I was on the porch after lunch. I didn't see her.'

'Isn't the road screened by your acacias?'

'Come and see for yourself.'

They went out on the porch where there were rocking-chairs and an iron table. The acacias screened the road to some extent but no one could have passed by the gate without being seen. 'In a place like this,' Marian said, 'you're more likely to hear people anyway, it's so quiet, particularly on Sunday afternoon. I'd even have heard her tyres.'

'You didn't doze off in the heat?'

'I may have cat-napped but I'll swear I heard every sound. The jays were a trial, no one could *sleep* through their racket. There had to be an owl about, or maybe a snake robbing a nest. And Kristen—oh dear, Kristen! Always quarrelling with her father, no wonder poor Ada takes to her bed.' Marian lowered her voice. 'You don't expect to retire to the country and have neighbours who act like it's a ghetto.'

Miss Pink was thoughtful. 'Tammy went to Pearl's place,' she mused. 'She made herself a sandwich there. I wonder—'

'She went on to Avril's?' Marian was intrigued.

'Possibly. Where was your husband?'

'I told you—birding: down on the river. He usually leaves his car at Clayton's farm and then walks downstream. There's a trail in the woodland. It's one of his favourite places. Even now.'

'You mean, in the heat of the day?'

'No, I don't mean that. I mean—since Veronica.'

'Is that where they found her?'

'Oh no, miles downstream; the river was high and it swept her down, but that's where she'd have gone in the water: from their own property. It was the only place she knew. They didn't allow her out on her own.'

'How did she get away that time?'

'She walked.'

'Someone saw her?'

'No, but she must have done; she couldn't drive and she didn't take a horse or a bicycle.' There was a long silence. 'It sounds like history repeating itself, doesn't it?' Marian said uneasily.

CHAPTER NINE

'I think Tammy went to town,' Ada said, 'to Palomares. She called some friends and they came and fetched her. She walked down the road to meet them.'

Miss Pink considered this. She was in a room which was gloomy in contrast with the bright patio. When Ada had called to her to come in from the veranda, she hadn't been able to see the woman until she moved. She was sitting in an armchair wearing a sombre dressing-gown. Only her face was discernible

157

and that was shadowed.

'Would you like me to turn on a light?' Miss Pink asked.

'Please don't.' Ada laughed apologetically. 'I'm sensitive about my appearance. I should be dressed but I didn't get around to it yet. I must have done too much at the fiesta, although I did enjoy myself. I think Pearl had fun too. You should have come.'

'Another time. Tell me, did your husband see anything of Tammy yesterday?'

'No, he would have said.' There was a faint movement of the lips, like a grimace; Miss Pink wondered if the woman was in pain. 'He's worried,' she said. 'He's thinking of snakebite, you see.'

'Is he still searching the creek?'

'No. He's gone to the Markow place, see if he can be of any assistance there.'

Miss Pink was surprised. 'We didn't pass him. We came down from there.'

'That's where he said he was going.' Ada sounded tired. 'Did you see Kristen?'

'No, the three of them: Kristen, Daryl and Jay, are out searching. We talked to Maxine. She's worried because she feels Tammy was her responsibility.'

Ada nodded. 'She mustn't take on; she has to think of the baby.'

'It's Tammy who's being irresponsible.'

'They don't think—and she's very young. Her folks should have taken her with them.'

'I must go back and see if there have been any developments. May I go out the back way?'

Ada stared. 'Of course. Was there something you wanted?'

'I'd like to walk up the creek.'

'Oh no, don't do that. There are rattlesnakes.'

'I thought people used the creek as a trail.'

'On horseback, not on foot. That's what Scott was worried about: that Tammy trod on one of those big old diamondbacks. They're deadly poisonous, you'd never stand a chance.' She stopped short. 'There, I don't want to alarm you. Most likely you'll never see one in the heat of the day but there are boulders and burrows where they lay up—'

'That's all right.' Miss Pink was reassuring. 'I'll go home by way of the street, the last thing I want is to meet a rattlesnake.'

She walked up the street, past the two unoccupied houses stopping to study each one—and the old grain store on the opposite side of the road. She'd forgotten to ask Marian if Michael had found anything in the building but of course he hadn't or she would have said.

Beyond the grain store was Marge's house: an L-shaped adobe on a corner lot with a weedy drive running from the street to her barn. Miss Pink turned aside and walked along the end wall of the house to find the patio on her right beyond a sagging fence. Marge was on her back porch watering fuchsias in pots. At the sound of Miss Pink's voice a fat grey poodle appeared, yapping hysterically. Marge shouted at the dog to no effect and directed the visitor to a gap in the fence. For the sake of quiet Miss Pink, who detested small poodles, gave the animal her attention, a proceeding which Marge observed with approval and then offered tea. Miss Pink declined, admired the fuchsias and remarked casually, 'No one saw Tammy yesterday afternoon.'

'Come and sit down,' Marge said, and subsided on a garden chair. She sighed heavily. 'Another hot day,' she breathed, fanning her flushed face and staring at the barn.

'What's worrying you?' Miss Pink asked.

Marge licked her lips. 'What a peculiar question.' The tone was too light, contrived. Miss Pink said nothing. 'I'm not worried,' Marge said.

'You were bothered about Tammy yesterday afternoon. What she did, who she was with—'

'She was alone—'

'Well, when she rode past your bedroom window—'

'Heavens, what have I done?'

'Both you and Maxine: you didn't like her being out alone.'

160

'She always is. It was that dress. And heels four inches high: at her age!'

'Not the red dress?'

'You saw her in it? I forgot. Do *you* think it's right? I tell you, if she'd been wearing that dress when she went missing I wouldn't have been surprised one little bit!' Miss Pink was silent for so long that Marge began to fidget. 'If it had been a larger size I'd have thought it was an old dress of Pearl's,' she said.

'It's a tacky dress; Pearl is elegant.' Miss Pink was neutral, stating facts, and Marge's response was startling.

'Elegant! You're talking about my neighbour, Pearl Slocum?'

'She has style.'

'No doubt.' Marge's eyes were snapping. 'In a *certain* way.'

'Are you upset about Tammy—Tammy wearing that dress, or because she was in Pearl's house yesterday afternoon?' Miss Pink paused, thinking. 'While Pearl was away,' she added.

'It's what she was doing there!' Marge had lost the last vestige of her serenity and was furiously angry.

'She was eating—' Miss Pink prompted.

'And the rest. What I don't understand'— Marge started to speak rapidly—'is why she comes down here wearing that dress which in the normal way of things wouldn't be seen

161

outside of a brothel and she comes straight to Pearl on a hot Sunday afternoon, like a bitch coming home. How long was she there? What was she doing?' Miss Pink was immobile. Marge's shoulders dropped and she started to breathe deeply. After a while she said in a hollow tone, 'I don't feel so good. This heat. Old people are old-fashioned. That dress puts you in mind—well, it's no dress for a little girl.'

She grimaced and blinked, as if trying to relax her facial muscles.

'What could a little girl be doing in an empty house?' Miss Pink was fully aware of how disingenuous was the question, but Marge rose to the bait.

'How do you know it was empty?'

'You're suggesting she met someone there?'

'I'm not suggesting anything. You said the house was empty. I asked how you knew, is all. Of course,' she added offhandedly, 'Pearl is in a far better position to tell you who has the freedom of her house than me. And now, if you'll excuse me, I have things to do.'

She rose, wheezing with the effort and, as she passed, again serene with a smile on her lips, Miss Pink caught a strong smell of brandy, which told her something about Marge's mood, but didn't explain everything, by any means.

There was a note on the kitchen table: 'Gone to Avril's. I saddled the sorrel for you. Leave word which way you go. Pearl.'

Miss Pink changed into boots, walked across the corral, climbed through the rails, and paused on the bank of the creek. A narrow path descended the bank which was at an easy angle, with widely spaced trees and rampant undergrowth. A bronze butterfly wafted through the sunshine but no birds called. It was too hot.

She dropped down the path to the creek bed which was composed of varicoloured stones with pockets of mud, and water gleaming in the cracks where it was free of a spongy green scum. She started to move downstream, her feet scrunching the stones. Weeds had sprung up as the water level dropped but the depression seemed devoid of animal life except for insects—and tracks. On larger patches of mud there were the prints of a shod horse and of a riding-boot. She didn't relate this last to the print in Slickrock Canyon because this must be Scott's track made as he searched for Tammy, whereas the one in Slickrock was presumably Jay Gafford's, and there was surely no connection between a print in a canyon five miles away and Tammy's disappearance from the Markow ranch.

Shrieks stopped her in her tracks, and her heart continued to thud even when, a moment later, she knew it was only scrub jays shouting their alarm. She should have been prepared for that and if she was so preoccupied that she could be shocked by jays, would she have noticed a diamondback in the shade of a clump of arrow-weed? She went on, edging round bushy plants like a nervous horse.

She had followed the creek for about two hundred yards when she came to a break in the vegetation on the right bank, the village side. Here old horse tracks were indented in dried mud and there were rails at the top of the bank. She climbed the slope and looked across an empty corral to a wall of bamboo. She had reached the Scott property.

She retreated to the creek and continued downstream for some distance. There were no more tracks, which was what one might expect. The Scotts' was the last house east of the village and the creek bed was used by no one other than Kristen, except in abnormal circumstances, such as when people were looking for a missing child. She thought about this, loitering on the return, considering the other villagers. Michael Vosker could well come here because there would be birds to watch in the cool of evening, and small mammals and snakes, but no one else would be interested. She had been thinking of the dry creek as a thoroughfare but it was nothing of the kind, except for the animals which needed to come and go without attracting attention to themselves. Her pace quickened. She returned to Pearl's house, ate a sandwich, mounted the sorrel and rode along the track to Las Mesas.

'No, she didn't come here, and I haven't laid eyes on her for weeks. We're isolated at this end; I got no idea what goes on in the village.'

Avril stood stiffly at her front door giving the effect of barring access to the house. Miss Pink said quietly, 'People are concerned; she's been missing for over twelve hours.'

'So why come to me?' In the face of the other's cool regard Avril swallowed and her eyes shifted sideways. 'I mean, if I haven't seen her—I mean, what could it have to do with me—us?' The last word was whispered, her eyes fixed on a point beyond Miss Pink who turned, but saw nothing more than the escarpment. 'What are you afraid of?' she asked curiously, turning back.

Avril gasped, then her face set. 'I don't believe this. You wouldn't act like this where you come from. How dare you!' She gave a furious laugh. 'You're forgetting your manners. You all make the same mistake, English tourists, you reckon ranchers—

165

people owning thousands of acres—they're no better'n farmers back home: lower class. Let me tell you: a rancher in this country is looked up to, they got their own clubs in town, they're like—like gentry! This country was built on cattle ranching, it still depends on people like us, never mind the depression, we're doing all right. I got eighty-five cows up on the mesas and I own all my land and my house, and that's a sight more than you own, I'll bet, with all your high and mighty airs.'

Miss Pink said pleasantly, 'It's an achievement to emigrate and work hard and end up with your own ranch. You can be proud of yourself. But suppose you tell me why you're so upset about Tammy.'

'You got no right to talk to me like that, coming here asking questions—'

'I'm asking everyone about Tammy.'

'Why?'

'She has to be found.'

'Why you? Why you poking your nose into something as don't concern you? You got no right—'

'A missing child concerns everyone. Including you.'

'It don't, it don't, it's got nothing to do with me!' Her arms were clutched defensively across her chest. Her eyes wouldn't remain still, darting from the escarpment to the visitor, rolling sideways as

166

if she wanted to turn her head but daren't.

'Let's sit down and have a cup of tea,' Miss Pink suggested.

The eyes were still. Avril stared at the skyline. 'I don't know nothing,' she muttered. Miss Pink took a step forward and the woman turned and walked along a passage to a neat kitchen. 'Fill the kettle,' Miss Pink ordered, and automatically Avril did so and switched it on. She took cups and saucers and a silver teapot from a cupboard, switched off the kettle, warmed the pot, switched on again, reached for a tea caddy.

'Where can you buy loose tea?' Miss Pink asked.

'Safeway's.'

'And the teapot?'

'I brought it from home last time I was over.'

Miss Pink drew out a chair and sat at the table. Avril made the tea and sat on the opposite side.

'Of course it has nothing to do with you,' Miss Pink said. 'It's not on your land.'

'What are you on about?' It was listless.

'The marijuana.'

Avril showed no surprise. Her elbows were on the table, her chin on her fists. She stared at the teapot.

Miss Pink poured the tea. 'Milk?'

'In the fridge.'

'You're a narcotics agent,' she said when

Miss Pink sat down again. 'I knew you weren't a tourist. No one'd ever come here, there's nothing to see.' She sipped her tea and her expression sharpened. 'I didn't even know it was there. Like you said: Slickrock isn't on my land.'

'No one's land? But Lloyd's in a different position, you could be held responsible for him.'

There was a tense silence. 'I'm not responsible for what my hands get up to,' Avril said tightly.

'Not for Ramirez?' Miss Pink mused.

Avril stared at her without subterfuge. 'You reckon Ramirez was growing it?'

It was Miss Pink's turn to be silent. Avril recovered some poise and said carelessly, 'I'm not bothered who's growing it; Lloyd, Ramirez, Gafford, you can't involve me if it's not on my land. What's a few plants anyway? There's far more people die of alcohol poisoning.'

'I don't think the grass is important either—unless there's some connection with Tammy's disappearance.'

'How could there be? And why are you interested in Tammy? Oh, I get it: there *is* a connection.'

'I'm not with Narcotics.'

'You said—you tried to make me believe you were! What are you?'

Miss Pink put down her cup. 'Which way

168

did Lloyd go?' Avril's eyes were jumpy again. 'Up to Badblood,' Miss Pink stated. 'Why would he think she went up there?' Avril stared at the table. 'Pearl too,' Miss Pink murmured. 'What sent her up there?'

'Pearl Slocum didn't go after him this time,' Avril said viciously. 'That makes a change. She went to the cabin out by Massacre Canyon.'

'Why?'

'She said as how we should look everywhere there was shelter. The kid wouldn't have stayed out in the open at night, she said.'

'Tammy wouldn't walk to Massacre, it's over six miles. Was she on a horse?'

'How would I know?'

'Why did Lloyd go up Badblood?'

'I didn't ask him. He's a cheeky sod, that Lloyd; I'd sack him but it's difficult to get experienced labour these days. He can do his job and he doesn't drink but he's a surly bugger when all's said and done, no respect for who's paying his wages. This time he never even gave an excuse like going to move the cows into Rastus. He acts like he owns the place. Even the horse he's on is mine.'

'You ride?'

'I mean, I own it. I have three horses.'

'But you don't ride.'

'That's nothing to be ashamed of! I can go anywhere in a pick-up a horse can go.'

'Not on the mesas, surely.'

'I pay a man to do that.'

'Did you send him up there yesterday?'

'He took some salt up to the cows.'

'On Sunday afternoon?'

'Ranchers work all hours. Why, did you see him? I knew you were up there; I saw you pass.'

Through the open window came the sound of a horse's hoofs. They looked up and saw a pinto turn in under the crossbar. Pearl pulled up at the hitching rail and slid down.

'Nothing,' she said, entering the kitchen. 'No sign of her at the Massacre cabin. What about this end?' Miss Pink shook her head. 'What do we do now?' Pearl asked. 'I guess at some point we have to call Thelma and Ira. And what about the police?'

'We can't call the police before the parents are told,' Miss Pink said. 'Let's go back to the Markow place. Kristen and the others must be back by now.' She looked meaningly at Pearl and stood up. 'You'll let us know if Lloyd discovers anything,' she said to Avril.

*　　　*　　　*

'Lloyd's gone up to Badblood,' she said as they rode towards the village.

'I know; Avril told me. Probably gone to look at that grass in Slickrock. He wouldn't

170

go down there yesterday with you there.'

'I don't see him going halves on the crop with Avril.' Pearl stared in astonishment. 'It crossed my mind,' Miss Pink added. 'She's so hostile; she seemed to think I had something on her, she even thought I was from Narcotics. She knew about the grass.'

'I told her that you found it, but she knew already—that it was there, I mean. Fletch must have told her.'

'She's not bothered about the grass itself.' Miss Pink was following her own tack. 'It's not even on her land.'

They continued in silence for a few moments then: 'It can't be to do with Tammy,' Pearl stated as if clinching an argument. 'You must have stroked her fur the wrong way.'

'I asked her if she'd seen Tammy, of course, but she was hostile before I arrived, or frightened; I mean, before she opened the door, and she fought so hard to distance herself from Tammy that it was obvious, as if she were disengaging herself from some other situation. In doing that she appeared to be callous about Tammy but she didn't care. Something else is more important to her.'

Pearl grinned. 'A time like this people's skeletons start to rattle in their closets. She was very rude about you when I called earlier: new money, she said, jumped up. Back home you'd be a cleaner.'

'How curious.' Miss Pink was fascinated. 'Could it be the mix of two cultures? Upwardly mobile people are usually proud of their achievements; does she think she's sneaked in by the back door, or that other people think that of her? So what?' Miss Pink shook herself and the sorrel laid back his ears. 'It's immaterial how she worked her way up, what puzzles me is why she was scared when she opened her door.'

'If it's not the grass and it's nothing to do with Tammy, and if you made it clear you knew about her background and didn't care, what else could it be? Maybe she has a lover?'

'Lloyd?'

'Of course not! Didn't you realise? Fletch took a shine to me.' She laughed. 'But it sure ain't physical. I'm just a mother-figure.'

'I don't believe that.'

'It's certainly not sex. Poor Fletch, if he ever touched me it was by accident. Times I wonder if he's gay.'

'Really? How interesting.'

'You say the weirdest things.'

'But—oh, never mind. Did you see anyone else on your ride—besides Avril?'

'No, did you? Where is everyone? You were going to the Voskers when we came back from Maxine's.'

Miss Pink told her about her visits to Marian Vosker, to Ada and to Marge.

'Fruitless,' she commented, 'so far as last night is concerned, and we still don't know where she went yesterday afternoon. Those women swear it wasn't to their houses—Ada was with you anyway, but she says Tammy didn't go to the Scotts, so after Marge saw her pass we know nothing more except that she came in your kitchen and had something to eat.'

'I guess she came to see me and forgot I'd gone to the fiesta, if she ever knew.'

'Wait a minute.' The sorrel halted. The pinto stopped and turned. 'Was *that* where she was going, in the red frock and the high heels?'

'What! She was wearing that rag? I thought Kristen took it off of her. You think she went to Palomares: rode to the interstate and hitched to town? But she was at the Harpers' in the evening so she came back safely. You don't think she met someone there, at the fiesta—oh my God, is that what you're thinking?'

'We have to find Kristen,' Miss Pink said grimly. 'As quick as we can.'

The sorrel leapt away and the pinto followed. They slowed at Pearl's place only because the horses wanted to turn in there, but the riders pushed them on and they didn't check again until they saw a solitary horseman riding towards them on the Markow track.

'Clayton Scott,' Pearl grunted but Miss Pink had already recognised the horse. 'Any news?' Pearl called as they drew near.

He shook his head. 'This is a bad business. We have to contact Ira; I don't think there's any question of it now.'

'We were just wondering if she could have gone to the fiesta,' Pearl said eagerly. 'She was dressed up, you see; Marge saw her go by in the afternoon, and she didn't visit with anyone so she has to have gone down the street to the interstate, and she was on her bike.'

He eyed her speculatively. 'She was back at Maxine's last evening.'

'She went and came back. But she coulda met someone there at the fiesta and he brought her back and then she went out again at night and met him outside the village.'

He was staring at her. 'Do you realise what you're saying?' He shifted to Miss Pink. 'Do you, ma'am? This is a little child!' She shrugged helplessly. 'You mean, like a schoolfriend?' he asked, with a glimmer of hope.

'We hadn't got that far, Clayton.' Pearl was embarrassed. 'We only just thought of the fiesta angle because of the clothes she was wearing, like party things.'

'I don't like it.' He shook his head. 'I would prefer to think she's just being

174

mischievous because she couldn't go to Texas: deliberately stirring up a hornets' nest. I'm praying she's holed up somewhere. I'm sure she is. Maybe she did meet a schoolfriend, even called one to come and fetch her, another little girl maybe.'

'Little girls don't have cars, Clayton.' If he was trying to reassure them he was failing miserably.

'Have all the barns and cabins been visited?' Miss Pink asked.

'Jay Gafford was up to an old shack in Scorpion. I've done the buildings at my farm.' His face set and he stared stonily towards the river. 'Michael Vosker was down there too,' he added dully.

'We'll ride on and talk to the Harpers,' Pearl said. 'And then I guess we have to call Thelma and Ira.'

He sighed heavily and nodded.

'Do you know where Kristen is?' Miss Pink asked.

'I haven't seen her. Did you want her for something special? I'll tell her if she's home when I get there.'

'Tell her to give us a call. And there's Daryl, he might have some ideas.'

'He doesn't. He found nothing in the river meadows.'

'He's obsessed with the river,' Pearl murmured as they rode on. 'Do you wonder? Hell,' she burst out, 'why is all this happening in one place: Veronica, Gregorio, now Tammy?'

'Tammy's only missing. What makes you think otherwise?'

Pearl glowered, her hat brim shielding her eyes. 'Because *he* does?' she ventured, jerking her head, indicating Scott.

CHAPTER TEN

'Kristen, can we have a word?'

'For Heavens' sakes, she only just got in! Let her eat.'

Maxine glared at Pearl across the kitchen table where Kristen sat before a plate of steak and chips. The girl was drawn with fatigue; she had been on the go for twelve hours, by now she must be running on nervous energy.

'What d'you want?' she asked listlessly.

Pearl hesitated and glanced at Miss Pink. The men had come back before Kristen and were sprawled on the sofa in the living-room, drinking beer.

'You got something private to say to her?' Maxine asked coldly. 'You want me to go?'

Kristen sighed and pushed her plate away. Pearl's eyes widened. Miss Pink asked pleasantly, 'Where's Tammy?'

'Safe,' Kristen said. 'I hope she's safe in

Palomares. That's where I think she is—or on the way to Texas.'

'That's what we reckon.' Gafford had approached silently and was leaning against the door jamb. 'She's nowhere here,' he added, his eyes on Kristen. 'We looked everywhere: between the cliffs and the river, up Scorpion—why, we searched much further than she could go on foot, and we was calling all the time. She's not here.'

Harper appeared at his elbow. 'If she was hurt,' he said, 'like in a fever 'cause of some bite, she couldn't call out. And we couldn't look in all the draws and arroyos, the weeds is so thick. If she was laying in one of them places—' His frightened eyes sought Maxine's, shying away from the responsibility which had suddenly descended on them.

Gafford was putting up a better front, all the same he was on edge; they were all on edge but where the Harpers were frankly terrified, Gafford and Kristen seemed to be in control, alert and purposeful—which was remarkable in the case of Kristen who was plainly worn down with fatigue.

'You gotta eat,' Maxine said desperately as the girl picked at her food.

'I'm not hungry. I'll put it in a bag.'

'You're coming back with us,' Pearl said. 'You need some sleep.'

Kristen's eyes narrowed and her mouth

177

set. She stood up and went to fill her glass at the tap. 'Look at you,' Pearl scolded, 'you're dehydrated: out in the sun all day—'

'Everyone was. So what?'

'Something I don't understand'—Miss Pink was persistent as a terrier—'last night you said Tammy was terrified, that she was frightened of the dark—'

'It was true.'

'Rubbish,' Pearl said hotly, while Maxine gaped. 'I said so then, and I say so now: Tammy was not—'

'What was she scared of?' Maxine asked, her eyes going to her husband.

'It was what *she* said,' Kristen shouted. Gafford's eyes were like a wolf's: watching, careful. 'She wouldn't tell me why,' she said more quietly, staring at her plate. 'I get the picture now, she was planning it already, planning to run away, try and get to Texas.'

'Why would it be easier to run away from my place than from here?' Pearl asked.

'Oh, for God's sake! I can't see into the kid's mind. If I could, I'd know where she was now.'

'You reckon she's in Texas,' Pearl reminded her. 'There's one way to settle that'—she looked round in triumph—'we call Ira.' She realised what she'd said and frowned. 'Do we?' she asked Miss Pink.

'I think you should,' Maxine said stoutly.

'And me,' Harper said. 'Her folks have to

178

be told.'

'Yeah,' Gafford was watching Kristen. 'I'm all for that.'

'Where'd she get the money for the plane ticket?' Pearl asked. 'And how did she reach the interstate? Her bike's still here. Would she call a cab?' Her voice rose.

'It's easy enough to find out,' Maxine urged. 'Either she's arrived and she's with her folks in Big Thicket, or she's still on the plane. Wayne Spikol can ask at the airport if a kid of twelve flew to Houston early this morning, no one could miss her in those clothes.' Heads turned slowly and she looked thoughtful. 'Maybe she wasn't wearing them, she was in jeans when she went to bed.'

'What clothes?' Kristen asked.

'Well, sweetie'—Pearl remembered Kristen's disapproval 'she seems to have hung on to that frock, remember, the one we all thought was so unsuitable? And the heels?'

Maxine said doubtfully, 'I don't think she'd have worn it to go to Texas.'

Kristen said, 'What *is* this? When *did* she wear it?'

'It was nothing.' Pearl was playing it down. 'She probably went to the fiesta is what we think. She was wearing it when she went out on her bike—both Maxine and Marge saw her—but she was home again for supper-time, wasn't she, Maxine? She must have gone to her own home and changed.'

'So who's going to call Ira?' Maxine said loudly.

Pearl looked at the attentive faces. 'I guess it has to be me,' she said.

The call was painful, particularly as the listeners guessed what was being said at the other end. Pearl asked to speak to Ira, not Thelma, and it was obvious, when he came on the line, that he had no idea where Tammy was, moreover she hadn't contacted her parents. Pearl's tone became increasingly artificial as she tried to be reassuring. She told him they had searched everywhere, or everywhere that was a likely place to find a child, but the corollary hung in the air: a child who was incapable of calling for help. There was a chair by the telephone and she sat down suddenly. Ira must have mentioned the police. 'I'll call Wayne now,' she said weakly, 'if that's what you want.' She cleared her throat and repeated it loudly. The morose mood of the listeners deepened.

Miss Pink leaned towards Harper. 'Would you have any whiskey? Or brandy? She could do with it.'

Pearl put down the receiver. 'He's going to talk with Thelma and call us back. He flipped. How awful for him; his old dad's sinking, he says, and now his kid—it doesn't bear thinking about. Why, thanks,

Daryl'—as he handed her a shot glass—
'sweet of you. I need it.'

'That was difficult.' Miss Pink was
admiring.

'I felt so sorry for him.'

'I know. I'll ring Spikol. It's my turn—' as
Pearl made to protest. 'If he wants to speak
to you, then you can fill in the gaps. I'll do
the groundwork.'

To her surprise no one else protested but
had anyone done so, then he would have
been forced to inform the police himself or
herself—and no one seemed inclined to do
that. The Harpers were blatantly expectant
as if, having relinquished responsibility, it
was of no account to them whether Miss
Pink was a resident of Regis or a country ten
thousand miles away. As for Gafford, he was
concentrating on the whiskey Harper had
poured for him. Only Kristen looked
doubtful but she made no move to speak.
Too young, Miss Pink thought; all of them:
they were relieved that the adults had taken
over.

Spikol's initial reaction was predictable:
Tammy was with a schoolfriend. When Miss
Pink pointed out that a friend's parents
would have insisted that she call home, that
her bicycle was still at the ranch so either she
had left on foot or been picked up—the
implication being by an adult—there was
silence at the other end of the line. At length

he asked what they had done so far to try to find her. She told him, and told him that Ira had asked for the police to be informed.

'Have you called the hospital?' he asked.

'No.' She was surprised; in this case it hadn't been the first thing they'd thought of. 'I don't think she could drive'—she mimed inquiry at the others—'they're dubious, but no vehicle is missing anyway.' There was no sign of contradiction in their faces.

'I'll make some inquiries in town,' he told her. 'Who were her friends here?'

'I'll put Kristen Scott on.'

The girl came to the phone and took the handset. 'She didn't have any friends in town, sir, living way out here...' She listened, and started to list Tammy's teachers.

'He's going to try to contact the parents of girls in her grade,' she said when she replaced the phone. 'And the hospital. He'll come out in the morning. He doesn't think she's here, he reckons she's in Santa Fe.'

'Why Santa Fe?' exclaimed Pearl.

'Because that's where runaways go.'

The telephone rang. It was Thelma saying that she would return tomorrow, just as soon as she could get connections. She had persuaded Ira to stay in Texas.

Kristen was upset. 'It's her dad that Tammy needs,' she said. 'She's his princess, everyone knows that.'

Pearl said gently, 'It's Ira's father is dying, Kristy; he can't leave right now.'

Kristen bit her lip. Harper, apparently needing something to do, poured whiskey for everyone.

Pearl and Miss Pink guessed that Spikol's inquiries in Palomares would take a long time—not the hospital, he would ascertain almost immediately whether Tammy had been admitted—but tracing teachers and other children in her grade during the summer vacation. They decided to go home. Kristen elected to stay with the Harpers. 'Then I'll be on hand in the morning,' she said flatly. 'I'll call Mom, tell her where I am.'

They rode home in the shadow of the cliffs. Miss Pink regarded the bright desert mountains thoughtfully. Large birds were wheeling above the river.

'What are you thinking?' Pearl asked, turning to see what the attraction was.

'Nothing.'

'Vultures,' Pearl said idly. After a moment she gasped and shivered.

*　　*　　*

'No,' Marge said. 'I've heard nothing. Have a glass of wine and tell me what happened at the ranch. I saw you come home.'

Miss Pink related the bare facts of her day,

including the recent developments: the contact with Tammy's parents and with Spikol.

'Good,' Marge said with satisfaction. 'Now something's being done.'

'Can you think of anything we left out?' Miss Pink was curious rather than tart.

'You missed some people who could tell you a thing or two.' She nodded sagely and poured herself another glass of wine.

Miss Pink, at the right stage of perceptiveness, knew that the old lady was well past it. 'Oh, I don't know,' she was airy, 'I spoke to you and the Scotts. And there was Avril and Marian. We've been everywhere, seen everyone.'

'You missed Fletcher Lloyd.'

'I saw Avril. Same thing. What he knows, she'd know.'

'He's just the hired hand. Now if you was to ask Pearl, that's a different matter. She'd tell you what Lloyd was doing and thinking. Avril Beck couldn't.'

Miss Pink's eyelids drooped and snapped open. 'Lonely bachelors need a motherly soul to talk to; what's the term: letting it all hang out? They talk to me too.' She nodded solemnly.

'Fletcher Lloyd don't visit across the road to talk, my dear. He has animal appetites, same as all the men. Pearl is'—she smiled sweetly—'she provides accommodations, as

184

the English would say.'

'Really?' Miss Pink was nonplussed. 'Well, no harm done. Live and let live.'

The silence stretched. 'He was across there Sunday afternoon,' Marge said wildly.

'Sunday afternoon. Yes?'

'So was Tammy, remember?'

'There's some connection?' The question was sharp but the speech was slurred.

'She's disappeared, hasn't she?'

'What time Sunday afternoon was he in Pearl's place?'

'The same time as Tammy. I saw her.' Marge's eyes were like pebbles. 'She was undressed.'

*　　*　　*

'I couldn't get any more out of her; she becomes increasingly wild, trying to convince you of her argument, until she goes too far and then she retreats, pretends she's drunk.'

Pearl strained the spaghetti and laughed. 'She never got over Sam's death. All the same, that's way over the top: suggesting Fletch and Tammy were in here together. D'you mind opening that can of tomato paste? She's going senile'—she returned to her theme—'sitting there all day brooding ... I guess the thought crossed everyone's mind but to name someone—and Fletch at that! I

185

wonder'—she stared out of the window—
'was he here, did he call?'

'Good Heavens no! It was fantasy on her
part—'

'How can you know?'

'He was on Midnight Mesa, looking for
me in Slickrock.'

'Of course he was. Poor old thing, she's
going out of her mind.'

'Why does she suddenly turn on you? It's
not so much that she's crude about you and
Fletcher, what's more unpleasant is that
she's hinting this is, well, a brothel, really:
saying Tammy met Lloyd here.'

'Surely you've come across this kind of
thing before: old women living alone,
younger women close by, neighbours. And
then senility; they've always gossiped, it puts
a bit of spice in their dull lives. I just hope I
don't go like it, is all, but I don't think I will,
I enjoy myself too much.'

They were drinking coffee on the veranda
when Michael Vosker arrived and Miss Pink
realised that here was another person whom
she hadn't seen today. 'Marian told me you
were driving the tracks between here and the
river,' she said, after they had told him about
their own day.

He nodded. 'And I was along the river
bank, about a mile in each direction. I'm
glad the police have been informed; after
twenty-four hours there was no more we

could do. We're only amateurs.'

'Twenty-four hours.' Pearl sighed. 'I guess it's about that since she must have gone as soon as she went in the bedroom. What do you think happened, Michael?'

He was silent. Miss Pink rephrased it. 'What do you think is the most likely explanation?'

'I think she holed up somewhere.'

'You mean, voluntarily?'

'I hope so.'

Miss Pink looked out at the dark patio and lowered her voice. 'If it were not voluntary, would you be thinking in terms of a stranger or a local person?'

'That's wild,' Pearl said.

He ignored her. 'There are only six men in Regis,' he said, 'including me; four when you exclude Ira and me. There are the three ranch-hands and Clayton Scott. So it has to be someone who's not from Regis, and since she left the Harpers' place voluntarily—it has to be voluntary, doesn't it?' Miss Pink nodded. 'Then I'm inclined to think she's holed up with a friend, like a schoolfriend. She's not a stupid child and not particularly adventurous, not like Kristen, so I don't see her running off with a boy. I reckon she's with another young girl.'

'What about the kid's parents?' Pearl protested. 'Why don't they call the Harpers to say she's with them?'

'There's an obvious answer: parents could have gone away—on a vacation, or been called away, like the Markows, and they left the other little girl with relatives or friends. But the kid's house is empty, locked up. She takes Tammy there and agrees not to tell anyone. Bound to be food in the freezer and canned stuff.'

'It wouldn't work,' Pearl said. 'She'd be bored stiff.'

'It's a possibility.'

'You're thinking in terms of a house in town, or at least some distance from here,' Miss Pink said. 'How did she get there after she left the Harpers?'

'She walked down the road and the friend met her in a car'—the women were shaking their heads—'they learn to drive early here,' he persisted. 'They learn in the desert. It's not an impossible hypothesis.'

'I just hope you're right,' Pearl said gloomily. 'And now, if you'll excuse me, I have to take a shower. You stay, Michael, visit with Miss Pink a while.' She went in the house but was back immediately with a bottle of Drambuie and glasses.

When they could hear the shower running Miss Pink said conversationally, 'There are two plots of marijuana in Slickrock Canyon.'

'There are? Who's growing it?' When she didn't respond he answered the question himself. 'Jay, I guess; maybe with a hand from Kristen. Small plots, of course?'

'There were no more than twenty plants in the bit that was left. Peccaries had trampled the other; they've probably destroyed the second by now.'

'You were up there yesterday? Birding? I envy you. I've no head for heights so I've never been able to go down into Slickrock. What did you see?'

'There's a cabin in the bottom.'

'Is there indeed! Now what would that be for? You can't get cows into that canyon.'

'It was Sam Dearing's place. His mine is close by.'

'Sam. Of course. How did you know that?'

'Pearl told me.' Now it was his turn to be silent. She went on: 'Relationships are extraordinarily intricate in a village: like onions; one is constantly peeling away layers. If you're a social anthropologist you know all about that. And the top layer is this skin of convention. Pearl and Marge: next door neighbours, ostensibly old and tried friends—and Marge, somewhat drunk, implying Pearl is a whore.' He started, stared, and reached for his drink. 'Pearl employs a child as a maid,' she went on. 'Why is she allowed to work here? Thelma may be careless, but Ira adores his daughter.'

'You're not suggesting Pearl knows something about Tammy's whereabouts?' He smiled, almost teasing.

'Oh, you're back to that—'

'You mentioned Tammy.'

'By accident. Incidentally, but then everything comes back to her. No, I don't think Pearl knows anything—about Tammy. I was pondering relationships.'

'But not idly, I'm sure. How does Pearl explain Marge's hostility? I'm sure you asked her.' And now he was definitely teasing.

'As an old woman's fantasy.'

'Exactly. There are people like this in every community: widows, spinsters, you name it. Marge was too dependent on Sam; no children either. And she had no interests. He had his mine, and hunting; Marge had nothing to do except keep house for him. She used to go out with him when she was young, a lot of young wives hunt but as they get older, eat too much, don't take exercise, they seem to stiffen up.' He looked surprised, as if something had just occurred to him. 'I mean, mentally, I guess; they lose their sense of enjoyment.' He nodded earnestly at her. 'That's what Pearl never lost: her sense of fun.'

'I didn't? So what?' They turned at the sound of her voice. She was standing in the doorway, wearing a pale silk robe and holding a red rag. 'What d'you make of this? I found it pushed down the back of a drawer.'

Vosker didn't react, he merely waited for

an explanation, but Miss Pink stared in dawning recognition as Pearl held out that part of the rag which was still whole: two overlapping flounces. The bodice hung down, ripped from neck to flounce. 'It's her frock.' Pearl stated the obvious. 'Thank God she was seen afterwards.'

'I'm not with you,' Vosker said. 'Whose frock?'

'You never saw Tammy wearing this thing? Well, she did; Kristen said it made her look like a hooker and she wasn't far wrong. She wore red heels with it too. What I'm saying is, if she'd disappeared wearing this, and we'd found it ripped, what would you have thought?'

'How do you know she wasn't wearing it when she went?'

Pearl gasped and turned to Miss Pink who said slowly, 'She was wearing it on Sunday afternoon, and you found your sweatshirt and Levis in her bedroom at the ranch. So she changed here. Why?'

'Because this got ripped.'

'How?'

The women stared at each other. Vosker removed the drinks and they spread the dress on the table. 'There are no stains,' Miss Pink observed. 'Just a clean rip as though she'd torn it off in a great hurry. The zip is still closed. If she'd hurt her arm she wouldn't be able to undo that. No one said anything about her arm being hurt.'

Pearl said quickly, 'This can't have anything to do with her disappearance; she was alive and well in the evening.'

Miss Pink wondered if she realised what she'd said. 'The point is, we can't find any explanation for her disappearance, apart from her just wanting to make trouble, so we have to consider any unusual behaviour before she went missing, because there could be a link. And this'—she fingered the rent in the dress—'is the most unusual thing yet.'

They stared at what remained of the dress. 'God!' Pearl breathed. 'I hope she just ran away.'

'It doesn't *matter*,' Vosker insisted. 'She was all right hours later.'

CHAPTER ELEVEN

Wayne Spikol arrived in the village at eight o'clock the following morning. He went to the Harpers first and then came down to talk things over with Pearl. Miss Pink was present, eating breakfast in the kitchen, and it was obvious to her that the deputy looked on Pearl as an important source of information, although in this case she could tell him little more than he had gleaned from the Harpers. She did tell him about the discovery of the red dress and the theft of her clothes but as soon as he realised that this must have occurred hours before Tammy vanished he dismissed the incident. For his part he told them that inquiries in Palomares had come to nothing. There were no young girls in the hospital, no reports of accidents, or of a twelve-year-old being picked up by police, and those children in her grade whom he'd managed to trace had seen or heard nothing of her. He was flummoxed and he was looking to Pearl, even to Miss Pink, for inspiration.

'But you're the professional!' Pearl protested. 'We thought as soon as the police were called in things would start moving. Where are the rest of them: forensics, fingerprint guys and that? Where's the sheriff?'

He was amazed. 'You reckon there's been foul play?'

'Of course not! Well, I hope not. What makes you say that?'

'We've had too long to speculate,' Miss Pink put in. 'By now the possibility of foul play has occurred to all of us.'

He shook his head. 'She went voluntarily, ma'am. Either Harper or Maxine would have heard if there'd been a struggle.'

'Granted, but did she stay away of her own free will? Suppose the person she went to meet turned out to be a wolf in sheep's clothing?'

'You got someone in mind?' She sighed. 'Kristen Scott is riding back in the forest,' he went on. 'She says Tammy could be using the old cabin up the head of Scorpion Canyon. She coulda hid in the woods when the men was there yesterday but at night she'd go back there for shelter. So they're in Scorpion this morning: her and Gafford and Harper, when they done the chores.'

Pearl looked at Miss Pink. 'Kristen knows how Tammy's mind works,' she conceded. 'And when you think: the Scorpion cabin is the most likely place if she never left the area; we picnic there sometimes so it's familiar country to her. It's around five miles to walk but if she was mad with everyone—you know, like feeling rejected, she coulda rushed up there in a temper. If Kristen thinks so that's good enough for me. Why don't we ride up to Badblood and work our way across in case she makes a break for it? If she runs ahead of them we might catch her on Midnight, or see her in Slickrock. Give us something to do. If Wayne's going back to town we can't sit here all day doing nothing.'

'You in back?' came a harsh shout from the front of the house, and Marge appeared in the doorway: an angry Marge in crumpled slacks and a blouse with food stains down the front. 'Saw your car,' she flung at Spikol. 'I been robbed! Someone was in my house

194

last night. He took around three hundred dollars!'

'No,' Pearl said flatly. 'Pedro would have barked.'

Marge hesitated, then came back furiously. 'So it was someone he knew!' Her face was dangerously flushed.

'Sit down,' Pearl said. 'Have a cup of coffee.'

Marge said through gritted teeth, 'Who's so short of cash they gotta rob their neighbours?'

Pearl drew in her breath sharply but Spikol got there first: 'Maybe you mislaid it.'

Marge snarled. Miss Pink said brightly, 'Tammy?' They were silenced. 'Tammy needs money,' she went on. 'She doesn't know Thelma's coming home today; she could be taking money in order to buy a plane ticket to Houston.' Marge subsided a little. 'If your dog didn't bark,' Miss Pink prompted.

'Had to be someone the dog knew.' Spikol picked up his cue. 'Dog's all right, is he? Not drugged nor nothing?'

'He's all right.' Marge was grudging.

'Little devil,' Pearl said thoughtfully. 'I wonder if anyone else suffered. Better look in your billfold,' she told Miss Pink.

But their cash seemed to be intact, at least, no large sums had vanished. They rang round. Marian, who had left her handbag in the Vosker living-room, had lost a hundred and fifty dollars. The Voskers hadn't closed their patio door and the thief had only to unhook the screen and walk in. Ada had lost nothing. She told them incidentally that Scott had gone up on the mesas today; both Kristen and her father thought Tammy could be hiding out in the forest. She seemed relieved to hear that Pearl and Miss Pink proposed to go on the plateau as well. 'She needs to be found,' she said, 'before any harm comes to her.'

'Were you thinking of something in particular?' Pearl asked carefully.

'I was thinking of the dangers up there, and of Gregorio. Accidents happen so easily.'

★   ★   ★

'If Tammy did steal that money—and it has to be her, who else could it be?—did she come all the way down from Scorpion and go back there to sleep?' Pearl was incredulous. 'That doesn't sound like Tammy. No one round here hikes—all except Michael Vosker, and you. Everyone else rides.'

They were on the Las Mesas road, the horses moving slowly as the riders talked. 'Perhaps she didn't go back.' Miss Pink looked about her as if she might catch sight of Tammy dodging behind a bush. 'With such a huge expanse to search, so many places where a youngster can hide, she could be anywhere, and moving around at that.'

'You think we're wasting our time going on top?' Pearl looked up at the sunlit rim.

Miss Pink didn't say anything for a few moments but when she spoke her voice was firm. 'No, I don't think we're wasting our time.'

'So who else was robbed?' Avril asked, coming to meet them as they approached her house. They had telephoned her earlier but after the theft of her diamond ring she locked her doors when she went to bed. She had lost no money.

'Only Marian and Marge,' Pearl said, looking round. 'What happened to Fletch?'

'He's up in Badblood again. He left about an hour ago. And Clayton Scott went up after him. What's with this sudden interest in my land? I take it you're going up there too. Lloyd said he had to go and see if there was pink-eye among the cows. Herefords don't get pink-eye, do they?'

'I wouldn't be surprised.' Pearl was staring absently at the trail climbing the escarpment. 'People are more interested in Markow land than yours; Kristen thinks Tammy's holed up in the old cabin in Scorpion.' She looked at Miss Pink, hesitated, then went on lamely, 'We'll cut her off if she makes a break for it this way.'

'You sound as if you're hunting the kid!' Avril protested. 'And she's on foot, she can't cross Slickrock; there's a precipice on my side.'

'You reckon?' Pearl grinned. 'The only way she can cross Slickrock *is* on foot.'

'That woman don't know where she's at,' she observed once they were out of earshot. 'If anything happened to Fletch she'd have to sell up.'

'She could get Mexican labour.'

'She wouldn't trust 'em. She thinks all Mexicans are out to rip her off.'

'Why did she employ Ramirez then?'

'Oh, Greg was all right; she got on well with him. Everyone loved Gregorio. There I go again! Suppose I'd said that to Ada!'

*   *   *

They were crossing Midnight Mesa when Pearl remarked that for all the signs they could be alone up there. 'Do you think we missed the men?' she asked. 'They went up Badblood or Rastus?'

'You reckon they're together?'

'You mean, if Clayton caught up with Fletch? I'd expect them to stay separate: they'd cover more ground that way.'

'How do they get on usually: Lloyd and Clayton Scott?'

'Fletch keeps clear of him; he had a very strict daddy himself. Ask me, Clayton frightens Fletch, but then Fletch is frightened of most people, except me maybe. Funny thing,' she mused, 'so is Clayton. What a lot of fear there is around.'

'What's Scott frightened of?'

'Women.'

They parted at a grove of pinyons and when they came together again Miss Pink said, 'Yes, that makes sense, but how did you discover it?'

'Isn't it obvious?' Pearl was surprised.

'I wouldn't have said so. It wasn't obvious to me, but you know him much better than I do.'

They rode on, through the glaring sunlight and the deep shadows. The heat seemed to shrivel the brain and their thought processes were slowed down as they conserved their mental energy.

'Why do I keep thinking Tammy is his daughter?' Miss Pink asked.

'Whose daughter?'

'Clayton Scott's. Who are we talking about?'

'Tammy's Ira's kid. Tammy Markow.'

'I know.'

'It's because I told you Kristen acts like she's Tammy's big sister. You think of Tammy as being family: Scott family.'

'But Ada doesn't like her.'

Silence. Click, went the hoofs on bedrock, slap, went big feet in the sand. A scrub jay watched them from a pinyon, too somnolent to move. A lizard scuttered from one patch of shade to the next.

'It's because of Veronica,' Pearl said. 'Tammy's childish, so Ada sees Veronica in her. That makes her miserable so she discourages Tammy. Kristen's different—and they're very close: Ada and Kristen, like Kristy was grown up. Of course she is, she's seventeen. But she never was a kid, never childish.'

'What's she going to do?'

'Find her if she's here, bring her home. Tammy will come down with her.'

'I mean, what's she want to be? Is she going to college?'

'Kristen? All she wants is Jay Gafford—oh, and horses, nothing else, except for her mom to be happy.'

'She's that serious? She means to marry Jay?'

'Marriage or whatever. She's still passionately in love; once she calms down a bit, she'll find a house, move in with him. That's what she wants and that's what she'll have, and no one's gonna stop her.'

'Not her father?'

'Least of all her father—'

A horse neighed. The sorrel threw up his head and answered. They came on two horses tied in the shade. 'Clayton and Fletch,' Pearl said. 'You know where they are?'

'They've climbed down into Slickrock. Are you game? Shall we follow?'

Pearl dismounted and tied her horse to a branch. 'I'll have a look at it,' she said grimly, loosening her cinch.

They stood on the rim and looked down the line of descent into the canyon. So far as they could see there was no one on the wall, nor anywhere else. They could see much of the mesa on the other side but there were innumerable depressions where horses and people might be hidden. As for the canyon, Miss Pink regarded the green canopy absently, not expecting it to reveal any secrets. 'All the same,' she murmured, commenting on her thoughts, 'you should be aware of them; birds would take fright, or those pigs.' She looked upstream to where she thought the marijuana plots must be. The cottonwoods were bright and immobile and oddly sinister. Pearl licked her lips. She seemed tense. 'Yes?' Miss Pink asked gently.

'I was wondering who was down there.'

'We hope it's Tammy. Don't we?' Pearl shook her head stiffly. 'Shall *I* go down?' Miss Pink asked.

'No, we'll stay together.'

'What's the problem?'

She didn't answer immediately and her

eyes wandered. 'I'm scared of heights,' she said.

Miss Pink didn't believe her. 'How curious'—she was looking at the ribbon of woodland below—'there may be five people down there, six if you were to count Tammy, and not a sign nor sound of them.'

'What bothers me,' Pearl said tightly, 'is are there more, like one or two strangers?'

'Poachers?'

She shrugged and stepped towards the edge, then held back for Miss Pink to show the way. Whatever was bothering her it wasn't the descent; she climbed down the wall almost as nimbly as a mountaineer, hampered only by her smooth-soled boots.

As they approached the level of the trees Miss Pink noted again how the canyon, which had seemed so quiet and unpopulated from above, was in fact full of life. Sound increased with the heat, which was steamy where it had been dry, and if you looked closely, there was movement in the canopy, but only in the canopy. If there were people on the ground they were as quiet as deer.

They reached the bottom. 'Now what?' Pearl asked.

'We'll go to the cabin first.' Miss Pink stooped to tighten a bootlace, aware that Pearl turned automatically and glanced down-canyon, but as she straightened, the woman said casually, 'You lead on, you've been here before.'

Miss Pink started to work down the canyon outside the trees where the going was rough. After a few yards Pearl said, 'I wish I'd worn trainers now; surely there must be game trails in the trees?'

'There was a proper trail once but it's overgrown.' There was no response from the rear.

They came to the yellow towers and Pearl's pleasure was obvious; she might have forgotten the reason for their presence in Slickrock. 'Fabulous,' she observed as Miss Pink looked back to see why the other had stopped. 'Is the cabin near?'

'Keep your voice down; she may be here.'

They approached the cabin from the side so it wasn't until they were almost at the entrance that they saw the door was open. Miss Pink stopped short and heard Pearl catch her breath. Nothing moved inside. They could see a corner of the interior; Miss Pink could even see the dark patch that was the gopher's hole. She couldn't see the bed or the cupboard, only a shelf with cans on it. There was a flash of reflected light on the wall. She tensed, and knew that Pearl had seen it too. The silence was palpable. Something else was showing now, halfway up the opened door: something long and slim and black. Their eyes were fixed, then Miss Pink exhaled on a long breath and said loudly, 'It's Melinda Pink and Pearl. Who's that?'

Clayton Scott stepped into view, lowering his rifle.

'Clayton!' Pearl gasped. 'Who did you think we were?'

'You could be anyone.' He emerged from the cabin, his gaze shifting from one to the other. 'You seen her? You heard anything?'

'Nothing.'

Miss Pink stepped forward. 'May I?' He was in her way. He stood aside, opened his mouth, and closed it again. Pearl moved up.

'You're blocking the light,' Miss Pink said.

Pearl slipped inside and looked round in silence. Miss Pink stared at the bed which no longer held the hollow made by the big snake. Someone else had been there and left the print of a different shape: long but shallow, and at its head was a carton that had contained chocolate-chip cookies.

'She must be just ahead of you,' Miss Pink told Scott. 'Think back: did you hear anything, like an animal in the undergrowth?'

He laughed. 'You're imagining things.' He indicated the carton. 'That's been here days; it was left—' His face changed. 'Poachers,' he spat out. 'Like that Ramirez. His kind used this cabin.' He glared at Pearl.

She ignored him. 'It wasn't here before?' she asked.

'No.' Miss Pink turned to Scott. 'Have you seen anything of the others? Kristen and Gafford are about.'

'I've seen no one except Lloyd, he's somewhere down here. Are you saying you been in this cabin by yourself—before today?' His eyes bored into hers.

'This packet wasn't here two days ago, and someone's slept on that mattress, a person who doesn't weigh much.' She turned to Pearl. 'It has to be Tammy.'

'Then she couldn't have stolen the money, not and got back here in the time; I mean, Tammy'd never walk and climb in the dark, she's only—'

'What money?' Scott interrupted harshly. 'Who's stole money?'

'Last night someone broke into Marge's place and the Voskers', stole several hundred dollars.'

'Not broke in,' Miss Pink demurred, 'but entered, certainly.'

'Who?' He was vehement.

'Why, we thought it was Tammy.'

He blinked. 'We have to find her,' he muttered. 'Someone's about—' Standing in the doorway now, blocking the light, his eyes were fixed on the mattress. 'Alone?' he asked. 'Was she alone here? Or'—he stared at Miss Pink—'was she with someone? That little kid?' He turned away and looked at the trees. 'He's got her down here,' he muttered.

'He can't get out, he's trapped.'

'And her,' Pearl pointed out. 'You guessed, didn't you, Clayton? That's why you came armed. What made you think a man was involved?'

His gaze returned to her. He looked demented. 'If you was the father of young girls and one of them was violated ... after a time, lying awake there in the dark, when another's gone missing, you remember, you can't help but recall the other time, fearing the worst: where is she, who's she with ...? Is he—' He turned away again, unable to meet their eyes. They stared at his profile. 'Last night,' he went on, 'I thought, there's another monster at work in the village. This morning I said it was only my imagination, but I felt it was better to bring my rifle. Men like that should be—they're like rabid dogs, they infect everything they touch.' He wiped his mouth with his hand. 'And now'—he looked at them almost carelessly and his lips stretched in a thin smile—'if I find him with her, I'll ask questions after I fire.'

'Now wait a minute,' Pearl protested. 'Jay Gafford's out there, searching, and Fletch, maybe Daryl, any one of 'em coulda found her and be taking her home. You could shoot the wrong guy.'

'Maybe. Maybe not.'

'Look! Clayton—' but he was gone, striding into the woodland as noisy as a bull in the undergrowth. 'My God,' Pearl exclaimed. 'What a mess!'

'And Tammy's in there somewhere.'

'Oh, to hell with him. He doesn't mean it. He's thinking about Veronica, not Tammy.' She ran her fingers over the hollow in the bed. 'It's odd about that money all the same; I don't see how she could have stolen it.'

'Perhaps a stranger came in from the interstate—oh no, Pedro didn't bark. Anyway, it's not important. We have to find Tammy, she can't be far away.'

'Where do we start?'

'We start with the premise that she was here last night. And she's frightened of snakes, so the gopher wasn't here, or it left quietly when she approached the cabin, but it came back—when she was asleep? She must have been terrified.' They were outside now. She peered in the open door. 'I'll swear she was here alone; that depression was made by a small, light body. There wasn't a man—' Pearl gasped. Miss Pink ignored her and continued to voice her thoughts. 'Surely she knows we're here? Maybe not, if she's in the trees; the sound of running water could drown voices. There's more noise down here than you'd think: birds, insects ... but she doesn't shout, she's not trying to attract attention. Is she still hiding, after all this time?'

Now she did address Pearl who said

grimly, 'Maybe she *is* with someone, and he's forcing her to keep quiet.'

'He wouldn't bring her here. It's too far.'

'They do! They take their victims miles into the forest; you don't know these mountain men: there were two killers in Montana kidnapped a girl out jogging—'

'I know about that,' Miss Pink said shortly. 'Here we have to assume we've found Tammy, at least where-she was until recently. Now, which way would she go from here?'

'Scott went upstream, but then he doesn't know any better than us; he's only guessing.'

'It's the way she'd go. She came downstream to here. And which way did she enter the canyon?'

'That's easy. She'd come in from the Markow side; she's used to riding over her own land.'

'So I suppose she'd go back the same way if she wanted to get out again.' But Miss Pink sounded doubtful.

'Of course she would. Why not?'

'Yes, well, in which case we'd better follow.'

They looked wryly at the dense undergrowth. 'At least he's made a trail,' Pearl said. 'More or less.'

'The thing to do is force our way to the creek and work up its bed. We'll see tracks too; she has to cross the stream to get back to

Markow land.'

Evidently Scott had had the same idea; he had trampled a path through the vegetation to the creek which was quite close. There were the marks of a man's boot in the fine gravel under the bank and there too, when they looked carefully, were the tracks of a small foot in trainers.

'You were right,' Pearl said. 'Here are prints going down to the cabin and coming back, and here's a different trainer; that will be Kristen.'

'So she's here already. Well, why not? They'd come on here from Scorpion.'

The going was rough with rocky rises and long pools, and fallen timber where they had to make wide detours. Scott was moving faster than them; they were still on his track but there was no sign of him ahead. It was a narrow creek, and the cottonwoods interlaced above their heads so that they moved through chequered sunlight, and visibility was confusing. There was a current of air in the depths and the foliage was in continuous motion, giving the impression that others were keeping pace with them. Despite the proximity of the water—and much of the time they were splashing through it—the air was sticky. Miss Pink was considering whether to leave the creek and look for a passage close under the canyon wall when they heard a scream.

They stopped. It wasn't one scream but a prelude. Shrieks rose: uninhibited, terrified, startling jays and doves. It was a young girl's voice. Without a word they plunged up the creek bed only to halt again as a shot rang out, and another.

Pearl moaned and went to leap forward. 'No!' Miss Pink hissed, grabbing her wrist and holding on. 'Wait! Listen.'

Something was hurtling through the woods. Pearl clung to Miss Pink. They heard squealing then, and above the squeals, shouts: 'Tammy! Tammy!' The peccaries were racing downstream in the direction of the cabin, and behind them a man continued to shout urgently.

'That's Jay,' Pearl gasped, relinquishing her hold on Miss Pink's arm. 'And we found Tammy, thank God! Was that Clayton shooting? Of course, he shot at the pigs. They musta charged him, took him by surprise. He's trigger-happy.' She gave a sickly grin. 'At least we know he didn't shoot Jay.' She lifted her voice. 'We're coming, Clayton, don't shoot us. Jay! Where are you? Tammy! We're here!'

Gafford came plunging down the stream bed. 'Did she come your way?' he called.

'We didn't see her,' Pearl said. 'Is she all right?'

He grinned. 'Not much wrong when she can yell like that.'

'What's she got to say for herself?'

'I didn't even see her, only heard her. Who's doing the shooting?'

'Why, Clayton Scott.'

'Who was he shooting at?' Miss Pink asked, adding meaningly, 'Tammy's stopped screaming.'

'He shot her?' Pearl's voice rose.

'No.' Gafford looked bewildered. 'I thought the pigs—yes, that had to be it: he shot at the pigs. I was at the foot of the trail there'—he seemed embarrassed—'over there,' waving vaguely towards the Markow side of the canyon. 'I'd agreed with Kristy I'd wait there, stop Tammy if she came that way. But those pigs come out of the creek and they didn't see me till they was right on me. I was sitting quiet and they sees me and they up-tailed and went charging back into the trees and then Tammy starts screaming. I saw the last brutes swerve off the trail and dive into the wood so I knew Tammy had been coming towards me. And then the shooting starts. Clayton—starts—shooting.' He stared at them. They said nothing. 'He didn't hit her,' he said. 'I went along the trail. So where did she go? And what happened to him?'

'There he is,' Pearl said. 'Listen! He's shouting to her.'

Again they heard Tammy's name being called. Pearl shouted: 'Clayton, where are

211

you?'

'That's not Scott,' Gafford said.

People converged, guided by voice, but before they met they knew it was Fletcher Lloyd who had been calling. They met on a game trail and Lloyd looked hot and angry and confused. The first thing he wanted to know was who was doing the shooting, and the second: the whereabouts of Tammy. He'd taken up the call himself after he heard Gafford shouting to her. He wasn't surprised to learn that Scott was armed and, once he was satisfied that Tammy had been frightened only by peccaries, he didn't seem bothered that she had run away again. 'She's tired and hungry,' he said, 'and someone starts shooting. I don't blame her.'

'He wasn't shooting at her.' Pearl was tart. 'And where did you come from anyway? You weren't down the canyon or we'd have seen you.'

'I was upstream. The pigs were running ahead of me. Know what they were doing? They found some plots of grass; they been eating it. It's ruined.'

'Why tell me?' Gafford's eyes were slitted.

Pearl sighed and started to speak when her eyes focused beyond him. Daryl Harper was coming along the trail from the direction of the creek. He had been coming down into the canyon when he heard the commotion below and thought it prudent to wait until he

212

thought the shooting was over.

'Why were you coming here?' Miss Pink asked, when events had been explained to him.

'Kristen told me to come once I'd finished chores.'

'That's right,' Gafford put in quickly. 'We're searching the high country today and it was her said we should come and look at Sam's old cabin.'

'And did you?'

'Did we what, ma'am?'

'Look in the cabin.'

'Kristen did.'

'Was Tammy there?' Harper asked, while Miss Pink and Pearl exchanged looks; they'd been right about the tracks in the creek bed.

'If she was in the cabin she'd be with us.' Gafford was cutting. 'She musta been in the woods someplace. She's in the canyon. That was her screaming.'

'So where is she now?'

Gafford glared at him.

'And where's Kristen?' Pearl asked brightly. 'Come to that, what happened to Clayton, him and his hair-trigger gun?'

They started to move along the trail in the direction of Midnight Mesa but very soon the path diverged sideways, heading downstream. They took to the undergrowth at a place where it had been trampled by someone ahead of them.

They were working their way round a tangle of brambles when they heard the rifle again. It seemed to come from higher up the canyon but in that place, with people crashing about, they couldn't be sure of the direction.

'Did he follow the pigs?' Pearl wondered, looking downstream. 'And he's shooting at them again?'

'Why would he kill a pig when he's searching for Tammy?' Gafford asked. 'He's not interested in pigs.'

'What's he shooting at then?'

'Or who,' murmured Miss Pink, but the men were gone.

'You're still thinking she isn't alone?' Pearl asked. 'But who—who could she be with?'

Miss Pink made no response. They moved after the men.

It was very hot and their discomfort was intensified by their emotions. They had lost control. Events were moving of their own volition. It was as if the canyon was no longer background but a participant in the drama, and the people were no more than puppets. As they approached the fringe of the woodland and saw the bright rock wall through the trees, they came on young Harper slumped like a doll against a tree trunk—but his face was rigid. He was staring at something on the ground.

They crept forward and stood beside him.

A body lay at the foot of a tree. It was hatless, the hair clotted with blood, the face pressed into blood-soaked grass, a rifle close to his hand. It was Clayton Scott.

CHAPTER TWELVE

'He's alive,' Pearl whispered. 'Look.' The fingers of one hand were curling. They pressed forward.

Lloyd said, 'There's someone else around.' It was a warning.

'Yeah,' Harper agreed. 'He's been shot in the back of the head, like an execution. Could be the Mafia.'

The women ignored him as they knelt beside Scott. Parting his hair gingerly, feeling the skull, Miss Pink looked up and caught them unawares. Harper and Lloyd were staring at each other, Gafford was studying the skyline, only Pearl was concerned with the injured man. Miss Pink's eyes fell on two branches lying by the rifle, one branch really, broken in two pieces.

Scott groaned, reclaiming everyone's attention. The fingers clawed the ground. 'Can we get a helicopter in here?' Miss Pink asked generally.

'They can fly anywhere,' Harper said. 'You think he's going to live?' He sounded disappointed.

'He hasn't been shot, and I can't feel a fracture. I think he's just been knocked out, probably by that branch.'

Lloyd picked up the pieces. 'Who hit him?'

Scott was mumbling. 'Don't—' he said clearly, but the rest was incoherent. He scraped his face on the grass and groaned again.

'We don't need a chopper,' Gafford said. 'We can't get a horse down here, but if he's only knocked out he could maybe walk after a while. Fetch some water, Daryl.'

'How will I carry it?'

'In your hat. That's what they do in the movies.'

Miss Pink looked at him sharply, and then she remembered that this was Kristen's father, there wasn't much love lost between Gafford and Scott.

He was trying to raise himself so they propped him against the tree and waited to see if he was going to vomit. After a minute he did, and they got him to his feet and moved him to a more salubrious spot. Harper returned with a little water in his hat and carrying his dripping shirt. Scott stayed on his feet to drink, and Pearl wiped his face but left the scalp alone. Awareness was returning to his eyes as he looked at them in turn, concentrating on Gafford. Miss Pink handed him his hat. He put one foot in front of the other. 'Rest a while,' she urged. 'You had a nasty knock.'

'I'll walk out.' He was still staring at Gafford. 'But not with him.'

Gafford gave a tight smile.

'We were all together,' Miss Pink said.

'I don't—' He stopped. 'Were you?' His eyelids drooped and he winced. They edged forward to catch him as he swayed but he put his hand on a tree trunk and after a moment he stiffened and said calmly, 'You had to've seen the guy. Didn't he come past you?'

'We've seen no one,' Pearl said. 'No one else. Who was here? Who attacked you?'

'I didn't see. He got me from behind. I knew someone was around and I had my finger on the trigger. I sensed something, a movement—someone behind me, and that's the last thing I remember, except—there was a noise.'

'That was your own rifle. You fired a shot.'

'Did I? Yes, I suppose I would have. I was ready for him but I wasn't quite quick enough.' He tried to smile and winced again.

'We'd better get you to a doctor,' Miss Pink said. 'We'll take it slowly, and once you reach the rim you can ride.'

Gafford stayed in the canyon—they still had to find Tammy and Harper said he would go as far as the rim and then return to help look for her. The party moved slowly up the scree to the foot of the wall, Lloyd and Harper on either side of Scott, the women following.

'Who hit him?' Pearl whispered, holding back.

'God knows. It's weird.'

'You can say that again. And where is the guy? Still in the canyon or up on the rim?'

'At least he isn't armed; no one else is doing any shooting.' But where was Tammy, and why did she keep running? And why was Scott attacked? Because he was searching for Tammy and someone had to stop him finding her?

The wall rose above them, baking in the sun. Miss Pink gave her mind to the climb, thankful that there were two able-bodied men there to assist Scott; she wouldn't care to be the person shepherding him across those unprotected ledges, or below his heels as he climbed the vertical pitches. She watched from a distance; he seemed to be fully recovered, neither stumbling nor wavering, and apparently unaffected by the heat.

'Watch it,' Pearl said, treading on her heels as she stopped. 'You all right?'

'I'm fine. I was looking at Scott.'

'He's fit for his age.' The tone was grudging. 'But I guess he lives a clean life, so far as drink and drugs are concerned anyway. I thought he was dead, all that blood!'

'Most of it was from his nose—but he'll need some stitches and he should have a tetanus jab.'

They crawled over the rim and trailed after the men, bumping into each other as if their legs were made of rubber. Tension had been high in the canyon and on the wall; on the level mesa they felt it was safe to relax. So it came as quite a shock to realise that one of the horses was missing and that the flaps of the saddle-bags were unbuckled.

It was the sorrel that was missing. Pearl started to swear. Lloyd said, 'He'll look after it; he has to, going down that trail, or he'll be off—'

'Don't you believe it. If he can ride well he'll whip it down that old trail.'

'Whipping won't hurt it,' Harper said. 'Funny thing: how'd he get here if he didn't come on a horse?'

Scott seemed uninterested, he was leaning against his own mount, waiting to move on.

'What did he take from the saddle-bags?' Miss Pink asked.

'He couldn't have got anything from mine,' Pearl said. 'I didn't bring any cash, only a sandwich.' She lifted the flap on the nearer bag and felt inside, then walked round and felt the other. 'The bugger's taken my sandwich!'

219

Lloyd stared at her, did a double-take and looked in his own bags. 'I had a coupla buns and a sausage. They're gone.'

They looked at Scott's bags but his were still buckled.

'He was hungry,' Pearl said superfluously. 'God, I hope he doesn't hurt the sorrel.' Then she remembered and looked at Miss Pink with contrition. 'I'm terribly sorry. You ride the pinto.'

Miss Pink started to protest but Lloyd said his horse could carry two riders, and the four of them set off across the mesa on three mounts, leaving Harper to go back and rejoin Gafford in Slickrock.

There was no sign of the horse thief on the mesa but crossing Rastus Canyon they saw the deep prints made by a horse in a hurry. Pearl's face set. At the escarpment she slid down from behind Lloyd, saying that she could move as fast as a horse on the steep descent. But she stopped on the edge and Miss Pink reined in beside her. They studied the ground below. No horse was visible on the zigzags and nothing was moving on the road to Regis, and there was only one vehicle between the village and the interstate so far as they could see. Las Mesas seemed abandoned; there were no trucks in the yard and the only living things were the steers in the feed-lot.

When the zigzags ran out at the foot of the

scarp Pearl mounted again and the horses, scenting water and feed, stepped out on the home stretch. As they approached Las Mesas the sorrel came trotting to meet them. He trod on a rein and snapped it but no one was bothered. Pearl jumped down and ran to the animal which was dark with sweat. 'He's all right,' she said. 'Isn't that great? Oh, my God, just look how he's been ridden! But he's undamaged far as I can see.'

The others were looking beyond her, at Las Mesas. She sobered and went to pick up the severed rein. She knotted the ends absently and stared at the ranch where nothing stirred. Even the steers were hidden from this angle.

Scott rode forward and the others followed, Pearl leading the sorrel. He turned in at the big road gate and walked up the drive. No one came to meet them and the house door remained closed. He dismounted at the garden gate, took his rifle from its scabbard and loaded it with shells he took from his pocket. Pearl gaped. Miss Pink got down and after a moment so did Lloyd. They stood at their horses' heads while Scott opened the screen and tried the door. It was locked. He turned and looked past them. The others turned and surveyed the empty yard.

Lloyd said coldly, 'He's taken the pick-up.'

'And Avril's out in the new one?' Pearl ventured.

'That'll be it. He jumped off the horse and took the truck. Keys would be in the ignition.' He didn't seem concerned.

A pick-up came along the road from the village and turned in at the ranch. It stopped and Avril got out, glaring at Lloyd. 'Who's driving the old Ford? I though it was you! Who did you lend it to, without asking permission?'

'Where did you see it?' Scott asked.

'In the village. He—whoever it was, was going like a madman. He couldn't drive neither.'

'Who was it?' Pearl asked.

'That's what I'm asking. Don't *you* know?'

Scott went to push past the others, moved too fast and staggered. They grabbed at him before he fell. His face was yellow.

'What's wrong with him?' Avril asked.

'We hope to get him to hospital,' Miss Pink said. 'Will you take him?'

Avril looked bewildered. 'I'll come with you,' Pearl said. 'I'll tell you about it as we drive, OK?'

'But—who's in my other truck?'

'God knows. Never mind about that now; Clayton's been hurt. I'll tell you soon as we get on the road. Will you take our horses home, Melinda? Fletch will see to Clayton's.'

Scott was helped into the pick-up, Pearl

222

squeezed in beside him and Avril drove away. 'Well!' Miss Pink breathed and, walking across the yard, pulling the sorrel and the pinto after her, she sank down on the ground in the shade of the bar.

'Let me see to these,' Lloyd said, 'and I'll give you a drink. Or you can go in the bunkhouse and fix one yourself. Fridge is on the porch.'

She raised her eyebrows, unaccustomed to Lloyd's being solicitous, but she didn't move. He took the other horses into the barn.

'You ought to be rubbed down,' she told the sorrel. 'I don't suppose it'll matter, it's far too hot to catch cold.' She leaned back against the planks and closed her eyes.

She dozed, still holding the reins, vaguely aware of footsteps as Lloyd unsaddled, of the clump of hoofs passing and fading as he turned the horses out. She woke with a start as the reins were eased out of her fingers. 'You've had a hard day,' he said. She realised that he was making overtures and wondered what he could want from her.

He took her through the barn to a frame bunkhouse. The door and window were open wide and the building was shaded by trees so that, with curtains drawn against the sun, the interior was marginally cooler than the air outside. She looked round the neat and folksy room: patchwork quilts on two

223

beds, a plastic check cloth on a table, Remington prints on the walls. 'You'd better look at your cash,' she said. 'And the food. Did he take any food?'

'He wasn't here. I looked while you were asleep.'

He went out. She sat on a bench and stared in surprise at a plate and mug, knife, fork and spoon set neatly on the opposite side, and sparkling clean. At the other end of the table was a pressure lamp with a box of matches beside it, and a book: Beryl Markham's *West with the Night*. He came in with a pitcher of iced tea. She indicated the book. 'You're interested in flying?'

He sat down slowly, seeming to need time to orientate himself. 'In the author,' he said. 'She was great. Did you read that? I'll lend it to you.' He didn't wait for a response, his eyes were alight with enthusiasm. 'She was a free spirit.' He stopped as if suddenly switched off.

'We all admire free spirits.' She took a long draught of tea. 'What can Tammy be frightened of?' She wasn't looking at him but, drowsy with heat and fatigue, she could have been talking to herself. 'She *likes* Pearl; the child's not really a maid, Pearl's befriended her, she understands her— probably a lot better than her own mother does, and there has to be some antidote to Ira's spoiling. And yet she ran away when

Pearl approached the cabin.'

'There was a snake—but you knew that! You told Pearl.'

'Yes, but Tammy knew we were in the canyon; why didn't she come to us?'

He shrugged. 'The kid's got her own reasons. Pearl'd know more about that than me.'

'You don't think Tammy being in Slickrock could have had anything to do with the marijuana?'

'No.' He showed no surprise that she should raise the subject. 'She's too young to be mixed up in anything like that.'

'But if she'd seen the plots and Gafford knew she'd seen them?'

'By the time she got there the pigs had ruined that crop. Besides, Jay would never touch her. Kristen'd kill him.'

She regarded him blandly and he fidgeted with his glass. The words hung between them. 'Pearl told you about the red frock?' she asked.

He raised his eyes slowly. '*And* that Marge Dearing said I was in that house around the same time as Tammy Sunday afternoon. Prove it!'

She blinked. 'Prove you were there?'

'Prove I go after kids.'

The sweat was trickling down her ribs. She fingered the edge of the tablecloth. 'Of course,' she said, 'we all had the thought.

225

Marge merely put it into words—'

'You all thought it was me?' It was said quietly, with a hint of curiosity; there was no anger, no bluster.

'You couldn't help but think of a man, a deviant, but no one discussed it, at least to my knowledge.' She raised innocent eyes. 'But Tammy seems unharmed—and yet terrified. You think there's a man in this somewhere.'

'You don't believe Marge.'

'Of course not.' She shifted impatiently. 'You were on Midnight Mesa at that time. Marge is jealous of Pearl.'

His face softened. It was a remarkable transformation and she looked away to hide her astonishment.

'One of your free spirits,' he said, and glanced at the book. 'Like her.'

'No, not like Beryl Markham. Pearl has principles.'

'Of course she has'—indignantly—'so did she!' He snatched up the book as if it were a child in need of protection.

'She was fearless,' Miss Pink conceded, 'a fine aviator, but totally amoral.'

He was speechless. She could have dealt him a personal insult.

'She was like an animal,' she explained pleasantly, 'without—'

'We're all animals!' It was a shout of rage.

'Pearl is in a different league.' It was the

tone she would use to a fractious horse. 'I like Pearl; I wouldn't have any time for Beryl Markham. May I have some more tea?'

'Help yourself.'

He turned the pages of the book, not reading, just doing something with his hands while he tried to make sense of what had been said. 'Pearl's a very special person,' he muttered. 'She's young and pretty and she can ride, and she's great company. You see the problem?'

'Jealousy and resentment.'

'You got it.' He nodded eagerly.

'So Marge made a wild insinuation about you in order to involve Pearl in Tammy's disappearance and—to drag Pearl down? Incriminate her?'

'She fantasises.'

'Exactly.' And not the only one to have fantasies, she thought. The conversation ground to a halt. She looked round with simulated interest and focused on the beds. 'Of course,' she murmured, 'you shared with Gregorio.'

He followed her gaze. 'Yeah, that was his bed.' He was casual.

'He was something of a lady's man.'

'Not really. No more'n any other hand. He was engaged to a girl from Casas Grandes.'

'Pearl didn't tell me.'

He shrugged. 'Maybe she kept quiet about

it 'cause she was fond of him. But that's why he left. He wanted to get married and he couldn't live here with his wife. He asked Mis' Beck would she bring in a mobile home for 'em, but she wouldn't.'

'So you knew he was planning to leave.'

'Eventually, yes. Not sudden though, while we was away. The cattle was left without food.'

'Where did Veronica fit into this? Are you telling me he was engaged to marry a Mexican girl, and he seduced Veronica?'

'How would I know?' He was angry again. 'He wasn't the kind of guy would boast about women, just the opposite.'

'What kind of guy was he?'

'Very polite to women; he always called 'em "ma'am", and he'd open the door for Mis' Beck when she got in the pick-up and like that.'

'How did he treat other women?'

'Pearl and the kids, he'd hold their horses for 'em when they got on and off; he seemed to enjoy doing things for folk.' He thought about that. 'I *liked* the guy,' he said defiantly.

'So you must have been shocked when you learned the truth.'

'He didn't steal that ring. I'll tell you what happened there: it rolled down a crack in the floorboards and she didn't know. She only discovered it missing after Greg took off, so she blamed him. She's like that; always

228

blaming people for something.'

'And Veronica?'

'Yes, well'—he was embarrassed—'she was a sweet kid but—you know—defective? And Greg, he'd go out of his way to be kind, see what I mean?'

'You're saying she made the running.'

'It's all I can think.'

'But he never said anything about her to you.'

'Never, but it need only have happened the once—just a chance meeting in the creek or somewheres. Come to that, he never mentioned a friend in the locality neither. I knew he'd worked in Arizona before he come here, but he never told me he'd met up with someone locally, a guy I mean.'

'What makes you think he did?'

'After he left here he had to stay with someone—because he came back, didn't he? He wasn't alone up in Rastus, we know that.'

Miss Pink stood up to stretch her legs. She walked to the doorway and stared through the screen at the corrals. 'Has it occurred to you that he could have had someone staying here while Mrs Beck and you were away, and that they went up to Rastus from here; there was an accident and Gregorio was shot, and his companion came back with the two horses?'

'I don't see it matters how he was killed.' She said nothing and he blinked, thinking it through. 'If they was poaching,' he said slowly, 'as they had to be—it was out of season—then it could happen that way, particularly if this other guy was illegal, like a wetback. But then'—he swung round and surveyed the cabin—'he took all of Greg's gear too!'

'Pearl said he didn't own much. No saddle for instance.'

'All he had went in one old backpack. It were gone when I come back. I was fishing in Colorado. That other guy musta been dirt poor if he had to steal Greg's stuff. But then probably he was.'

'He had a vehicle.'

'How do you know that?'

'One assumes he had. How did he arrive and leave otherwise?'

'Greg coulda picked him up—no, wait! We only had the one pick-up at that time, and I'd taken it to Colorado after I dropped Mis' Beck off in town. There was no truck left behind. You're right; if Greg had someone staying here, that guy had to have his own wheels.'

CHAPTER THIRTEEN

'You'll look after her?' Lloyd had his hand on the sorrel's neck detaining Miss Pink, who said diffidently, 'Pearl?' Then, more firmly, 'Pearl can look after herself.'

'She's scared.'

'Who's she scared of?'

He ran his hand over the sorrel's shoulder and studied its leg.

'Who's after Tammy?' she pressed.

'Well, that's it! Who is it?'

The man was a mass of emotions interwoven with this prickly anger, the latter accentuated by his fierce stare. 'Anybody'd be scared,' he said. 'Someone putting the fear of death into little kids, like having a mean bull running loose.'

'Who is it, Mr Lloyd?'

Her quiet persistence reached him and his face set. He stood back. 'You all got to be on guard,' he told her, and stopped, and stared at the escarpment as if he saw something, but not there on the skyline; he was contemplating something a long way back: in space or time or the recesses of his own mind.

She started home, leading the pinto. As she turned south on the dirt road the world darkened, and she was so preoccupied, so accustomed to the continuous day-long sunshine that she cringed. But the sorrel merely flicked an ear and she glanced up and saw it was only a cloud that had reached the sun.

Eastward the desert mountains were

washed with a deeper gold than was usual in late afternoon. The sky beyond them was still clear and bleached by the heat but above her, boiling forward above the cliffs, still very high, rose splendid thunderheads: grey deepening to graphite in the depths, and the leading edges dazzling as clotted cream. Far back in the high country there was a growl and a crack. It was the crack that alerted her and sent a chill down her spine. Her thighs tightened and the sorrel broke into a sharp trot.

By the time she had attended to the horses, had showered and changed, she had recovered from her initial relief that Pearl was absent and that no one came visiting, and she had started to wonder where everyone was, particularly Marge. It was gloomy now and no light showed in the house across the street. At long intervals there were claps of thunder but as yet there was no rain. She went to Marge's front door, opened it and called. There was no reply.

She stood on the front step looking down the street where nothing moved except dust lifted by a vagrant breeze. From the creek came a sound like rain but it was only a current of air stirring the cottonwood leaves.

She moved into the road. There were vehicles outside the Scott house and there were lights in both the Scott and Vosker places. She relaxed; it had been disturbing to realise that no one was about—and the storm coming, and the situation unresolved ... What situation? Which situation? And there was Lloyd's warning that kept returning to puzzle her: to look after Pearl. Surely it was Tammy who needed protection?

'Did you find her yet?' Thelma cried as Miss Pink entered the Scotts' crowded living-room. Belatedly she remembered that Thelma had intended returning from Texas this morning.

Tammy's mother looked older than she did three days ago, which was hardly surprising considering what she'd been through emotionally, not to speak of the plane journeys which must have been a strain in themselves, not knowing what awaited her at either end.

The Scott place wasn't really crowded, it merely appeared so after the emptiness of the rest of the village. Marge was there, and Ada, of course, but only the three of them. It transpired that Thelma had reached home, talked to Maxine and come rushing back to the village. Marge couldn't tell her anything so the two of them had come to Ada. They knew nothing of the events in Slickrock Canyon and all they had seen of activity down here was Avril's old pick-up go past, the driver grinding the gears. Avril had been with them at that moment and she'd been furious; it was only afterwards that they

233

wondered why Fletcher had come down from the canyons.

Miss Pink told them what had taken place in Slickrock. Thelma was bewildered, Ada was shocked. 'The good news,' Miss Pink said, stretching the truth, 'is that Tammy's safe and well, and that Clayton's just got a flesh wound. They'll release him as soon as they've stitched him up and given him a tetanus jab. Oh yes, and the person responsible has left the area. The old pick-up you saw go past: he was driving that.' Still dehydrated, even after pints of tea, now drinking beer and eating nothing, she was in a state of euphoria. She beamed at them. 'Tammy will come down now,' she assured Thelma. 'Kristen will tell her the man's gone.'

Ada telephoned the hospital. When she put the phone down she said quietly, 'They've released him; I guess that means he's coming back with Pearl and Avril, so he'll be here soon.' She smiled weakly. 'All's well that ends well.'

'I don't have Tammy,' Thelma said meaningly.

Marge, who had kept quiet until now, perhaps feeling that, with no dependants, she was outside the drama, suggested that the police should be told of the attack on Scott.

'But he'll have told them himself,' Miss Pink exclaimed. 'Or the hospital will have done so.'

'We should report it,' Ada put in firmly. 'He may be suffering from concussion, he could just forget; everybody could leave it to someone else. Maybe you should do it,' she told Miss Pink, 'since you were there.'

Put like that, Miss Pink had no alternative, but when she got through to the police she was relayed to an excited woman who told her that she could speak to Spikol when he was free. At the moment he was with the doctor and Tammy Markow.

'With—' Miss Pink checked and turned her back on the company. 'Is everything all right?' she asked, with as much deviousness as she could summon at short notice. 'Why the doctor?'

'What would be wrong?' came the voice—ironic now. 'You mean: was she raped, drugged, whatever? That kid's got nothing wrong with her a good spanking wouldn't cure, ma'am; she's just a naughty little girl wants to join her daddy in Texas, never mind they got a death in the family; all she thinks of is herself. She knows her mom's home but no way can they get her to come back to Regis. You ask me, she's scared of a whipping. Ah, here's Wayne now—'

'Miss Pink?' came his gravelly voice. 'I can't do nothing with this kid. Where can I find her mom?'

Thelma took the telephone as if uncertain

that it was the right thing to do. 'Tammy's all right,' Miss Pink hissed, and pushed a chair forward. Thelma sank into it, her expression changing from wariness to intensity as she listened. 'I'll come,' she said, adding quickly, 'You keep her there, Wayne; lock her up, don't you let her go again.'

A pick-up stopped outside the house and Kristen got down from the passenger seat and walked towards the passage. The truck turned and went back up the street. Jay Gafford was driving.

'Tammy's safe,' Ada said as her daughter came in from the patio. Kristen sighed. Her mother regarded her benignly. 'She's in Palomares with the police. You look hot; you got time for a shower before your dad comes home. They've released him from hospital so he'll be coming back with Pearl and Avril. They took him there.'

Kristen looked at Miss Pink. 'Who hit him?'

'He didn't see his attacker. We missed you in Slickrock. Did you hear the shots?'

'Distantly. I was looking for Tammy in some old caves at the head of the canyon. I started back when I heard the shooting, thought you were trying to attract my attention, but by the time I got down you were all nearing the top of the wall, except for Jay. I found him eventually and he told me what happened.'

Miss Pink had sat down at the table and now, looking up at Kristen, she tried to visualise the head of the canyon. There was the marijuana that had been trampled by the peccaries, but were the caves at ground-level, accessible? Her chin was in her hands, her elbows on the table, and she became aware of a tense silence broken by Marge: 'Why are you staring at Kristen, Melinda?'

She sat up, blinking. 'I've had too much to drink, and no food since breakfast.' Immediately there was a bustle of activity: 'Why didn't you *say*?' 'I'm so sorry. Marge, come and give me a hand, we'll fix some sandwiches...'

Thelma said, 'I have to fetch Tammy.' She sounded a little lost.

Miss Pink caught the wistful note and started up. 'I'll come with you if you'll wait a moment.' She turned to Kristen. 'It was Tammy,' she said clearly—and the women stopped what they were doing in the kitchen. 'She climbed out of Slickrock ahead of us,' she went on, 'and rode away on Pearl's sorrel and then she took Avril's truck. She took the food from the saddle-bags too; the child must have been starving.' She beamed. 'More proof that she's fit: yelling like a banshee when the pigs came charging along the trail, stealing all our food—and of course she was fit enough to gallop out. We saw the tracks. There's not much wrong with

237

Tammy.'

'Good,' Kristen said. 'So when you pick her up, watch she don't go again.'

'I don't need you telling me how I'm to look after my own daughter, miss.' Thelma was snappy. 'You coming?' she shot at Miss Pink.

'I'll come—' Kristen began.

'You stay here,' came Ada's voice from the kitchen. 'Your father'll be home any minute.' It sounded like a warning.

*   *   *

'I'm at the end of my rope,' Thelma confessed as they drove out of the village. 'Wayne Spikol said Ira's father died this morning so I'll need to go back for the funeral, and here's Tammy—what do I do about Tammy?'

'Take her with you,' Miss Pink said.

'You mean I should give in to her!'

Miss Pink sketched a shrug. Ahead of them the desert was grey under a dark slate sky and the cottonwoods were a black ribbon across their road. There must be a window in the cloud and through it the sun came slanting to light one patch of trees which shone, achingly brilliant, like emeralds in a pit. 'There's nothing to Texas,' Miss Pink said, and then adjusted it a little: 'It has nothing to do with Texas.'

'Her behaviour?'

'Yes, her terror.'

'She's never been left on her own before.'

'She had Kristen and Pearl. They weren't enough. You have to talk to her.'

'Now it's you telling me how to raise my child.'

'Of course. I'm drunk.'

It was a neat withdrawal and Thelma was unable to handle it so she lapsed into silence and allowed Miss Pink to enjoy the scenery. When they passed through the woodland the cottonwoods were as sombre as a cathedral and the river was a leaden lake shattered by sooty terns fishing the evening rise. The patch of sunshine moved ahead of them, lighting the desert as it went: yellow sand, glittering quartzite, a cactus flower richer than claret.

They came to the interstate and a pick-up stationary in the creosote bushes. 'I guess that's Avril's,' Thelma said.

'Where did Tammy learn to drive?'

'Her dad lets her drive in our pastures.'

The interstate was almost clear of traffic. 'They'll be broadcasting a Storm Watch,' Thelma said. 'Our radio's broken.'

There was a flash in the west and a spiky range was silhouetted like a theatre set. Long curtains of rain were drifting across the valley of the Rio Grande and as the weather moved eastward storms engulfed successive ranges,

239

lightning striking their peaks with white fire that ran along the ridges to be drowned in gloom. Wind rocked the car and the windscreen spotted, was momentarily obscured by mud as Thelma switched on the wipers, then battered by hail. 'I hope we can get home again,' Thelma shouted.

The first fury of the storm passed and by the time they reached the sheriff's office in Palomares the rain was a thin drizzle but the back streets in the town were flooded and the storm drains were running red with mud.

'No way,' said Wayne Spikol, 'no way could I convince her to come home, but her mother won't stand no nonsense.'

Tammy and Thelma were alone in an office behind a closed door and he was talking to Miss Pink in a large room dominated by computers. Miss Pink was in an office chair, the deputy perched on the edge of a desk, his thighs straining his uniform trousers.

'Did she say why she won't go home?'

'Because she insists on going to her daddy in Texas.' He lowered his voice. 'There's nothing wrong with that family?' It could be taken as a statement but she knew there was a question mark at the end. 'I guess some girls are their daddy's favourite ...' She said nothing. He tried again. 'It was the same at the airport. They were on watch for her, of course, so there was no problem about

240

holding her. Just between us, and no witnesses, they had to lock her in—and who cares about the law, she's only twelve.'

'You mean they had to restrain her, they forced her into a room?'

'No other way. One of the staff went in with her: big powerful lady. No one hurt her, they just held her arms. She was screaming. Something got to that kid.'

'They did right. She couldn't be allowed to escape again. She hitched up the interstate. Eventually she was going to meet someone who wasn't a friend.'

'You'd think she did already. Who was this guy knocked out Clayton Scott? And if Tammy was the one took Pearl's horse, then that guy is still in Slickrock canyon, except he'll have come out by now. He'll have gone in and left by the top road.'

'The top road? And who told you about the attack on Clayton? I meant to when I called you earlier but your telling us that Tammy was here put it right out of my mind—and then you asked to speak to Thelma—'

'Pearl called me from the hospital. I didn't see Clayton yet because I had to go to the airport and fetch Tammy, but I'll have to see him, take a statement. Pearl says he didn't get a sight of the guy who hit him, and none of you did neither. Why do I think this guy went in by the top road? We had that same argument when we were up to Rastus last week and we found the bones. There's only two ways into that high country from the bottom: past the Markow place and at Las Mesas, so anyone up to mischief has to use the top road.'

'What sort of mischief would anyone be up to in Slickrock?'

He was fiddling with a stapler. She wanted to tell him to put it down before he injured himself. 'Pearl says you came on some old marijuana plots,' he said. 'All destroyed now by pigs,' he added hastily. 'There's an occupational hazard to growing that stuff: getting ripped off by your competitors—like guys who can't be bothered to grow it themselves. That guy who hit Scott coulda been after the grass and he thought Scott were the grower.'

'How does Tammy come into it?'

'Coincidence. She holed up in Slickrock at the same time as this guy comes in to steal the crop. Of course, he wouldn't know the pigs had destroyed it. You don't believe that? Look, ma'am, it had to be a stranger attacked Scott. There was no way it coulda been anyone else. There's—what?—five men in Regis not counting Scott himself, and you're not going to suggest he hit himself on the back of the head! Now one of those five is in Texas, and three was under your eye, so Pearl says. There's only one guy, we don't know where he was: Professor Vosker. You going to tell me it was the professor attacked Scott? Now what's on your mind?'

She wouldn't be rushed. After a pause she said, 'You're right, it couldn't have been any one of those four—assuming Ira is still in Texas—and Michael Vosker is so obvious, I can't believe ... apart from the fact that he has no head for heights—although that's only on his evidence. Why does it have to be a man?'

'Oh, come on! How could—' There was a thunderous explosion. The lights flickered and went out. 'Oh, shit! Excuse me, ma'am!' The first hail hit the windows like bullets. Through the gloom Miss Pink saw a door open. Thelma and Tammy approached.

'We're staying,' Thelma shouted above the racket. 'We'll book in at a motel and fly to Houston tomorrow. I have my bag in the car and Tammy can buy clothes in Houston. You take my car back, Melinda, if you're happy to drive it.'

Miss Pink nodded absently, her eyes on Tammy who was so close to her mother as to give the impression that she was clinging to her. Then there was a fresh clap of thunder and Thelma flung an arm round the child. 'Use your phone?' she cried to Spikol, and moved to a desk, Tammy shadowing her like a dog at heel. Miss Pink took a step forward and was blocked by Spikol. 'I'm glad to see you safe, Tammy,' she shouted into an unexpected lull. Tammy's eyes were like a terrified colt's; Thelma, dialling, regarded her bemusedly. 'I'll be on my way,' Miss Pink said, moving towards the door.

'Go and fetch my bag.' Thelma addressed Tammy but the girl shook her head vehemently.

'I'll get it.' Spikol advanced between desks, giving the appearance of driving Miss Pink before him.

By the time she was back on the interstate the rain had stopped and she looked down on a town blazing with lights although it was only a little after sunset. Westward, beyond the badlands that fringed this stretch of the Rio Grande, the mountains were shrouded in night except for one torn patch of palest lemon.

The lull was temporary. Before she reached the Regis turn-off, another storm was crossing the valley and her wipers were finding it difficult to cope with a deluge sluicing down the windscreen. Occasionally she was aware of lights creeping by on the northbound carriageway and she felt a peculiar kinship with these other travellers, all of them united in a struggle with the elements.

The rain eased a little by the time she came to her exit and now, with the desert and the river ahead, she thought about real bad floods, and flash-floods, and then she thought that the flash-floods might have passed by now, water would have found its level. She drove on, forgetting to see if Avril's truck was still in position; it hadn't shone in her lights but it wouldn't show up in the creosote bushes, and no way was she going to drive over and look, the desert would be a quagmire.

The old dry arroyos were now brawling torrents and where they crossed the road (beyond the signs telling motorists not to proceed if flooded) she edged forward gently, careful not to swamp her engine.

She came to the woods on the river bank; here the wind that drives ahead of the storm had taken its toll and dead branches lay shattered on the road. The rain was heavy again and twigs were hitting the roof of the car, making her think of whole trees coming down. Headlights passed—it was only the second vehicle that she'd encountered since she left the interstate; she wondered who could be abroad on such a night, and then remembered that this was only evening, it was not yet nine o'clock.

She crossed the river bridge but her lights showed only the parapets; there was no way she could judge the level of the water, except to know that it wasn't over the road. Then came more arroyos, more shallow floods, and the gentle rise to the village, and lights showing under the escarpment. The rain had stopped.

There were no vehicles in the street other than the Voskers' car. There was a note on Pearl's kitchen table saying she'd gone to fetch Avril's pick-up from beside the interstate. That explained one of the cars she'd passed on the highway. She called Maxine to bring her up to date with events only to learn that Thelma had phoned from a motel in Palomares. Maxine told her to keep the Markows' car until the morning; she shouldn't attempt to reach the ranch tonight, there had been flash-floods everywhere and there was water over the road. Miss Pink was relieved not to have to make the journey; she could hear the creek at the back of the corral. She thought she should go and see how close the water was to the top of the bank. The horses could be at risk.

Taking a slicker and a powerful flashlight she squelched across the patio and through the corral. The torch beam found the horses, their coats gleaming wet, sheltering under a walnut tree. She approached the far side of the corral, treading gingerly although it was obvious that the rails were still firm. The noise was awe-inspiring, not loud, not a roar but a menacing rush. She shone the light through the undergrowth and could see nothing but movement, as if an enormous throng of animals were hurtling past. She looked down and saw water shining very close, among the vegetation, about two feet down. She thought about snakes leaving their flooded holes and threw the beam round wildly like a weapon. Shadows danced on the periphery and sent her hurrying back to the house.

Pearl came home late: breathless, apologetic. 'No damage so far,' she announced, shrugging out of her slicker. 'Did you eat? Good. My God, what a day—and night! No trouble on the way back? So Tammy's safe; if they'd only taken her to Texas in the first place, none of this would have happened.'

'You got it out all right?' Miss Pink asked.

'What? Got what out?'

'The pick-up. You left a note saying you'd gone to collect Avril's pick-up. I must have passed you on the road.'

Pearl stared and blinked. 'Oh, that was you? Of course—yes; we were on our way to get the pick-up: several of us, make sure no one got stuck. Coulda been there all night if we had to drag it out and got bogged down ourselves. Fletch came. Well, he had to, didn't he? I couldn't drive two trucks back.' Seeing Miss Pink's expression she gave a high peal of laughter. 'Imagine: like riding two horses in the circus, one foot on each back. God, I'm dying for a drink; do you realise we were on the mesas all day, climbed

247

down into Slickrock, out again, all in that blazing heat, and then: the hospital, and the storm—what a day! Are you sure you're feeling all right? Don't you want to go to bed?'

'I'm fine. You were gone so long I was worried.'

'No, no, nothing happened. I mean, apart from getting it out of the desert: the pick-up. It was mired a bit, we had to put a rope on it, drag it free. Everything takes longer in bad weather. I'm soaked. Shall I have a shower, or am I too exhausted? I think I'll just fall into my bed. We both should. You're asleep on your feet.'

It was the second time that evening that Miss Pink felt she was being driven away. It had been reasonable of Spikol to assume that she would want to question Tammy—he had Miss Pink's measure and was aware of her insatiable curiosity—and he could feel that, in default of her father he should protect the child—but if Pearl was driving her to bed, was she too protecting someone, and why?

CHAPTER FOURTEEN

The mockingbird was singing his heart out but the morning light was pale and watery. Miss Pink parted her curtains and saw dim rock rising into cloud. But for the mockingbird she could have been in Scotland.

She showered and dressed and went along to the kitchen. The coffeepot was on the stove and through the window she could see Pearl in the corral. She stepped out on the veranda and saw that the cloud had retreated until it lay in a long band below the rim of the escarpment. Above the cloud the cliffs rose like fairy castles touched here and there with gold, and glittering wet. The sun was breaking through the overcast.

'Come and see!' shouted Pearl. 'Look at the waterfall!'

White water was pouring over the rim from the mouth of Slickrock, vanishing behind the cloud, reappearing below it to come tumbling down the screes.

'Great, isn't it?' Pearl's face was streaked with dirt and there were ragged plates of mud on her boots. The horses stood stiffly as if stuck to the ground. 'Monsoon weather,' she said. 'I love it.'

'Does this happen every year?' Miss Pink asked. 'As bad as this?'

'As good as, you mean. Where would we be without it? What's a bit of dirt? "Listen to the mockingbird",' she sang.

Miss Pink thought she was a little hysterical. 'There'll be no riding today,' she said in a calming tone. 'A good thing we were searching the canyons yesterday.'

'Yes.' Pearl sobered suddenly. 'This is clean-up day. We seem to be all right but I have to call people, see if anyone needs help. Marge first, I guess; she's on her own. Ha, someone's about.' They heard a truck pass down the street. 'Markows,' she said. 'From the Markow place anyway.'

On the phone Marge said that she had suffered terribly: all her fuchsias smashed flat, the four o'clocks ruined, Pedro had to be washed before he could be let back in the house ... 'She's all right,' Pearl said. 'And everyone else has men around, so that's our duty done. Now folk'll start calling us, see if we need any help. It's great fun, living in a small community; everyone helps everyone else. Why is it I have this feeling you're not with us this morning?'

Miss Pink poured herself a second cup of coffee and took her time replying. She sighed and blinked, aware that she was spoiling the mood but unable to do anything about it. 'Difficult to say,' she murmured. 'Something appears to be not quite in order: out of synch, as they say. How did we change so suddenly—was it too sudden? This time yesterday we were searching for a missing child who—let's face it—could have been injured, raped, even dead—'

'But we found her—'

'I know, and everything's all right. The

child's safe and well and with her parents, or one of them at least, so all the terrible hypotheses were just that, and can be forgotten. I *saw* Tammy, I know she's all right.'

'Well, don't sound so doubtful about it.'

'I'm getting old. At my time of life it takes time to recover from traumatic events. And you Westerners, you're much more accustomed to high drama—like that storm. You have resilience. I thought the storm was terrifying. You *liked* it.'

'Not all the time. Thunder terrifies me. But it's over now, no trees fell on the house, the horses weren't struck by lightning, the creek didn't top its banks and flood the corral; we're back to normal.'

She spoke too soon, and although an hour went by without further communication with the neighbours, when it came it was disturbing. Pearl was tying up damaged plants when the telephone rang and Miss Pink answered to find Kristen on the line. She sounded subdued and apologetic. 'I don't want to bother you but I wondered: could Pearl—and maybe you—come down and—er—give me a hand here? I could do with some advice.'

'Of course.' Miss Pink glanced out of the window but she couldn't see Pearl. 'I'm not sure where she is, but I'll find her. Is someone ill?'

251

'I don't know. I don't even know if it's urgent, but the pick-up's here and not him. We can't find him. I mean, what could have happened?'

'Who are you talking about?'

'I wish you'd come!' It was distraught. 'The road's clear; you won't have any trouble.'

'Where are you?'

'At the farm of course. Didn't I say that? My dad didn't come home all night and I can't call Mom and tell her I haven't found him—'

'Here's Pearl.' She was working off her boots on the step.

'Just *come!*' The line went dead.

'Who was that?' Pearl asked, opening the screen.

'Kristen. She sounds frantic. She's at the farm and can't find her father. His pick-up's there but he didn't come home last night.'

'Jesus! What does Casey say?'

'Casey?'

'The hired hand. He lives on the place.'

'She didn't mention him. She wants us down there: for advice, she says. And she doesn't want Ada to know.'

Pausing only to put on their boots they piled into the truck. 'But Ada must know,' Pearl said, as the pick-up slid crabwise round the corner and started down the street. 'She'd know if he didn't come to bed all

252

night. Or would she? Maybe not.' She pursed her lips. 'Road's slick,' she added superfluously.

There was no sign of life as they passed the Scotts' house but one could never tell who was watching from behind the screened windows.

The farm was close by the river and approached along a track that was marked by recent traffic and the hoofs of a horse. It was a small farm, Pearl said, less than two hundred acres, under corn and alfalfa except for a pasture which Scott sometimes let for grazing. The whole place was nothing more than a clearing in the riparian woodland, and so enclosed by trees that for all that could be seen of the desert and mountains, it might have been in an Eastern state.

At the edge of a cornfield, dwarfed by the trees, were a barn and a cabin with a smoking chimney. Outside the cabin stood a pick-up and an old Army jeep. A man appeared, aged about forty and clean-shaven. He was large and powerful with the blurred features of an old boxer, and he looked nervous.

'Hi, Casey,' Pearl called, climbing out of the truck. 'Where's Kristen?'

'Down by the river, ma'am.'

'What happened? Where did he go?'

'I wasn't here!' It burst out of him as if he'd been harbouring a grievance. 'I never

253

saw him, I was in town. I come home this morning and there's his pick-up, and that's all I know. I didn't even know he'd been here all night until Kristen come and told me! I left before the storm—'

'OK!' Pearl checked the flow. 'We'll find Kristen.' Miss Pink said nothing. There was nothing to say.

A track led round the edge of the cornfield and a ragged pasture to a wire gate in a fence. 'This is his boundary,' Pearl said. 'Between here and the river is a kind of no-man's-land.'

'I wonder why she's looking here.' There were prints of shod hoofs in the mud.

'Poor kid, looking for him all on her own.'

They unclipped the gate and walked along a low dike following the hoofprints. The sun was hot now and the swamp steamed. Vultures were perched in a dead tree, all facing west, warming their backs. At water level black and yellow turtles basked on a log.

'This is where Michael Vosker comes,' Miss Pink said suddenly.

'That's right; the river banks swarm with wildlife.'

'Why would Scott come here?'

'I guess Kristen has looked in all the likely places.' Pearl stopped and stared at her companion. 'It's Tammy all over again, isn't it?'

'I was more concerned about Tammy. She was vulnerable.'

'Yes, of course. Clayton can look after himself.' But the glance she threw at Miss Pink implied doubt.

They continued until the track ran into water. 'She turned back,' Pearl said, glancing sideways. Willows stretched across their line as far as they could see in both directions and beyond the willows the river slid by very fast carrying branches and rafts of sedges and unidentifiable rubbish. A bulging sack swept past and they followed it with their eyes but made no comment. Pearl swung round suddenly. A horse was splashing towards them with Kristen on its back, her jeans soaked to the thighs. She looked drawn and wary.

Pearl said when she came up, 'What did he tell you when he left home?'

'I wasn't there. He told Mom he had to come down, see if anything was wrong. He called Casey after the storm started and couldn't get any reply. So Dad left to make sure everything was all right: you know, if Casey had gone to town—which he had—to see all the doors were closed and stuff.'

'What time was this?'

'Around seven. I was up at the Markow place.'

'And you heard nothing since. So why didn't he call you—Ada anyway—from the

255

cabin?'

'Why should he? He'd just make sure the barn was closed and nothing left loose to blow away, then I guess he meant to come straight home.'

They thought about this. Pearl looked at Miss Pink who said, 'I suppose you tried the pick-up to make sure it would start?'

Kristen was surprised. 'I didn't, but if it wouldn't run, he'd have phoned for someone to come and fetch him. The cabin was open and the phone's working because Casey called us soon's he got home this morning. After he looked around for Dad, I mean.'

They went back to the cabin and tried the pick-up. It started at the second attempt. Miss Pink proposed that they search the corn but Kristen said that both she and Casey had been round all the crops, herself riding, and if anyone had walked into the corn or the alfalfa their track would have shown.

Pearl telephoned Wayne Spikol. He was putting out diversion signs where a bridge had been carried away so she was put through to the sheriff. She didn't like that because it implied that the situation was serious and as yet no one wanted to admit that it was. The sheriff said that he would send someone down, and had they thought of snakebite or a knock on the head and amnesia?

'A snake?' Pearl repeated, replacing the

phone, turning to Miss Pink who was waiting in the doorway of the cabin.

'No. He's a healthy fellow; at the least he'd have been able to get to the phone and tell someone. Amnesia?' She turned and looked across the cornfield. 'I can't imagine a man losing his memory and just walking away from an empty truck.' She looked at the ground. 'Yesterday's tracks have been washed out by the rain. A pity. What did he do when he got out of the truck?'

Kristen rode round the side of the barn and stopped in front of the cabin. 'Did you cover all the boundary fence?' Pearl asked, staring fixedly across the corn.

'I said: I rode right round and there's no one, not even a deer, been in the corn, or the alfalfa.'

'You were looking inwards. Is it my eyesight or is that fence broken on the far side there, at the break in the trees?'

'Could be.' Kristen was casual. 'But there's no way out there, the river's immediately below and it's cutting the bank away—' She stopped.

'Get down!' Pearl ordered harshly. 'Give me your horse.' She moved but she was too slow. Kristen's horse leapt away and was galloping round the corn towards the gap in the trees. 'Oh, God!' Pearl gasped, her hand to her mouth.

The horse stopped but Kristen didn't

257

dismount, and she didn't return. Without speaking they started to run. They came up to her and saw what she was staring at. Two old posts hung down the eroded bank, held there only by strands of wire.

Casey approached. 'That's been like it for months,' he said calmly. 'Clayton, he were going to bring some new posts and fix it.'

They looked at him and back at the river, so close below that they daren't approach the edge. 'We drug that fence back twice already,' he said with a kind of satisfaction. 'That old river cuts the bank away more every season; it's not safe to bring a tractor down here no more, the whole lot could fall in.'

Pearl said, 'No way would Clayton come down here to move a fence during the storm. This is a cornfield; it's not like stock in a meadow that are going to fall over the edge if the fence isn't fixed. We should go home now.' She glanced at Miss Pink and saw agreement. 'Ada has to be told,' she went on. 'Don't worry about it, Kristy; your mother's a lot tougher than you give her credit for. Casey can handle things here; 'fact, there's nothing for him to do, he just tells the police what he told us. You start back and we'll overtake you on the road. Do you want me to tell your mom?'

'I don't know.' Kristen swallowed. 'I guess I ought to.'

'I don't like that broken fence,' Miss Pink said as they drove away. 'How reliable is that fellow?'

'Casey? He's speaking the truth, because Wayne told me he reckoned Veronica could have gone into the river at that point. The fence was already broken at the time she died so Clayton never got around to moving it back. I guess Kristen had that in mind when she galloped over there. What made you think he wasn't telling the truth?'

'I didn't—necessarily, but why was he away—'

'He said he was in town.'

'The police can check that. It's a coincidence though, that he should be away, *says* he was away when Scott disappears.'

'You know something? You have a very suspicious mind. Anybody'd think you were a detective. Clayton came down *because* Casey was away. Ask me, Casey's often away nights; who'd spend the evening down here on his own when he's got wheels, and a town close by? And no way is Casey going to push his employer in the river and do himself out of a job.'

'Ada could be a better employer than her husband.'

'Ada would sell—' She didn't complete the sentence.

'Which reminds me,' Miss Pink was smooth, 'why would Ada not know that

259

Scott was out all night? Do they have separate bedrooms?'

'How would I know? I assume so, with Ada being sick. Sick people like to sleep alone, don't they? None of my business.' It was a mutter.

Miss Pink stared through the windscreen at the steaming road. There was no sign of Kristen, who was moving fast to judge by the widely spaced prints in the drying mud. They came to the village and only glanced at the Scotts' house, not wanting to appear inquisitive. No one was abroad in the street. They turned the corner and turned again, stopping the pick-up under the gable-end of the house. The telephone started to ring as they were removing their boots.

'I'll go,' Pearl said quickly as Miss Pink opened the screen door. She went back to the bench and started to peel off her socks.

'So what?' came Pearl's voice. 'I'm not responsible for—Oh, come on, Wayne, it floated down from Santa Fe —Albuquerque then, the river's running high enough— What? You're out of your mind; she's a sick woman and to ask her to identify—You do that, Wayne Spikol, and you'll never set foot in this house again, never!'

The receiver was slammed down and Miss Pink's jaw sagged as the screen door crashed open and Pearl stood there, livid and speechless with fury.

'He's found a body?' Miss Pink asked. 'In the river?'

'That's not the point. He's going to fetch Ada to identify it. Head blown—well, that's an exaggeration maybe—gunshot wound in the face. I'm going to speak to the sheriff!' She swung round and the screen crashed to. Miss Pink listened, her face stony, her eyes bright as a bird's. 'You'll connect me, Tessy Silver,' Pearl hissed, 'if it's the last thing you do—Then I'll speak to a deputy—any deputy—But I was speaking to Spikol this very minute! He can't be—Listen Tessy, Ada Scott's a sick woman—' She stopped and listened, interjecting: 'You sure of that?' and, deflated, sullen: 'He should have *said*.' A few more grumbling remarks and long silences and she rang off. She came out to the veranda and sat down with a sigh. 'That girl says they've gone to pick up the body, but they wouldn't be asking Ada to identify it, she says, without the head was covered, or they'll clean it up first. It's an entry wound in the mouth apparently, and it's the back of the head is blown'—she grimaced—'isn't there any longer. Someone who brought it out of the river recognised it as Clayton. Of course it can't be; why should Clayton commit suicide?'

'Well, if he's done it at the same spot that Veronica threw herself in the river, there could be a connection.'

261

'You think so? Anyway, there's a watch so they won't be asking Ada to see the body; they'll take the watch to her first. There's no other means of identification; his billfold must have been washed away. I reckon it's a body floated down from Santa Fe. Wayne said it wouldn't have come as far in the time. That's rubbish; you saw how fast the river was moving.'

'Where was he found?'

'At San Juan. That's about five miles downstream. It got caught in a tree at high water. A farmer saw the vultures. Should we warn Ada and Kristen?'

'Spikol meant you to do that or he wouldn't have called you first. He was probably exceeding his duty; perhaps it was a good thing you didn't speak to the sheriff.'

'Now why would Wayne do that?'

'As I said: meaning you to warn Ada.'

'Then why couldn't he say so?' She went back indoors and Miss Pink followed to change her clothes. In her bedroom she reflected that she'd automatically accepted that she should accompany Pearl to the Scott house, which was curious since she was only a visitor but then, she shrugged, maybe she was a supportive presence.

While she was sponging her face she heard a screen door slam and thought nothing of it. In five minutes she was ready but Pearl had gone, had left the house without another word to her. She stood in the living-room that was full of muted sunshine and stared through layers of net at the shadowed façade of Marge's house. A supportive presence? She had been rejected.

CHAPTER FIFTEEN

Miss Pink drove the Markows' car to the ranch and walked back without seeing anyone. She was trying to interest herself in the local paper when a horse snorted and she looked up to see Michael Vosker lowering his binoculars. He peered into the willows at the creek's edge, then straightened and came towards the veranda. 'I thought it was a pygmy nuthatch,' he said. 'Couldn't understand it; we're too low for pygmies. It was a white-breasted, of course, an optical illusion on my part. Are you all alone? Shall I join you?'

'Do. I was about to make coffee.'

He sat down, his expression that of an enthusiast about to indulge in shop-talk. There was silence as she busied herself in the kitchen, a pregnant silence. 'I gather you haven't heard the news,' she said, emerging and handing him a mug. He regarded her with interest, as if she were a strange bird.

'Marian did remark on an unusual amount

of activity this morning. Did something happen—other than storm damage?'

'A body's been taken out of the river at San Juan. There's a gunshot wound in the mouth.'

'Oh yes.' He looked wary. 'Out here suicides prefer shooting to hanging, it's more reliable. This—can't have anything to do with Tammy.'

'No, no. She's on the way to Texas now with Thelma. It's a man's body, and Clayton Scott went down to his farm during the storm and he never came home. His pick-up's there, outside the cabin but he's not on the farm. We searched.'

'Good Heavens! What does Casey have to say?'

'He was in Palomares last night. When he came back this morning he found the pick-up. He alerted the family.'

He sipped his coffee. He seemed to have forgotten his companion. After a while she said, 'You're not unduly surprised.'

'It's a favoured method,' he repeated.

'He's guilty?' His head came round slowly, his eyes intent. 'He feels guilty for Veronica's death,' she explained.

'No doubt.' He looked back at the patio and eased his legs.

'And Tammy could have brought things to a head,' she added.

'In what way?'

264

'As it turned out Tammy's adventure was just a childish escapade, but until she was found everyone must have had the same thought, as the time passed and we became more frantic: that a man was involved. The sexual element must have reminded Scott of Veronica.'

'It could have.'

'He was very strict, particularly so for these days. He'd have been all right with sons; he couldn't handle young girls.'

He looked at her again and now she realised that he was deeply shocked. He saw her surprise and he stiffened, spilling his coffee. 'I have to tell Marian,' he said. 'She'll want to go to Ada.'

'Pearl's down there. We don't know that it's Clayton.'

'But that's the implication.'

'Someone in San Juan is said to have recognised the body. There's been no confirmation.'

'Unpleasant though.' He smiled, more or less in control again, and stood up. 'It's been nice talking to you. We must go birding some time. I'll look forward to it.'

Marge came over, clean and casual in apple green, her eyes flicking into corners as if Pearl's veranda held secrets. 'Such a coming and going,' she breathed. 'I called Marian Vosker and she'd noticed it too, it wasn't my imagination. She said Michael was out birding but he wasn't, was he? He was here.'

'He had coffee with me.'

'Well, that's no sin, dear, no need to be on the defensive.' She paused for protest but Miss Pink only smiled politely. 'Where is everybody?' Marge snapped.

'They've all gone into huddles—like us; that's my guess. A body's been taken out of the river.'

Marge sat down carefully on the chair vacated by Vosker. 'Who is it?'

'Someone said it was Clayton Scott.'

'Clayton.' A pause. 'How did it happen?'

'There's a gunshot wound in the mouth.'

'Oh.' She exhaled on a long sigh. 'Suicide.'

'What else could it be?'

The woman's gaze shifted sideways to the kitchen, her body seeming to soften where it had been stiff. Again she took time to reply. 'With anyone else,' she said at length, 'and a night like it was last night—drinking, working in an arroyo, it would have been an accident, like caught in a flash-flood. But Clayton didn't drink—and then shooting: no accident there, it had to be deliberate; unless he leaned his rifle against a bank and it fell down and fired. It happens.'

'It could have happened here.'

'I doubt it.' She considered this. Miss Pink had the impression of wheels turning. 'He had more than his share of problems,' Marge went on: 'two wild daughters, one of them defective; an invalid wife who—' She checked and pondered, ignoring Miss Pink. 'Where *is* Pearl?' she asked sweetly.

'She went down to Ada.'

'She would. Always the first to offer comfort. She's got a lot to learn, we're not quite so outgoing in these little communities as they are in a San Jose ghetto. Mind you, I don't hold it against her for what she was: where there's a demand there's always someone around to supply it—just so long as she leaves it behind. There's a time and a place for everything.'

'I don't see that a beauty salon could hurt Regis,' Miss Pink murmured. 'Might do some good.'

'Oh, so she tried it on you too? Said she was a beautician. That's a little wide of the mark. A massage parlour wouldn't have her. Miss Pearl may know how to fix her face to hide the wrinkles but she never did an honest day's work in her life.'

'Oh, come on! She put enough by to purchase a nice old house and a few acres—'

'Not as a beautician, dear.' The tone was honeyed but the eyes glittered. 'Pearl Slocum walked the streets, that's how she made her money.'

'I don't believe it.'

'And living right opposite'—the tone was

rising—'I couldn't entertain; imagine: Marian Vosker or Ada or Thelma sitting at my table, seeing 'em going and coming. Why you looking at me like that? They was coming in off the interstate! Why, in no time at all we'd have had truck drivers here, parking overnight! You don't believe me? I see you don't. Wayne Spikol used to come, still does.'

'Who else did?'

Marge stopped as if she'd been hit. Standing up, she smoothed her slacks and nodded. 'I have to take Pedro for his walk now. I'll see you later.'

Miss Pink poured herself a brandy. She needed it. A vehicle with a good engine went by but she couldn't see what it was because the house blocked her view except for a section of the Las Mesas road. The car didn't go to Las Mesas, but very shortly it returned. She assumed its destination had been the Markow ranch.

It was past noon when Pearl came home, full of information and apologies. 'But I knew you weren't on your own,' she said. 'Michael came down and told us he'd visited with you and I saw Marge cross the street while I was talking to Wayne. You should have come down—or maybe not, some of it was morbid. Did you eat? Good. I had a salad at Marian's.'

'I thought you were with Ada.'

'Oh, backwards and forwards, you know. Come out in the patio and I'll tell you.'

'It *is* Clayton,' she said as they settled themselves under the walnut tree. 'It's his watch. Wayne brought it out on his way from San Juan to the morgue, and Ada and Kristen identified it. Ada's gone to town to identify him formally. Michael went along for moral support and he'll be bringing her home. Kristen's gone to the Markows—oh, did you know Thelma and Tammy were back?'

'I heard a car.'

'They hired a cab from the airport. Thelma called Ira this morning and he said they weren't to go all the way to Texas for a funeral—and Thelma flying this way only yesterday. Ask me, he won't have his princess being exposed to all the horrors of a burial. Tammy had hysterics—just like yesterday again refusing to come home; she said they'd have to rope her to get her here. She refused to leave the motel to go anywhere except to Texas. Then Kristen stepped in, talked to her on the phone and she agreed to come home.'

'Just like that? How did Kristen manage to persuade her?'

'I've no idea.' Pearl was airy. 'Kristen did agree to go and stay with her; she's there now, at the Markow place.'

'What about Scott? Do the police have a

theory? Was it accident or suicide?'

'Suicide, Wayne reckons.'

'What about you?'

'Yes, I would think it was suicide; it's classic: gun in the mouth, hook the trigger with the toe.'

'Was he barefooted when he was found?'

'Of course. He couldn't put his boot back on afterwards, could he?' Pearl laughed angrily. 'Sorry, it's not funny. Graveyard humour. Anyway, one boot's missing, and his rifle. They'll have gone over the edge with him and been swept down by the river.'

'What was his man doing in Palomares?'

'Casey? Drinking. I didn't know he drank, and Ada says Clayton wouldn't have employed him if he'd known. She's not bothered about it; she's keeping him on for the present.'

'How is Ada?'

'Shocked of course, but she says she shouldn't be surprised; he's never been the same since Veronica died and—you see—he chose the same way to go.'

'He didn't.'

'Well, the river. The water must have been hypnotic for him, but it's more in character for a man to stand on the edge and shoot himself than to walk out into the stream like Veronica.'

'Is that what she did?'

'Either that or threw herself in from the

same spot—Heavens' sakes, what are we talking about? Tell me about your visitors. What did Marge have to say?'

Miss Pink, who had been about to ask after Kristen, was taken aback by this sudden change of direction, and Pearl's eyes sharpened. 'Marge has a theory?'

'I don't think she's interested in Scott's death but she's certainly got her knife into you. There's something very wrong there, Pearl; she couldn't have been more spiteful.'

'What was it this time?'

'The same, only worse. Sexually orientated, of course; she's bothered about truck drivers coming in from the interstate and parking overnight.'

'Well, I guess that's her fantasy: truck drivers. Poor old Marge. I suppose she said I'd laid every man in the village.'

'I think that was the implication.'

'Did she mention Sam? Her husband?'

'No, she didn't mention him.'

Pearl smiled wryly. 'That fits. He was a very macho guy: loved the outdoors, hunting, his little mine—I told you. We used to meet up there, on the mesas. I know that cabin in Slickrock like I know this patio. I think Sam was a little in love with me. I didn't encourage that, it could be disruptive; all right to meet up there'—she glanced at the skyline—'keep it discreet, but not down here.' She grinned. 'I never had Sam in my bedroom except the once and I wouldn't have had him then but she'd stopped him going up on the mesas and he came over and told me he didn't care to go on living if all he could do was sit in the patio all day and look at the cliffs. That's why he was drinking heavily. So he spent a while with me here'—she gestured at the house—'and went home and dropped dead. She'll never forgive me.'

'She knew about it?'

'We didn't think so. I like Marge and I'd never have let on I was a comfort to her old man. She must have found out somehow. Maybe she knew all the time.'

'So now she's having her revenge by accusing you of—loose morals.'

'She'll have picked up some gossip. Someone could have seen me in Santa Fe and recognised me. I ran a house in San Jose, that's how I made my money, such as it is.' She grinned. 'I was what you'd call a madame. Are you shocked?'

'No. I think you must have made a good one.'

Pearl stared, then laughed. 'You mean it as a compliment! You're something else, you know that?'

'We're getting a long way from Scott's suicide.'

'Why not? It's over, we don't want to stay with it. You got reservations? I can see it in

272

your face.'

'I'm bothered about Marge: so vindictive.'

'That'll blow over. You can't afford to be on bad terms with your neighbours in a place as small as this.' She stood up and stretched. 'You should go out this afternoon, it isn't too hot to take a horse, the storm cleared the air. Why don't you take the trail to Massacre Canyon, out beyond Las Mesas? Call on Avril as you go by.'

*   *   *

'For the funeral,' Avril said, tossing a sheet of macaroons on a cake rack. 'And how's everyone bearing up in the great metropolis?'

'As you might expect.' Miss Pink was vague, thinking of Marge's outburst. 'When did you hear?'

'After the police came and showed Ada his watch. She said she hadn't called me until she knew for sure. Terrible thing to happen.' She tested the oven with her hand and opened the chimney damper. 'Coffee?' she asked without enthusiasm.

'No, thank you. I've had so many visitors, I've been drinking coffee all day.' Avril licked her lips. 'A troubled man,' Miss Pink observed. 'It was to be expected.'

'Who've you been talking to?'

Miss Pink shifted her feet. 'Sit down,' Avril muttered, but it was a reflex, not a

273

courtesy.

Miss Pink pulled out a chair and seated herself at the table with a sigh. 'People talk to strangers,' she said apologetically. 'The assumption is that they'll never see you again; they unburden themselves and—could it be that there's some feeling that, with someone else to share it, the other person has lifted some of the burden? A trouble shared is a trouble halved?' Her eyes were childlike behind her thick lenses.

'All they got to do in a place like this is gossip,' Avril said contemptuously.

'I know. I live in a village myself.'

'England was never like this. You don't know the half of it.'

'People are happy to inform me though.'

'Not me; don't you go classing me with them.'

'No, you brought your English reticence with you. It must have been a shock when you realised that people gossip even more in rural America.'

'If you been listening to that Ada Scott you need your head—' Avril stopped, her mouth slack, then started again. 'Not just Ada,' she said shakily. 'All—several of those women: they gossip like old hens. A younger person, a widow, on her own up here with an unmarried hand.' She shrugged. 'They can think what they like, see if I care.'

'Ada doesn't gossip.'

'You picked up some tittle-tattle from someplace.'

'You found your ring.'

'My—' Avril sat down suddenly, her face blank then, as a thought struck her, she flushed and her eyes went to the door. 'That Fletcher Lloyd,' she grated. 'The ungrateful sod! Where'd he get work if I didn't employ him?'

'It wasn't him,' Miss Pink said, stretching the truth.

'Then who? Pearl. He'd tell her anything.'

'Women are careless with their jewellery. If Gregorio hadn't been missing at the same time you'd have searched until you found it, but as it was, you jumped to conclusions.'

'I did nothing of the sort! It was Clayton Scott who asked me was I missing anything and when I told him, it was him said Greg stole the ring, not me.'

'He would, wouldn't he?'

'I don't know what you mean. It *is* Ada Scott, isn't it?' Avril spoke slowly, watching Miss Pink's eyes. 'He talked it over with his wife. He was a worse gossip than any woman, and yet, you know'—she looked puzzled—'I wouldn't have thought Ada would believe him.'

'She'd never have stood for blackmail.'

'It wasn't blackmail!' Avril gave an angry snort of laughter. 'What use would that be? He knew Herb never had any cash in the

275

bank, all he left me was land. Scott just made accusations, is all, and not even that but inno—inn—what's it called?'

'Innuendoes.'

Avril nodded morosely, then glanced up and flinched, recognising compassion when she saw it. 'It's just the kind of thing a creep like that would think of,' she said fiercely. 'No one had any idea what he was like—'cept Ada, she had to know, living with him all them years. My mother was the same as Ada: strong but not strong enough. He had a filthy soul, that man.'

'You weren't the only person to suffer.'

'No, everyone as came into contact with him.' She fingered a piece of dough on the table, rolling and stretching it. 'I was fond of Herb—and I nursed Mrs Beck right up until the end, and it wasn't easy, I can tell you; cancer of the bowel it was, and she was in terrible pain. Had a spell in hospital but they brought her home to die and then she lingered on. Herb—that was when he had to drink—he couldn't stand to see her like that. No more could I sometimes. I tell you, it would have been a favour if I'd—if I done what that bugger said I done. And then what was more natural than Herb should marry me? Not immediately, we waited six months; it wouldn't have been right, marry right away so soon after Mrs Beck was buried. But Herb couldn't stop drinking; he was a born boozer, his liver musta been all rotted to bits, the doctor said. He died of a heart attack. She died of cancer, him of heart failure; it says so on the death certificates. Listen, I worked hard to get where I am now and look at me: I got a cattle ranch and I own my own house but what life is there here for a woman my age? I'm not old, I'm only forty-two! Would I have poisoned two people just so I could spend the rest of my life out here in the boondocks? I'd have been better off married to a trucker with a nice home in Santa Fe, and I could have done, I tell you now.'

'What did Scott get out of these silly accusations if it wasn't blackmail? Was it emotional?'

'What d'you mean?'

'Why, holding it over your head to try to force you to go to bed with him.'

'Scott! Go to bed with me! You're out of your mind. I wouldn't give him the time of day. Hell, if he wanted women none of this would have happened.'

'Someone else said that.' Miss Pink frowned, thinking back. 'No, it's gone.' She stood up and Avril pushed back her chair. 'Did you ever dare to retaliate, like questioning him about Gregorio?'

'Why—what would I say?'

'He was your employee, you had a right to know.'

'Actually, I woulda felt embarrassed about

277

that. I still do.'

'Embarrassed?'

'Wouldn't you be? Your own hand gets a girl into trouble and she goes and drowns herself? Hell, you're not going to talk about it with her father, are you?'

'You never had any doubt that Gregorio was responsible for her pregnancy?'

Avril returned the other's stare for a long moment and then looked away. 'I think this subject better be dropped; it can't do any good to rake it up again.'

'But you did find your ring.'

'It was in a box of papers, musta fallen off the night table.'

'So Gregorio wasn't a thief.'

'No, give him that.'

'And perhaps he wasn't the father of Veronica's child.'

'Like I said, forget it.'

A difficult thing to do, she thought as she rode on: three violent deaths in as many months, and the victims intimately connected in life. And in death? Oblivious to her surroundings she rode until her horse stopped of its own accord and she looked up in surprise to see that the trail was rising towards the mouth of a broad canyon that must be Massacre. She had ridden more than three miles from Las Mesas and couldn't recall one feature.

She turned and retraced the route through

foothills where arroyos were edged by crimson rock that was spiky with yucca and prickly pear. Coveys of quail were feeding in damp washes and a buck with magnificent antlers, all furred with velvet, glanced idly at the horse and went back to browsing on the willows. Quail and deer must have been there as she passed the first time but her mind had been busy—except that her subconscious may have registered a buck in velvet, and that had led her along a trail where the fixed points, the pointers, concerned hunting regulations and poaching and accidents involving loaded rifles.

There was no sign of life when she passed Avril's house and there was no one on the mesa trail. She wondered if anyone was trying to salvage the remains of the marijuana and who that might be: Gafford or Lloyd or even Kristen. She shook her head and walked on, reflecting that her horse hadn't had much exercise today, starting to trot—to check almost immediately as she caught sight of movement on the scree above the road. At first she thought it was a porcupine strayed from the woods but then she saw it had longer legs, and that what she had taken for quills was fat. It was Pedro.

Marge came hurrying round a bend in the road calling anxiously, worried about rattlers. Pedro ignored her and now he was circling something among the stones, giving little yelps of excitement. Above this point Rastus Creek dripped down the escarpment to fall on its own scree fan. The stones were in pale shades of red and as the women converged on the poodle the focus of its attention emerged from its background like the subject of a surreal photograph: a cracked old cowboy boot, the sole secured to the upper with strips of silver duct tape.

CHAPTER SIXTEEN

Marge was scolding Pedro. 'Coulda been a scorpion inside that old boot; one of these days you're going to get bit so bad it'll be too late to learn.' She clipped the leash to his collar and tried to pull him away. 'You been visiting with Avril?' she asked Miss Pink.

'And riding. I'll take the boot. Would you hand it to me?'

'What do you want with an old boot?'

'It's Gregorio's.'

'Never!' It was an expression of astonishment rather than denial. She stared at the boot and from that her gaze travelled up the course of the shrinking waterfall to the rim. Her eyes were thoughtful when they came back to Miss Pink. 'So now we know,' she said heavily.

'Hadn't people always assumed that it was

Gregorio—his remains—in Rastus Canyon?'

'Some folk might have preferred to think it wasn't.'

'Which folk?' Marge said nothing, her flat features inscrutable. 'It doesn't matter,' Miss Pink said, then added, 'You were mistaken about Fletcher Lloyd being in Pearl's place on Sunday afternoon. Have you realised since who it might have been?'

'Why wasn't it Lloyd?'

'He was on Midnight Mesa. I saw him.'

Marge looked away. 'So I made a mistake; she put a light on and I thought she was a man, with her short hair.'

'And you didn't see her undressed either.' Miss Pink was stern. She was surprised at Marge's reaction to this: embarrassment changing to a hard triumph.

'Didn't I? And how did she get out of that red frock and into jeans and a sweatshirt without undressing? Ask Kristen. They saw her, they had to have passed her between here and the interstate because I saw Jay drive by not long after Tammy went down on her bike. Did I say something?'

'Was he alone?'

'Jay? He was then. He musta dropped Kristen off at her place. They went to the fiesta together, remember: him and Kristen? But they had to pass Tammy so they'd know she was wearing jeans. Like I said, she changed in Pearl's.'

281

The sound of hoofs brought Pearl out to the corral. 'Something happened,' she said. 'I can see it in your face.' She unbuckled the bridle and Miss Pink pulled off the saddle. 'What's that?' Pearl asked, catching sight of the boot on the ground.

'Greg's boot.'

'Where did you find it?'

'Marge did, or rather, Pedro; it was washed down Rastus Creek and over the rim, I assume, to end up only half a mile from his home.'

'Except it wasn't his home. He left.'

'Not voluntarily.'

Pearl untied the sorrel and opened the gate to the corral. She loosened the halter and pulled it over his ears while Miss Pink trudged across the patio with the saddle. Pearl followed her into the old wash-house and hung the bridle and halter on their pegs. Miss Pink settled the saddle on a buck and spread the blanket to dry. They left the door open and walked to the house. 'I'll get the drinks,' Pearl said, and Miss Pink waited for her, seated at the table on the veranda.

She came back with glasses and frosted bottles. She passed a glass and a bottle across, the cap already loosened. She sat down and gave a deep sigh.

'How long have you known?' Miss Pink asked, but this brought no response. 'You knew it was Greg when you saw the bones in the ruin.'

'I guessed. That boot could have been his, the first boot, and the timing fitted.'

'So you knew what happened?'

Pearl shrugged. 'I don't expect I was the only one, but Veronica had died, so there was sympathy for the Scotts, not just for him but for Ada and Kristen. No one was going to talk—but I don't *know* anything; so far as anyone knew, Greg had just gone away, and we were forgetting, putting it out of our minds—until you arrived. You wouldn't let sleeping dogs lie.'

'I merely precipitated events—'

'If you hadn't gone into Rastus—'

'If Jay and Kristen hadn't been cultivating grass in Slickrock, I wouldn't have seen her climb out of the canyon. All I was after was a short-cut to the village, that's how I came to find the bones.'

Pearl changed tack. 'There's no way you can prove he didn't die by accident.'

'There's no point when his killer is dead.'

'You're guessing. And why are we having this conversation anyway?'

'Because when I leave here you're going to ask yourselves how much I know and what I'm going to do with it, if anything.'

Pearl stood up and went indoors. Miss

Pink listened for the telephone bell but all she heard was the opening and closing of the refrigerator door. She returned with more beer.

'So,' she said, with contrived gaiety, 'tell me what you think you know.'

'If Scott shot Greg then he collected the shells, but he could have hit him with his gun butt and pushed him over the edge. Whatever he did, Greg wasn't killed by the blow or the fall, because he crawled up into the ruin. Then Scott—'

'Wait. How do you know it was deliberate? It could have been an accident.'

'Then Scott would have brought him down.'

'You've no proof he was there.'

'What are you, devil's advocate?' Pearl looked away. Miss Pink continued, 'Someone was there: to bring Greg's horse down and remove his gear from the bunkhouse. And I suspect it was Scott who put the story about that Greg was the father of Veronica's baby.'

'At the time it fit. Greg disappeared after Veronica drowned.'

'Actually not soon enough. If he'd been the father he would have left immediately after the autopsy if he was going to leave voluntarily, even before. No way would he have waited several days before leaving.'

Pearl shrugged but her eyes were alert.

They drank in silence until she put down her glass with a crack and said, 'So Clayton talked Greg into poaching in Rastus. How could he do that if Greg was—' She stopped, disconcerted.

'There you are! He couldn't. If Greg would go into a remote canyon with Scott, an armed Scott, then Greg had to be innocent. If he'd had *anything* to do with Veronica, let alone been the father of the baby, he'd never have gone poaching with Scott.'

Pearl's eyes moved and Miss Pink turned to see Kristen approaching the veranda. The girl looked from one to the other. 'I'm interrupting something. Do I go away?' Pearl was hesitating. 'I stay.' Kristen grinned. She went in the kitchen and Pearl stared at the table. Miss Pink said nothing.

Kristen took her time and came back with a Coke. 'You're embarrassed,' she told Miss Pink. 'Tell me the worst.'

'Would you answer some questions?'

'About what?' It was said lightly but with a glance at Pearl that conveyed an element of doubt.

'About Tammy,' Pearl said.

'I haven't talked to Tammy.'

'You don't need to,' Miss Pink said. 'You knew some of what was happening and you guessed the rest.'

'She knows why your daddy shot himself,'

Pearl said. 'She pieced it together: about Greg. She just said that Greg would never have gone poaching with your dad if he was the father of Veronica's baby. We were starting to speculate who the father was.' Miss Pink stiffened. 'My guess,' Pearl went on, 'is your daddy discovered he'd made a tragic mistake, taking justice into his own hands, and he shot himself out of remorse. It's the kind of thing Clayton would do; he had such strong views on sin and punishment.'

'I think we should forget about my sister,' Kristen told Miss Pink. 'Someone made a mistake with her as well, and even if we knew who it was it wouldn't do any good. I want my mom to forget, and certainly I'm not after revenge. This thing only concerns my family.'

'I agree.' Miss Pink was quite composed. 'I understand *that*, but there are loose ends where Tammy is concerned.'

There was a pause. 'You said I knew some of what happened?' Kristen was polite.

'You didn't know everything that was going on because Tammy ran away twice and took you by surprise. She disappeared from the Harpers' guest-room and then from Sam's cabin.'

Kristen glanced again at Pearl who said sharply, 'I haven't talked to her about Slickrock.'

'It started when you met Tammy on Sunday afternoon,' Miss Pink said, watching Kristen. Seeing no denial, not even surprise, she went on, 'She was on her bike, riding down towards the interstate and she was wearing jeans and a sweatshirt.' Kristen frowned. 'She didn't tell you the whole truth then, she said that your father had taken her to task'—the girl's eyes were veiled—'she was lying.' The eyes widened. Miss Pink continued, 'But she told you enough for you to think it best to send her home with Jay. You put her bike in the back of the pick-up, and she crouched down on the floor of the cab so that your father wouldn't see her if he happened to be looking out, wouldn't know where she was—'

'How do you know all that?'

'That's simple. Marge saw Jay go by in the pick-up but she says that he didn't have a passenger. You weren't concerned about your father seeing Tammy but she was terrified. That says volumes. It means you couldn't have known what happened. She was too shocked to tell you.' Kristen was stiff, her knuckles white on the Coke can. 'Did he rape her?' Miss Pink asked.

Down in the bed of the creek the jays were mobbing an intruder. Miss Pink listened and nodded. 'Marian Vosker heard jays that afternoon as Tammy went down the creek and back, and she heard you quarrelling with

287

your father, although some of that could have been Tammy shouting.'

'I didn't know then,' Kristen said dully. 'I didn't know for ages. But it wouldn't have made any difference. The harm had been done.'

Pearl shifted in her seat. 'Tammy wasn't raped,' she said. 'But what did happen blew his mind, which is another reason why he had to put an end to his life. For a man of his calibre it was just as bad; he knew how his neighbours would look at it.' She was speaking to Miss Pink, seeming to exclude Kristen. 'This strict attitude with the girls: he used to whip them, did I tell you?' Kristen was watching Miss Pink's face. 'Both Veronica and Kristen were beaten,' Pearl went on. 'So was I, come to that; I've been there too.' She had told Miss Pink this, she was talking for the girl's benefit. 'What happened that Sunday afternoon was, he whipped Tammy.'

'Whipped her?'

Pearl bit her lip. 'He slapped her about.' No one spoke. 'All right! He handled her too—but there was no penetration.'

'That makes a difference?' Kristen asked.

'Well, she won't have a ba—' Pearl stopped short.

'And he tore her dress.'

'He said it was a whore's dress.' Pearl was staring at Kristen.

288

Miss Pink turned to the girl. 'You didn't know this at the time?'

She shook her head. 'Like you said, she was in jeans when we met her. She still thinks it was her fault, because of that dress. *He* told her that, he even said—'

'Tammy was full of guilt,' Pearl interrupted. 'She knew Kristen was at the fiesta, you see, and she was bored. I guess she wandered down to the Scott place just for something to do—' She trailed off.

'She had no idea of the danger,' Kristen said earnestly. 'How could she, at that age?'

Pearl threw her a glance. 'He said that if she told anyone he'd say that *she* approached *him* and everyone would believe him because of the way she was dressed. He probably said other things that she don't understand, and I guess we'll never find out because she'll block them out.'

'I see why your mother wouldn't have her in the house,' Miss Pink told Kristen.

'That was *before*,' Pearl said quickly. 'It was me wouldn't have her here on Sunday night, when Kristen came and asked me to take her in—'

'It wasn't your fault,' the girl said. 'I didn't know myself what was behind it, I thought she was just playing up because she couldn't go to Texas. When you wouldn't have her, I let it go. I thought she was all right with Maxine and Daryl. What happened, her

289

nerve broke; she was terrified he'd come and get her in the night and she knew Daryl and Maxine were only kids compared with him. They couldn't protect her. I guess she wouldn't go to Jay because he's—well, sexy, and that was the last thing she wanted.'

'She'd only feel safe with women,' Pearl put in.

'So she went to the cabin at the head of Scorpion,' Kristen went on, 'and that's where I found her in the morning, and I convinced her to let me take her to Slickrock, to Sam Dearing's old shack. On the way she told me more, but still not all of it, and anyway you know—I wasn't sure if it was true?' Suddenly she looked very young and helpless. 'But I thought it best to get her out, get her away to her folks, so I said I'd find money for the plane fare and I'd come up next morning and we'd take her to Palomares, Jay and me. She stayed in Sam's cabin overnight but in the morning she saw a big snake and she split. She got lost in the woods and when I arrived I couldn't find her, and I went up the head of the canyon, see if she was in those caves.'

In the ensuing silence Miss Pink knew they were waiting. 'By then you knew about the dress,' she said. 'You didn't know until the previous evening when we were all in the Harpers' kitchen. And that made a difference. So you hit your father?' She couldn't help but end on a query.

'I hit him because he was about to shoot Tammy. He'd fired at her already.' Kristen was grim. 'In the woods, remember, when you thought he was shooting at the pigs? She guessed he was in the search party so she didn't dare show herself. She was lost and in a panic. She came out on the Beck side of the canyon and started up the wall and he would have got her then but I'd been following him a ways and—yes, I hit him. Then I ran after her and we were both climbing the wall when you reached him. Jay saw us but you were too concerned with reviving him to look up.' Miss Pink was frowning. Kristen rattled on, 'I gave her the money for the plane fare and sent her down on Pearl's horse, told her to see if she could find a pick-up at Las Mesas and take that. You know the rest. I hung about in the pinyons until you'd all gone down and then I went back to Slickrock.'

'So Jay knows everything. And Daryl?'

Kristen shrugged. It wasn't important.

'We all know now,' Pearl said, and there was a trace of reproof in her tone, as if there was nothing left to conceal.

CHAPTER SEVENTEEN

At nine o'clock that evening Ada sent for Miss Pink. Pearl was obviously uneasy when she delivered the message. Kristen had gone to the Markow ranch and the two of them were alone. 'I think,' Pearl said, not meeting Miss Pink's eye, 'that she just wants to know what's going on.'

'I shall reassure her.'

'Oh? You haven't reassured me.'

'Kristen didn't want to talk about Veronica.'

'You think Ada does?'

'This is Ada's party.' Miss Pink smiled. 'She's calling the shots; you don't have to worry about her.' Pearl went to speak and stopped. 'Or me,' Miss Pink added, and hoped it was true.

Ada was wearing a yellow dress and a string of amber beads. She wore a touch of lipstick too and her hair was in a chignon as it had been when they met for the first time. Death had invested her with dignity and she received Miss Pink's condolences with poise. They sat in the dimly lit living-room with a coffee-table between them and a tray with cups and saucers, a china coffeepot and a plate of chocolate-chip cookies.

'You've been baking,' Miss Pink observed

as Ada poured coffee.

'Funerals are busy times. For the women.'

'So Avril said.'

'Was it Avril who told you about Gregorio?'

'Not in the way you mean. She found her ring so she admits he wasn't a thief. Otherwise she's willing to accept that he's guilty. It makes things easier all round.'

'In what way?'

'The accepted story is that Clayton killed Gregorio because the man was the father of Veronica's baby and so he was also responsible for her death. Then Clayton's mind became unhinged and he committed suicide.'

Ada had listened carefully. 'But you have another version; you say Gregorio couldn't have been the father.'

Miss Pink realised that this wasn't telepathy; if Kristen had gone straight from Pearl's house to the Markow ranch, she could have telephoned her mother from there. She spread her hands. 'The identity of the father is important? Pearl says everything is out in the open; by that she means it's confined to a small circle, to the village—and Kristen says that the family, that is, you and herself, want to forget. "It's a family matter," were her words.'

'She doesn't trust you.'

'Naturally, she doesn't know me as well as

she knows Pearl, but you don't have to trust me; all the evidence is circumstantial. The police couldn't build a case on it, and why should they? Murder was committed and the killer committed suicide. And Veronica's pregnancy? There's never been any suggestion of rape there; the police aren't going to look for a crime where there's no indication of one.'

Ada licked her lips very delicately. 'But there was Tammy.'

'It's over. She's safe. You're all safe.' Miss Pink smiled. 'Circumstantial evidence: your attitudes have changed completely, your own *appearance* has changed since he died. You're all overwhelmed with relief. The clincher was Tammy's terror, her adamant refusal to come back to the village, and her complete change of mood when Kristen spoke to her on the telephone. Of course, Kristen told Tammy that Clayton was dead.'

'It was all my fault,' Ada said. 'We should have—Kristen should have taken that silly dress away from her. I shouldn't have gone to the fiesta.'

'If it hadn't been the dress it would have been something else. After all—'

'He was very strict,' Ada interrupted. 'He wasn't balanced where some things were concerned and after Veronica he became even more obsessed.' She sighed. 'And there was Kristen and Jay, he was going mad with anger; he lost sight of the fact that Tammy wasn't his own daughter, she was just a—just any little girl, flaunting—what he thought was flaunting her, her—'

'Sex?'

Ada's jumpy eyes became fixed. 'You know what happened. Kristen says you know.'

'And then he had to kill her to silence her.'

Ada thought for a moment. 'That seems to be right,' she said cautiously.

'Kristen says he was firing at Tammy.'

'Don't you believe her?'

'I do. It was you who hesitated.'

'It's a terrible thing to admit: that your husband tried to kill someone.'

'It's more terrible to know why he needed to kill her.'

'You know that! To silence her.'

'But when he told Tammy she had to keep quiet after he attacked her, he said it would be her word against his.'

'He must have thought better of it; he was afraid Ira would believe Tammy if she told him.'

'In court, if it had come to a court case, Clayton would maintain that Tammy teased him. We all know she did, she thought it amusing to make him angry; why, Pearl and I were witnesses to that, when we were visiting you shortly after I arrived here. But if Kristen were to back Tammy's story, people would believe the two of them.'

'Kristen didn't know everything that happened that Sunday afternoon, not till much later.'

'She knew quite enough.' Ada stiffened. 'She didn't have to know much,' Miss Pink went on, 'only that Tammy had come in this house when there was no one here except him, that something had happened to frighten Tammy, she didn't have to know specifically what it was, it was enough to confront him—'

'He told Kristen—' Ada stopped.

'How Tammy was dressed?'

'No, she didn't know that until she learned it from you. What he did say was Tammy asked him to—to—'

'I know. He put all the blame on Tammy. They do that.'

'Oh. So—they quarrelled: Kristen and her father. Kristen was afraid of what might happen—not knowing that it had already.'

'She'd been afraid of it for a while.'

'Yes. She told you that?'

'And he repeated to her that it was Tammy's word against his, and Kristen said she could, would confirm Tammy's word. Because Kristen had always known he was obsessed with young girls.'

The hooded eyes closed and opened again. 'It was all in the past,' Ada said, adding, fighting to the last, 'whatever happened.'

'It's happening now.'

'How can it be? He committed suicide. Can't you let it go?'

'I accept that's the official version.'

'So what are you saying?'

'If it wasn't for the fact that Kristen has alibis all over the place, I'd say she shot him, although Jay had to help her get the body in the river.'

'That's pure fantasy—but it's clever. You're a clever woman. Tell me why you'd think Kristen would shoot her own father.'

Miss Pink looked thoughtful. 'Everyone—except Clayton seems to have liked Gregorio. Perhaps he was kind to Veronica—I mean *kind*,' she added sternly, 'I'm not for one moment suggesting that there was any sexual relationship. But Gregorio had been chosen for the fall guy and Kristen knew it. She shot her father because he was mad, and he was dangerous not only to Tammy and any other child who attracted him, but to you, because you *knew*. The reason why Kristen was helping Jay produce marijuana was so that they could get you away from here. She would do anything for money so that you could move right away, and growing grass was an easy way to get it. Why wouldn't you go anyway? Why didn't you—I'm sorry.' She'd lost her cool and tried to retract.

'People always ask those questions,' Ada

said. ' "You knew what he was like; why didn't you leave him?" And the wives, the ones who stay, can't answer—but they feel, they feel guilty. I did think it was all over, once she got older.'

'But Veronica was immature,' Miss Pink said quietly. 'So being older in years didn't count with her.'

'She was like a child.' There was a world of sadness in that. 'How did you know all this?' It was said without much curiosity but Miss Pink answered it all the same.

'I didn't. You asked me to come here so that you could find out how much I knew. It was just enough to be dangerous, and now you've told me the rest, but we're agreed: it's fantasy, women's gossip.'

Ada nodded. 'Like you said: there's no evidence, what I told you was the ramblings of a bereaved widow with a history of nervous complaints. But you don't know everything.'

'I don't *know* anything; it's all guesswork. I do know that for a girl to shoot her own father she'd need more compelling reasons than what she thought he might do in the future, and if she'd known about incest all along why didn't she act before? What brought things to a head at this time?'

'You did. And she didn't know.'

'*What?*'

'They forget what happens when they're

very young, or maybe they forget deliberately. Kristen was a feisty child and he had—there was Veronica to turn to and she never talked, not until near the end, and then Kristen didn't believe her. You have to understand that Veronica had all kinds of fantasies—and dreams; she thought her dreams were real. So Kristen didn't—couldn't believe what she was hearing, and she never told me; she tried to spare me trouble always. But when Veronica was taken out of the river and the doctor told us about the baby, then she knew that some of it, at least, was true, and she wondered about the rest. When you arrived and found what was left of Gregorio, I think at that stage she knew everything: knew, suspected, it doesn't matter.' Ada slumped in her chair.

'Veronica didn't drown herself.' It wasn't a question.

'I have to say this'—Ada was listless—'although it sounds dreadful with what we know now, but she seemed to be a happy girl, and she couldn't hide much.'

'But she did, didn't she?'

'No, she told Kristen!' The fine eyes closed in pain. 'And she didn't believe her.' She went on, in a voice drained of emotion, 'We never let her go out on her own, only way she could have reached the river was with one of us taking her, one night when Casey was gone to Palomares. She had to be killed because when it was seen that she was pregnant, he knew we'd find out who the father was.' The eyes rose to Miss Pink's. 'So now you know everything.' Slowly she seemed to regain strength. 'I'm not pleading,' she said calmly, 'and no way would I threaten you—not that I don't think killing can be justified. But the way I look at it is laws were made by men, and here was a man used his own child worse than a beast, and drowned her when his sin was about to be discovered, and then he killed another innocent to make that dead man take the blame. Then he starts over with the next victim and he tried to kill her when she became a threat. If someone kills that man before he can do more harm, that's justice. And who should take the responsibility except his own kin? But we're all in it,' she assured Miss Pink, 'Pearl, Jay and me, like you said: we're Kristen's alibis. And now you do know everything, what will you do?'

'Nothing. Lock the door and throw away the key. Although I shall remember some things.'

'Loyalty?'

'Yes, and confidence.' Miss Pink looked surprised. 'You all know where you're at.'

'Some of us do.'

★   ★   ★

The dust was soft and the street showed pale in the starlight. Under the brilliant canopy and the black-bulk of the cliffs the lighted windows looked like sanctuaries in the wilderness. Frogs were chattering in the creek bed, an owl called in the rocks, and behind the insect screens the women could be seen working in their kitchens, going methodically about their business of baking cakes and cookies for the funeral of Veronica's daddy.